Rembrandt Sings

Rembrandt Sings

Michael Johnston

akanos

Copyright © Michael Johnston 2012
First published in 2012 by akanos
2 Woodfall Ave
Barnet, Herts, EN5 2EZ

Distributed by Lightning Source

The right of Michael Johnston to be identified as the author of the work has been asserted herein in accordance with the Copyright, Designs and Patents Act 1988.

All rights reserved. This book is sold subject to the condition that it shall not, by way of trade or otherwise, be lent, resold, hired out or otherwise circulated without the publisher's prior consent in any form of binding or cover other than that in which it is published and without a similar condition including this condition being imposed on the subsequent purchaser.

With the exception of certain historical figures, all the characters in this book are fictitious and any resemblance to actual people, living or dead, is purely imaginary.

British Library Cataloguing in Publication Data
A catalogue record for this book is available from the British Library

ISBN 978-0-9542901-1-5

Typeset by Amolibros, Milverton, Somerset
This book production has been managed by Amolibros
Printed and bound by Lightning Source

For Anne

1

20050131

This is something I really do not need – somewhat of a cliché that, for the author of a dozen prize-winning books, but let it pass. The fact that I'm learning the news from a newspaper reporter who, somehow or other, has got hold of my ex-directory number, simply increases the feeling of irritation, annoyance; dammit let's be blunt, anger – and just a smidgeon of fear. I mean, what the hell does she mean by it? In truth, *she* probably doesn't know anything about it.

And the questions he asked. What an uncultured oaf! What would it 'go for?' Would I be 'flogging' mine too?

The trouble dealing with a lawyer who's also a friend is that when it comes to the crunch (another cliché), lawyers don't *have* friends. It was simply a mutual understanding, unwritten, that neither canvas would be sold in our lifetimes; hers or mine, and we were both young enough then. Now that lawyer and quondam friend is dead; his feculent son-in-law and his no less odoriferous wife are in charge, and they are on the make. And they could *make* tens of millions; not from this one item, of course, but from the whole collection, one of the most remarkable still in private hands. What's more, you don't need to be paranoid to feel damn-well certain they've chosen Shepherd's as the auction house because its place of business is just across the square from my office in the Contemporary Arts Foundation.

I told the reporter the painting would fetch what the market thought it was worth and that it was very hard to know what that would be now, many years after the event. Yes, it was one of only two in private hands and, yes again, I owned the other. I'd like to get my private hands on that son-in-law until I choked the life out of him, but I managed not to say so, nor even imply such a feeling; remarkable restraint in the circumstances. I'd like to get my hands on the painting too. I wonder if a private treaty sale is still possible.

After all, it would only be one item from a significant catalogue and, by any reasonable yardstick, the disposal of the wonderful Handschumacher Collection of German Expressionist paintings should be of greater significance than the sale of a single Golden. The Foundation's own funds for purchases are worth a great deal less than formerly but there are quite a few patrons of the arts who would not so much like to add a Golden to their collections as be known to own the painting. The trouble is this Golden comes with what my friends in television call a 'back story'. I don't know if I could survive its telling. Well of course I could, physically and even financially, but my reputation certainly wouldn't.

It's crass really, and typical of that man and his manners, to abuse his position as her trustee by slipping this painting into the disposal of his father-in-law's estate. If he thought to conceal it then his plan has spectacularly back-fired. The press and the art world seem to be regarding the sale as consisting of only two items, one entire Expressionist collection and one solitary Golden painting.

If Shepherd's follow their usual practice, they will ask the most appropriate independent experts to run their rule over the individual items and pass their highly respected judgement on the provenance and authenticity of each work. Amid all the auction house scandals of recent years, Shepherd's policy of ostentatiously making sure beyond all reasonable doubt that the *emptor* had rather less to *caveat* has stood the house in good stead. However, this means that it is almost inevitable – and never mind the 'almost' – that I will be asked to vouch for the Golden. Quite apart from being the Director, the youngest ever Director, of the normally very conservative Contemporary Arts Foundation and the owner of the only other Golden in private hands, I am, by design and by default, the world's leading expert on the paintings of Alexander Golden (1880-1938?), best described as a Scottish abstract expressionist – best described by me, that is. I placed the date of his death as 1938 (and most other scholars, in consequence, omit the question mark) but, in truth (that rare commodity), no one can be really certain when, where, or even how he died.

[The automatic back-up started up here and kicked me out for a moment while it burned all the past week's new data onto a CD which it then spat out. I have dutifully followed the on-screen instructions and put in a fresh disk. Can't be too careful with precious work.]

As I was saying then, all this means that they are bound to turn to the person one witty Australian art critic – *sui generis* – recently labelled 'the art world's Golden boy, who, after a *jeunesse dorée*, could now be thought of as a potential future Director of the Tate'. Who am I to argue? However, I am well past my youth and although some of the gilt still adheres I also feel a certain secret guilt that clings no less tenaciously. My next step must surely be to speak to (or as he would say 'with') Abramowitz. I have only met him a couple of times and the second occasion was after the funeral of his father-in-law. I'm not ashamed of the fact that I lost my temper, which was entirely justified, but I am annoyed now, in retrospect, because it's certain to complicate, it might even prevent, an amicable resolution.

20050201

As I predicted in yesterday's diary entry, Shepherd's have been in touch, by e-mail. Having had a moment or two to think about it, I explained I was 'unavoidably committed to a short visit to the USA'. Conveniently, I'd already arranged a spell of time away from the office, to work on the forthcoming package of television series and glossy book. (How I wish my producer would not badger me to write the television script then expand to book length, rather than abstract it from the narrative of the book itself, but that is another matter.) However, the fact Shepherd's intend to ask another of the Foundation's distinguished scholars to look at the German Expressionists, the man who was my only serious rival for the directorship, means (given how painstakingly, and Ye Gods how slowly, he works) that I can say I will get round to looking at the Golden in ample time for the auction itself. Besides, I know the painting intimately, even if I haven't stood in front of it for many years.

Having committed myself to the trip, I then had to book a flight to San Francisco and, gritting my teeth, speak with Abramowitz's PA to make an appointment. How that must be making the bastard chortle. I *must* keep my temper.

20050202

This flight contrasts in almost every detail with that first visit to the New World. Then I was squashed up in the back; near enough to smell the toilets but just too far away to get in ahead of the queue. Now? I think the young lady would even bring me a bed bottle if I asked nicely, and the one aroma I can detect is her perfume. Then, I had a notebook and pencil. (I also had a sharpener and what I had been warned by an American friend *always* to call an eraser.) Now, I have this top-of-the-line laptop with almost infinite storage capacity. It holds a whole gallery of paintings, from the Foundation's archives, and, of course, I have images of every Golden; including hers and mine. I even have the written transcripts and even the audio of my tape-recorded interviews with Joe and one or two facsimiles of crucial letters; a portable archive no less. It cost me a small fortune to have it done. By rights I ought to have deposited primary source material with the Foundation when I completed my thesis but, somehow, I never got round to doing so. The originals can stay where they are. The less said about Joe in the next few weeks and months the better, I think. We don't want an investigative journalist or, just as bad, some eager post-graduate art historian in search of a PhD (like I was once) working over *that* ground. However, since I am the Director it simply won't happen.

Despite everything, I can't help smiling whenever, and it's quite often, I think about Joe. Perhaps that's the real measure of his influence on my career, and on me as a person. If what one thinks about often makes one smile, can one be altogether a bastard? (According to Hamlet, yes, but what did he know about Modern Art?) Now, unable to sleep though cocooned in a comfortable First Class seat, I have nothing else to do but think which, in my case, means write and, with this box of tricks, I can switch from diary entry into memoir, or do I mean monograph mode; and I can do that in two clicks of a mouse's tail. [Click, click.]

I flew to San Francisco all those years ago after having written a short letter on Foundation notepaper but, with time pressing, I didn't wait for an answer. The first frustration had been to discover Joe's phone number was unlisted. However, some amateur sleuthing in the gaggle of galleries in Carmel identified the one he seemed to be associated with and, an innovation for the time, it had a bar and restaurant. By American standards I was nearer the net worth of one of Steinbeck's Salinas Valley characters than the cream of Carmel society but as I was still spending my way through my aunt's legacy I felt no great anxiety as I stood on the sidewalk contemplating the menu without first looking (as one does in Harrogate) at the prices. Hungry for the life-style as much as the linguine, I turned to go in.

Coming out in a hurry, the man in the loud plaid jacket simply didn't see me. I had to dodge aside or he would have walked straight into me. Short, squat and angry, he pulled a stubby cigar from his lips, spat copiously on the sidewalk and disappeared round the corner into the car park.

Giving it no more thought, I stepped inside, spotted the all-important sign and pushed open the door. As I took my first pace towards the urinal, the cubicle door flew open and slammed me in the face. Halfway between dazed and stunned, I slithered to the floor. Through watering eyes, I dimly saw the tall, white-haired, and very angry man charge out, yank me to my feet, put my head in a crushing arm-lock and begin to twist it off.

Then he saw who I was, or rather wasn't, and let go. I sank, sore, scared, bruised and breathless to the floor of the lavatory.

'Sorry,' he grunted and began to leave.

Whether I spoke or just wheezed I can't remember but it was enough to make him pause. God that worried me! I wanted to see the back of him. A solitary Brit in an American john: who wants to prolong such an encounter? As he reached down I cringed. He pulled me to my feet. His fists tightened on my lapels and he stared hard into my face.

'Owe you a beer,' he said and steered me to the relative security of the bar. I'd forgotten all about needing a pee. Needing the beer, even *American* beer, to give me the strength to flee, I let him prop me in a corner and deftly load our table with peanuts. He sat opposite me, obviously exhausted by the exertion himself, and we raised our glasses.

'Name's Rembrandt. Guess I owe you an explanation. Thought you were my ex-business partner. Just told him next time we met I'd kill him.'

'Somehow, Mr Rembrandt,' I said in my best Dashiell Hammett accent, 'I think we were meant to meet. And there's something else I'd quite like you to explain.'

Then, quite literally, the men in white coats (one man and one woman actually) came for him; and that was how, next day, I came to be sitting at the bedside of a dying artist.

To explain the jump cut from gallery to sick bed (and the almost Dickens-like coincidence), having found him, I just didn't want to lose him. As those two white white-jackets gently but firmly propelled him to the door, repeating some mantra about 'doctor's orders', I managed to blurt out who I was, and a one-line explanation of why I had flown eight thousand miles to see him. Joe stared at me for a couple of seconds, a slow smile came over his face and he grabbed my arm. I found myself sitting in an Edsel with Rembrandt between me and the starched white driver as we followed a Cadillac.

'Like the car?'

'I wouldn't have chosen it myself.'

'This beauty actually gets more valuable as we drive. Sure as hell don't make them like this anymore.'

'Mr Rembrandt, I ...'

'Joe!'

'Joe, I really need to talk to you but I hadn't any idea that ... well that you were ... I mean ... not quite well.'

'"Not quite well!" Haven't heard that limey understatement in a while. Listen son, I'm flattered. No one has come to visit me for a while. But if you want to talk, you'll have to move in; catch me when I feel like it.'

Joe Rembrandt was tall, spare, with weathered cheeks and thinning hair, cobalt blue eyes, Marlboro man's father. He lived in a sprawling ranch-type house in a hollow on top of a hill overlooking wealthy, arty-farty Carmel, south of San Francisco with what seemed, until you took a second, surprised look, a stunning collection of modern art; add to that a Cadillac in his car port, a 'collector's only' Edsel in his garage, some very potable white wine in his fridge, thick T-bone steaks in his freezer, and cancer in his prostate.

Wealthy enough to be able to undergo his chemotherapy at home, he still had to go into hospital for radiotherapy. When we met, he was in something of a remission, and was making life hell for his minders by ducking out to drive the Edsel downtown. And now I had been invited to stay with him! It seemed like a good idea at the time.[1]

Some weeks earlier than those events in Carmel, I had been summoned to the Director's office. He was scrupulously polite but did not let that obscure his message. If I, *Mr* William Maguire MA (Hons) History of Art, expected to continue working for the Contemporary Arts Foundation, beyond the term of my post-graduate scholarship, then I had better dissertate, or else. The streets of London might not be paved with gold, but they were richly carpeted with other Honours graduates in the History of Art, who regularly sent him their eye teeth by registered post, together with their impressive curricula vitae. True, I had shown promise but, so far, I had not fulfilled it. The appointment was there – Reader in Contemporary French Painting but, that irremovable *but*, it was reserved for a PhD. BA, nor even MA, need not apply. I had a modest fraction over twelve months left in which to complete it yet, to date, I had not even agreed the *subject*.

'There's no way I can make it any clearer, Maguire. No dissertation equals no doctorate – equals no job.'

What was the point in arguing? On the basis of the facts, none whatsoever; yet I passionately wanted that job. Unless you are now, or ever have been, in the grip of an obsession – a mild neurosis will not suffice – you cannot know *how* and, of course, no one would ever know *why* a Yorkshireman in his mid-twenties, a university graduate, wanted more than anything else to live and work in France, and to write and teach about twentieth-century French painting. I blame my father!

At the age of eighteen, with a clutch of A-levels and my place at University assured, he sent me to live with a French family in Roubaix, where no one spoke English and where – the crucial fact – the parents and *their* parents had been collecting modern art for most of the century, never mind a few pictures inherited from great-grandparents, mostly by Corot.

Until then, despite my lawyer father's Sunday painting, and compulsory visits with him to walk past the Old Masters hanging in the municipal galleries in Leeds and York, before the days when Harrogate had its own Mercer Gallery, my mind and eyes had remained (defiantly?) closed to the visual arts. Now, I was *living* in a gallery.

What's more, genuine, locally-living artists I'd never heard of were often to be found in animated discussion round the dinner table. A triptych by Roualt hung in the dining room. Three ugly judges with fat noses, shaped as well as coloured by the artist's palette knife, stared aggressively back at me, condemning me for my ignorance of Art, and the time I had wasted in not realising it was all that *really* mattered in life. An orchestra by Dufy played on and on in the salon, the golden background glowing while the musicians and their instruments were picked out in colourful semi-colons of bright red, blue, white, brown and amazing green apostrophes. To my surprise and utter delight, it made me want to dance for the sheer joy of it. Paintings covered the walls to such an extent that one often had to grope behind a heavy frame to find the light switch. There were evenings when I would do just that in order to sit and saturate my eyes with both the individual details and the sum of the parts. The whole family, teenage children included, spent their weekends making excursions to exhibitions within a 100 kilometre radius, not forgetting monthly visits to Paris. What is art for, the Philistines ask? It's for *me*, I thought, and sod the rest of you.

After three months, I was approaching fluency in French and coming to realise that I wanted to spend the rest of my life looking at paintings? In the grey light of London some years later, my Teenage Master Plan looked like it was coming off the rails. I had intended to graduate with honours (done), and pick up one of the scarce, well-endowed scholarships at the Contemporary Arts Foundation (done). The post-graduate school had a reputation second to none and, armed with their prestigious DPhil, I could certainly land a job in France. Already, on the strength of my good degrees and my French, I had been 'conditionally offered' a Readership at the Foundation, well worth doing for two or three years (maximum) while I plotted my eventual move to France but… But what? But I couldn't make my bloody mind up!

Either, I would light on an artist on the strength of one or two works I knew, then find there was less in them and in his or her *oeuvre* than would fill a postcard, far less a thesis, or, more often, I would find myself overwhelmed by the sheer amount that others had already written, leaving me little or nothing to add of scholarly value or academic originality – whatever that is. Should I write about one artist or a related group? Which artist? What group? Much effort and, more importantly, too much time had been frittered away on aesthetic indecision. My student counsellor, a brand new position in those days but already hard to get an appointment with, said it was 'fear of failure' that made me reluctant to start. Big help!

Hot favourite for my intensive and scholarly scrutiny had been Serge Poliakoff (1900-1969): his sombre but seductive polygons once hung in my bedroom in Roubaix and were, then and now, in all the best galleries, including the Tate. But what I had found out about him so far hadn't seemed enough to write a paragraph, never mind a monograph.[2]

It was in this make or break mood I found myself (yet again!) in the Orangerie on a despairing visit to Paris in search of that vital spark which, in combination with enough hot air, I might fan into a blaze of erudition. I had come to see a small exhibition of post-war French paintings by artists, some of whom, without realising my good fortune at the time, I had actually met in Roubaix – Manissier (1911- 1993), his *protégé* Bissière (I forget his dates), Maria Elena Viera da Silva (1908-1992), Nicolas de Staël (1914-1955), Maurice Estève (1912-2001) and a few others – but none of them seemed to fire me up and, apart from the so-called Catholic school which I was not taken with, there was no other common thread. Contemplating suicide, but *after* lunch, I took a short-cut towards the pleasant café.

And that was how I managed to walk through the annual outing of the much ballyhooed but then unfashionable and neglected works of Alexander Golden. Because the gallery, at the time of acquisition, had agreed always to exhibit them as a body of work and not individually, they came out for only four weeks, and spent the rest of the year either in the vaults or touring the world. For me, they were just a footnote to the History of Art. He'd painted in France, but he wasn't French. I'd only ever seen a few postcard reproductions. His early work was rubbish, almost photographic landscapes, personalised in the bottom right corner by a pretentious little cipher. Nothing had ever drawn me to them, or to him. But this display was a real *coup de foudre* and it was more than two hours before I finally made it to the café.

What the occasional postcard had simply not prepared me for was the sheer intensity of the fifty canvases and the way the colours, shapes, symbols and their arrangement, rearrangement, disarrangement, repetition and disruption made them such a complete and continuous panorama – no longer possible for me to think of as individual paintings but more like a twentieth century Bayeux Tapestry, in an artistic language as mysterious and tantalising as Linear B. Perhaps, but in a completely different way, only the paintings of Ben Nicholson – whose mistake, from my selfish point of view, was not to have been born French – had spoken to me so powerfully at first viewing.

Before the day was out, I had phoned my director – a fortune as well as a fiddle from a French pay phone – and he had agreed to make arrangements with the Orangerie for me to stay on in Paris, beyond the closing date of the Golden exhibition that weekend. I would have just over three weeks for intensive study, filling Moleskine notebooks galore and shoeboxes full of photographs, before the paintings were crated up and shipped off to São Paulo.

Despite all the fuss that had apparently surrounded their acquisition so many years previously, remarkably little had been written about him, and them, since the war. Apart from leaving the field wide open for me, it also meant I needed to spend every daylight hour in front of the paintings themselves, all fifty of them, contributing great dollops of what Gombrich calls 'the beholder's share'.[3]

As my research phase drew to a close, the patient Curator took me out for lunch and, over his *petite suisse à la crème* drenched in caster sugar, he just happened to mention – to this day, I cannot be certain just how casually[4] – the widow of an art dealer who came in every year on the last day of the collection's annual outing and who had recently told him a 'wildly improbable story' concerning Golden. So it was inevitable that, next day, armed with his letter of introduction, I should go to meet her.

In a tiny, elegant apartment, where else but on the Île St Louis, she perched like some slender grey dove painted by Picasso and dressed by Patou. Her manners were impeccable and I imagined that, as a younger woman, she must have presided over a *salon* thronged with characters from the artistic and literary worlds I only knew of from books and photographs but she had known personally, even intimately, in any sense of the word you care to use – this was Paris, after all. The walls of this apartment had a more eclectic and richer assembly of art than I had become accustomed to in Roubaix. A small light added a warm glow to a pen and ink sketch of her late husband with a signature that probably made it worth more than the apartment itself.

She pressed a little foot switch and, silently, Earl Grey was wheeled in, with a side order of *madeleines*, good for the memory perhaps. Then, after a few minutes of polite pleasantries, I was allowed to switch on the Foundation's Uher.

'It was in the fifties,' she told me. 'My first husband was responsible for his employers' business in the South of France. It meant frequent travel from Paris and I was most unhappy, for all the conventional reasons. We were *jeunes mariés*, he was passionate but, *hélas*, I knew him to have a roving eye. And we were very short of money.

'He returned from one *voyage* saying we were going to make our fortune. But he would have to keep it a secret from the gallery. Too big for *them*, he said. After another visit to Provence, he was even more excited but, *franchement*, more than usually *sournois*,[5] telling me he would have to go immediately to England to meet the client who was going to put up the money.

'Of course I asked and asked. And he didn't want to tell me anything which just made me more and more suspicious. I think it was simply to get me to leave him alone he said what he said.

'"I just might have found out what happened to Golden.[6] A rich American painter may have discovered his hideaway."

'I asked who this rich American was and he said, "Rembrandt". I was so angry. I thought he was mocking me. I threw things at him until he left the apartment.'

'But was it true?' I asked.

'I never found out.'

'Didn't he say anything when he came back?'

'How could he? He came back in a coffin.'

I stammered apologies. She shook her head.

'It was a long time ago. I married again. But I have taken a particular interest in those paintings ever since, and, for a while I think it was like visiting the grave of my first *grand amour*. That mood passed, but I have become attached to my annual ritual.'

So that was it? Scarcely worth a footnote, far less a mention in the Acknowledgements; or so I thought. As I got up to go, however, she casually handed me a copy of the latest glossy issue of *Connaissance des Arts*, suggesting I just might find it interesting. That night, leafing through it, I came, as she knew I would, on the article about 'The Illustrated House'[7] in the snob-art capital of California and the owner/artist with the distinctive name who had personally illustrated it; perhaps that very man her first husband had gone to meet, dying in the attempt.

So what did I do? Was it the Curator's Michelin-motivated joke, '*Ça vaut le détour*'? Was it that supposedly chance encounter with a French widow? A final throw of the dice? Or was it the bat-squeak of hope that this might just transform my rather earth-bound dissertation into a heaven-sent revelation?[8]

Anyway, I flew to Carmel.

[Two more clicks to 'insert a file' from the transcript of the interviews recorded in Carmel.]

'Mr Rembrandt, Joe! I'd like to begin by asking you about this house and the marvellous *trompe l'oeil* reproductions of masterworks that seem to cover the walls. Could you, perhaps …'

'Listen Bill, you want to hear the story, you need to hear *my* story and the whole story. Start in the wrong place, and you'll not see how this all hangs together.'

'Well, by all means, Joe, in your own way; in your own time.'

'Time, Jeez, that's rationed. But listen up. I never told anyone the *whole* story before.'[9]

And so he began. There were interruptions and enforced pauses. He would get tired, or the day nurse would throw me out. It took *days*. He started right at the beginning, walking round a depression-dead steel mill with his caretaker father. Where *he* saw tongues of fire, his Philistine parent could see only rust. Planning to go to art school encouraged by his mother, he came up against his father's attitude that 'all artists are faggots'. They had a fight which ended with Joe being thrashed and his father having a heart attack. Hearing Joe and his mother *still* discussing art school may well have caused the second, fatal stroke.

The Japanese attack on Pearl Harbour led to Joe being drafted into the Navy before he got started in Art School and while he had plenty time to draw, charging his mess-mates a dollar a time for lightning portraits, his painting was confined to the sides of battleships. At war's end, his mother now dead as well, he went to collect his 'inheritance' from the lawyer who was supposed to be keeping it in the bank. It turned out he'd kept it there briefly, in his own checking account. He looked up his childhood sweetheart and found she was already the mother of three children of 'somewhat doubtful provenance'. He socked the lawyer, kissed the girl goodbye, and went to seek his fortune in New York. It proved elusive.

Washing dishes in an Italian restaurant on 57th Street, living in a cheap room on the Lower East Side. One day, two three waiters took sick. Food poisoning at a guess – too busy to eat out. Only one in back who spoke English. Come to think of it, only one who wasn't some sort of relative, so Signor Spaghetti crammed me into a monkey suit. Sent me out to wait on table.

Usual lunch-time crowd. At one table curious mixture, sober suit and fancy dress, like they were forced to share, but they seemed to know each other. Arguing like New Yorkers. Polite as cab drivers.

'Whaddya talk,' says Sober Suit. 'If the client wants pig's wool and shit described like cashmere, I'll murder Webster's to give it him. I don't have to like his frigging product but I sure-as-hell have to pay the rent and buy groceries.' Fancy Dress came right back at him.

'Jee-zus,' he groaned, 'that's no problem for you. Nobody reading your frigging copy is ever fooled, leastways except the client, but one of my illustrators has to make your pig's ear prose into a silk screen print. Hey, d'y'hear that, d'y'hear that? I should be writing the goddam copy. Louie, can you draw as well as write? I really have a vacancy. I need someone who can draw dogs enjoying powdered brick like it was chopped liver.' Shame, but had to interrupt to take their order.

Caretaker where I lived had a Labrador puppy, colour of a wheat field. Drawn pastels of it all summer. Trouble was, caretaker had no taste, not even in his ass. And anyway, been too lazy, just too goddam tired, to try and sell him, or anyone, a sketch. But something got to me. Next morning, hauled the portfolio from under the bed. Put half a dozen of the best in an envelope with my name and address on the back.

Thought I'd be washing dishes again but they were still short of waiters so, as luck would have it, was out there when Mr. Fancy Dress came in at noon. Tell you something; what struck me most of all. He was wearing a *different* set of fancy clothes. Just didn't know anybody that time that had two of anything, except maybe socks. Wasn't alone, but seemed a quieter meal that day. Managed to be there as he got up to leave. Just shoved the envelope at him, saying something like 'You wanted dogs,' and ducked back into the kitchen. Don't know what I expected. Certainly wasn't to see the guy come bursting into the kitchen and come over to me like a cop.

'You draw these?'

When I nodded, he just said, 'You're coming with me.'

Went like a lamb. Never went back. Heard that Spaghetti figured I'd been arrested for selling porn. By evening, I'd drawn two more things: an illustration for a dog food advertisement *and* an advance twelve times what I'd been paid for washing dishes.

The agency was 'off Madison' like a theatre is 'off Broadway' but it was great training. And if I was getting less than I could have gotten elsewhere it took me a while to figure that out. Thought I was rich. Spent a lot of spare time in galleries, mostly MOMA; my second mother – joke, Bill.

Started going to an evening class. History of Art. Like I got religion. Suddenly, could *see* in every direction. Didn't drink or smoke for about a year, so high. Fancy Dress liked me but, when they lost the dog food account, he had to let me go. Took the train to Chicago, got a swell job within a couple of hours and stopped by the Art Institute – before I even found a place to live. Next three-four years, pretty much worked my way across America from one major art gallery to the next. Then sold a whole bundle of work to *Saturday Evening Post* – 'move over Rockwell', I thought – and reckoned I'd got enough saved to take a year out and 'do Europe'.

Joe started off in Paris but, after seeing the Mona Lisa, decided to 'go back to where it all began rather than where it was happening now'. Within less than a week of arriving in Florence, Rembrandt lost what was left of his money and his virginity, more or less coterminously.

In order to keep body and soul together, Joe turned his natural mimetic skill to use, and set up his pitch outside the Duomo where he was talent-spotted by a local entrepreneur who admired his reproduction of 'Venus on the half-shell'.

You'd have liked the guy, Bill. One part practical, one part smart-ass and, I guess, a dash of philosopher. Practical side was all about finding materials the right age; paper, wood, not so much canvas for the earlier stuff. If he couldn't lay hands on it and there was a client hungry for the stuff, he knew how it could be crumpled, soaked in all kinds of stinking stuff, smoked, burnt, pricked full of holes, the whole treatment. Listen, even Michelangelo did it.[10]

Even had a code of conduct. Called it his frigging philosophy. Actually painting an Old Master, he kept telling me – to keep me sweet and feeling safe – *that's* no crime. Otherwise every artist is a criminal, right? What sails closer to the wind is selling it. Depends what you actually say. If it's the client who believes it's genuine or, better still, if the tame expert he's paying money to for the collection he's building can be coaxed into saying, 'reasonably satisfactory provenance', then you're probably in the clear – with a good lawyer. And if that expert always happens to get the best table and some *genuinely* aged wine at the restaurant he's been recommended to take his client to – need I go on.

Another thing; he never overcharged. Reckon that was the real smart bit. Price, especially some of the crazy prices paid at auctions, says something about a painting. So, if there's a hint of a bargain in what he asks there's the chance to say later the discount was some sort of implied, unspoken hint that it just might not be, but then again it had *seemed*, so genuine. He was surely some kind of Old Master himself.

By the time I'd gotten back to the States around five years later, I'd aged ten years mentally, and I knew more about painting, and about art forgery, than maybe just a handful of the 150 million others in the US of A. Didn't quite know why I'd come back, except, perhaps, that my *padrone* had just died of lead poisoning – from a Beretta.

Fascinating stuff. An eye-opener. But this was not getting Bill Maguire nearer to useful knowledge and the loud clock in Joe's bedroom, which he couldn't hear, reminded me every second, every cuckooed quarter of an hour, how time was running out. Although he seemed stable, I had a horror of him dropping out of his pulpit before he got to the crucial part of his sermon. My various reasons for being in Carmel were beginning to look of rather 'unsatisfactory provenance'. Still, there were his pool, his amazing paintings – how would 'previously painted by Picasso' read in a sale room catalogue? – his porterhouse steaks, which I drank with white wine because to me, then (and now), most Californian reds were *non potable*. Like those tame experts in their recommended restaurants, I wanted to believe there was a good reason for my being there and that my knowledge and hard work entitled me to enjoy myself. Inside every honest man, there's a dishonest man; perfectly content to be there.

Joe picked up his story at a point 'some months later'.

New York winter grim. Heard from some guy Fancy Dress was Creative Director of an agency in Miami and, for no better reason than that, went down to Florida. Simply turned up in his office. Seemed pleased to see me. Didn't have a job to hand out but, for old time's sake, gave me some freelance work. Just so happened one of the assignments was for a cruise line. One time, when I took in some drawings, met their Vice-President of Promotions.

Fancy Dress had managed to double book lunch. Told this guy he'd get more pleasure out of lunching with 'my brilliant new Art Director, Joe Rembrandt'. Besides, his ulcer was playing up, and so on, and so on. Slipped me a hundred bucks and whispered not to go to the diner across the street. I took the guy to a real swell Italian place. Tell you the best bit. *He* insisted on picking up the tab and I got to keep the C note.

The veep began to tell me all the ideas he was dreaming up to make cruises interesting 'in a cultural sense'. News to *me*! Hell, always thought cruises were the interesting way to get laid – 'in a cultural sense!' But when he told me he wanted to organise *art* lectures and *painting* classes and the company was buying another ship for round-the-world cruises, I flagged down the wine waiter.

By the time we left, one well-oiled veep thought *he* had persuaded *me* to give up a well-paid job at the agency to become his new Director of Cultural Programmes.[11]

To begin with, hired experts but, after one cruise, seen enough of aca-frigging-demics. Could do a better job myself. Told the veep I was going to experiment. A course on – chose the title as I spoke – 'Ten Paintings that shook the World' in which – made up the program in my head – folks would not only learn about the paintings, the artists and so on but have the chance to paint their own Old Masters!

Ridiculous? Sure. Vulgar? Don't mind. But they were a great success. Not only that, sold the idea to Fancy Dress – Create your own Canaletto! Marketed it pretty damned well. Got myself a percentage of the gross, and a fee for designing the numbered canvases, then painting half way across each one so he could photograph these for the kits. Said on the box illustrations showed just what could be done 'by an *untrained* artist'. Told him preferred 'self-taught', but he told me to leave the copy writing to the experts! Got a raise from the veep too. Not all bad, was it?

When other cruise lines began to copy our ideas, Chairman and his wife decided to check it out. Booked themselves onto the two-week cruise that lets passengers ashore in Venezuela to buy their hash and then staggers back through the Islands while they smoke it. Both of them joined my class but pretty obvious he'd rather have his turpentine straight up with a twist. Found myself spending more and more time guiding her brush.

If there hadn't been some unexpected rough weather might have been okay, but we picked up the tail of a hurricane. When the bar came up too suddenly underneath it, Chairman broke his elbow, and spilt his drink. While the ship's surgeon had him sedated, she came to my cabin for personal tuition. Figured this was one shipboard romance better not survive the walk down the gangway.

At first, seemed I was going to be lucky. Didn't call me like she said she would, so dropped my guard. Turned down a job with Fancy Dress. He'd moved the painting kit business to California, his home state where his kid brother was in construction or something. Just gotten that letter in the mail when the veep called me into his office. Told me she'd booked herself on the next cruise, travelling solo.

So O.K. Remember I told you the cruise line was buying another ship? That was what saved me, for a while anyway. Told the veep didn't want to lose my job – not just yet anyway. Guess he liked me. Knew it wasn't all *my* fault. Sailed away before she found out. Now where did I learn to be so devious?

Much as I'm sure you'd enjoy Joe's account of the journey through the Panama Canal, the stop-over in Tahiti where two husbands deserted their wives and how Australia, in his (forgivable) view, is a cultural desert, it would get in the way of the point of his telling me all this, which was to let me know that one member of his steadily dwindling art class was a younger woman, younger than Joe certainly, and, unlike almost everyone else. For a start she didn't seem to be Jewish and she wasn't from Florida or New Jersey but Scotland; something altogether new in Joe's experience. It wasn't so much, he claimed, that he concentrated on her but that, as numbers melted away in the heat, she was the only one who seemed genuinely interested and, what's more, knowledgeable. Let me tune Joe in again somewhere in the Indian Ocean, approaching the Red Sea.

Finishing my nightcap and stubbing out my daily cigar when the barman placed another balloon in front of me and, this time, unstoppered a decent cognac. Poured a pretty generous gill and told me this was with the compliments of the lady at the table in the far corner. Now that had never happened before, well not on this cruise, and I liked it. Picked up the glass, turned round, took not my first but my first *serious* look at Margot Orr, and walked over to say thank you. She invited me to sit down and, in a sociable kinda way, said, 'Tell me about yourself.'

And when I got up again it was nearly dawn. She'd heard my entire life story. Seemed especially interested in my Italian experiences; *painting* experiences! And all I knew about her was she'd been ill for a while and this cruise was part of her rest cure.

It had been about the second or third week of the cruise before I'd really noticed her existence. Wasn't pushing herself forward, or complaining, like some of those rich American bitches, that I was spending too much time with the others. Actually seemed to know something about art too, especially modern art. When I'd mentioned a couple of artists and didn't have a picture to show on the Epidiascope, she'd urged me to 'paint something in their style' so they could all see what I meant. Of course I liked that, rising to the challenge.

Could see she was *almost* attractive. Close up, and after two cognacs, almost *very* attractive. Curly, red hair she pulled right back and that lay like a shag-pile rug on her head. Squarish chin and thin lips. Grey-green eyes. Nose had a dark freckle on the tip. Could have covered it with make-up like an American would, but she hardly even used lipstick. Complexion a bit too pale. Am I giving you the impression

I liked the look of her? Tell you, by the time we anchored off Naples, and probably because she was the only woman on the boat younger than me, I think I'd convinced myself I could fall in love with Margot Orr and her Scottish burr.

She'd said nothing encouraging, but, after our very respectable all-night session, there was some kind of relationship building. Could hardly wait to take her off and show her Florence, Siena and San Gimignano.

That art excursion was an optional extra. Turned out only five passengers, two couples and Margot had signed up. The rest had streamed ashore to eat pizza, 'just as good as any you could find in Paterson, New Jersey,' as one blue-rinse remarked.

Jeez, Tuscany was truly wonderful, like coming home. I was enthused about the place, the paintings, the ink-stained pasta, the stylish people and, in the process, getting to be somewhat besotted with Margot. We'd gotten into the pattern of walking around like three couples and, on a starlit night in a cobbled medieval street in San Gimignano, found myself arm in arm with her, dropping back a little behind the others.

'Professor Rembrandt,' she said very quietly, 'this is wonderful.'

'Please, it's Joe.'

'Joe.'

It had to be the moment to strike, or, if it wasn't, it seemed pretty much like it. Either that or I just got frigging carried away.

'Margot,' I said, 'would you ever consider marrying me?'

Appalled at what I'd just heard myself say. Have to admit I'd been thinking of something more basic. She turned, looked up at me, like she was weighing up the odds. Didn't speak. Didn't answer. Just put her arms round my neck and kissed me gently, like she was submitting to her destiny, or, more like, sealing my fate.

Even so, from then on, couldn't imagine a more decorous pair. Dinner together, of course, but always with the other couples. Besides, company policy against dating. Back on board, walked Margot round the deck, never touching her, then, if there was no one around, pecking her on the cheek at her cabin door. But, oh boy, how we, well *she*, talked and planned. Told me she'd been working in London in an art gallery, and had a little cottage up in Scotland some place. Sounded romantic, especially when she asked me if I'd mind going up there to get married. Could do that in Scotland after only three weeks residence. Now *she* was the one cracking on the pace.

What was amazing was how much I still didn't know about her by the time we reached Southampton. Somehow, when we talked, she was always getting me to tell her about my painting and how I managed to 'reproduce' famous paintings so accurately. Happy to talk. Wanted to impress her. Wanted to see her eyes widen with amazement. With that sort of appreciation, adoration even, it did seem a little bit like I was falling in love.

Night before we docked, wrote out a short cable to the veep, resigning with effect from the end of the month. Handed it over before breakfast and was washing down my scrambled eggs with the last decent cup of coffee I expected to get for months when the Captain's steward brought me a note. Seems the Captain had gotten a cablegram from the Chairman telling him to throw me overboard or, failing that, put me ashore at the next port. Paid me *three* month's salary in lieu and asked me to leave quietly at Southampton. Didn't tell him I was already packed. Lucky too; managed to catch my own cable and tear it up.

Joe's doctor arrived at this point, bringing that session to a close. I have to say it took some serious internal debate to persuade me to stay any longer and listen to what was fascinating but, to all intents and (my selfish) purposes, irrelevant – and excruciatingly time consuming if one has a thesis to write against a deadline. Yes, it was a neat little story; but there was nothing I could quote in my thesis with the swanky footnote, 'Personal interview – no, call it "private conversation" – with the artist.' My grand plan was slipping again. In fact, I had more or less told myself that the next session would have to be the last, and either, in the words of my favourite Sunday newspaper, I would have to 'make my excuses and leave,' or just slope off and leave him to wonder – grimly, I thought, it wouldn't be for long – what had become of me.

Mind you, I was already fond of Joe. I *wanted* to be there with him and, if that was what he wanted, let him unburden himself. He did seem to want to get things off his chest and the story had me hooked. It was just the time thing; the longer I stayed, without digging up useful nuggets of Golden, the less time I had for writing and refining my dissertation.

As it happened, I met the doctor coming back out of Joe's room and he made a point of thanking me for spending so much time with him, saying it was taking his mind off the pain and he hoped I could keep it up. If I had really wanted to go, I should have gone at once because, the next minute, fate fired a barbed harpoon.

Behind the doctor's back, and he didn't turn round to look, a bold-as-brass blonde swung along the corridor toting an expensive leather brief case, glanced appraisingly at me, and disappeared into Joe's room. At first glance, she seemed like the kind of awesome American that is reputed, among libidinous academics who circle the globe attending conferences, to eat art historians for breakfast – except they probably wouldn't be invited to stay for breakfast, nor even, to translate this into English idiom, to come up for 'a quick coffee *but nothing else!*'

That was all that happened, outwardly, or so I thought at the time. Inwardly, I think I was quite stirred. In England, we weren't quite as used to professional women and the sight of her that day, in a 'business' suit, with *trousers*, might even have been as much a turn-on as if she had appeared in a too-short gym slip and pigtails, suggestively sucking a lollipop (not that that wouldn't have been worth seeing too).

The next session with Joe came and went. He took me through his first week or two in Margot's flat in Hampstead, her sketchy account of her work in a Cork Street gallery and the fact that she seemed to have, as we used to say, 'private means'. As the basis of a long-term relationship, it seemed barely adequate. But Margot *was* interested in modern art and as the days went past they seemed to find more and more to share.

Joe boasted how he had painted a 'Turner' for her that might have been the same scene done by the Master, maybe an hour or so after the very similar one they'd just seen hanging in the National Gallery – more convincing and more saleable as a forgery, he explained, than a straight reproduction – and how this seemed to excite, even arouse, his fiancée.

Margot had been somewhat at a loose end after an 'illness', never specified and Joe was too polite to probe; but, despite a relatively lowly job, seeming to have resources more than sufficient to let her make her own choices. She'd finished up on the cruise, attracted, she said, by the prose poem about the 'Art History and Practice' cultural programme, and no less intrigued by the lecturer's very apposite name!

She wanted them to get married in Scotland and although Joe, brought up on the instant gratification that is America – witness Las Vegas weddings and Reno divorces and the shuttle bus that ferries people between – couldn't get his head round the three week residence requirement, they made it up to Edinburgh and checked into the 'best hotel'. I liked his one-liner about using a sun dial to measure the time it took the hot water to come. His description of her lawyer, with his Morningside accent, pinstripe suit, bowler hat and tightly rolled umbrella, spelling out politely but euphemistically the details of what we'd nowadays call a pre-nuptial contract, made him seem very real. The man didn't want to actually *say* he wouldn't get a penny if he didn't behave himself, and wouldn't inherit either, in the unlikely event of a much younger Margot dying first but, when Joe read the fine print, every such angle had been covered.

They married in an Edinburgh Register Office and honeymooned in her cottage, in the Scottish Borders. He spent some time painting, but not the gentle grandeur of the Borders, Scott's view from Bemersyde, the Eildons, Ettrick and Yarrow. Instead, she seemed intent on putting him through his paces, turning out convincing copies of other men's views. It was there they had their first row.

Think Margot was just a tad drunk. Told me ought to be glad I had the gift; being able to create such 'genuine' reproductions. Should be *proud* of it. Then she hit below the belt, saying I ought to be grateful she was able to support me and indulge me to do it all, just when it suited me.

Spent some of the night sulking. But when the only fire died and I was nearly frozen, remembered I was supposed to love her and went to bed. She forgave me! In the morning, she actually suggested we go south, somewhere warmer. That had to be appealing. Cottage had what realtors call 'charm,' but sure as hell didn't have central heating or anything like decent plumbing.

Couple of days later, we were off. She drove. Me, I was too nervous about narrow roads and cars coming towards you on the wrong side but, by the time we'd gotten halfway to the airport, was ready to take even that risk. She had this ability to look round at me, take in the view *and* talk; all at the same time.

Then, sitting right there on the spot where Cézanne painted Mont St Victoire, not only painting the same scene but exactly as *he'd* done it; gave me a real buzz. Margot was delighted, until she saw I'd signed it 'J Rembrandt after the style of P Cézanne'. Damn cross about that. Said it cheapened a perfect example of the talent I'd been given. What the hell, I thought. Painted out my own name. Guess it did look better after that. Less cluttered.

Took several weeks of sun, Cézanne, and sex, in a small hotel in Arles, till I felt it was time to move on. Oh, and another thing haven't told you. Margot spoke perfect French, real fast, and made sure we were really well looked after. Even so, having to use a second bedroom as a studio wasn't ideal. Didn't have a north light for a start. Margot got busy; on the phone a good deal but I couldn't follow a word of it. Came back one afternoon with someone else in tow. Took an instant dislike.

'Sweetheart,' she said, 'this is Monsieur Sauteret, one of the local realtors.' The guy looked down at his boots and tried not to look smug. 'He thinks he might have just the perfect place for us. He'd like to take us there. I said we'd go straight away. You don't mind, do you?' Thought about saying I had a 'meeting' but, what the hell.

Piled into his car. He and Margot gabbled away. I looked at the scenery. Some scenery! Ever wonder how Nature made something as frigging beautiful as an olive tree? Silvery green leaves, tortured branches, light and shade. Wonderful!

After about twenty minutes, civilisation disappearing in the rear view mirror, we pulled up outside a decent-sized farmhouse. Walked round the back and there, facing north, was a huge skylight; imagined it straightaway as a studio.

Sauteret saw I was interested and waggled the keys kind of suggestively. Followed him round the front and he unlocked the door. Door was so attractive Marcel Duchamp could have signed it, hung it in a gallery and got 50,000 bucks. Made a mental note to practice *his* signature. Margot was dashing around opening shutters and windows and running round like she owned the place.

On the way back sat beside Sauteret, with Margot poking her head between us chattering. Could hardly take it all in. Seemed the building had been lived in once by an artist, some 'Englishman' who'd licked the property into shape, and put in that window. Light was superb. Back at his office asked Sauteret who was this English artist and he pulled the file.

'It seems that we have received our instructions from the lawyers,' he said. 'The owners have never been here but the letters are always in French so it is all very straightforward. We maintain it but the property has been empty for many years.'

'But what's the owner's name?'

'The lawyers refer to it as the *Propriété Golden*,' he said. I nearly fainted.

He nearly fainted! Jesus Christ, the mother lode! And then, just when it all seemed to be coming out, Joe winced a bit and the day nurse spotted it. I was sent out while he had some medication and then she came after me to say she'd sedated him and, all things considered, it wasn't a good sign. She'd have to ask the doctor if it was sensible for him to be talking so much. So much! Hell, he'd only said *one damned thing*. If I had to go in there and slap him, I wanted more and I wanted it now. And then things got even worse.

I'd intended to fly back in a couple of days, on the Laker Skytrain, and that meant being at their offices to queue for tickets on a first come, first served basis and, once allocated, the tickets were non-refundable. Decision time: it wasn't so much my whole life that flashed in front of my eyes, rather my whole career. Even if I had to kidnap him and beat it out of him, I wanted more. *Then* he could die. Yes,

I'm ashamed of what I thought then, but can you just imagine the frustration? I told the nurse how much I appreciated the way she was looking after Joe, how I would take it easy but I was sure his talking with me actually helped him. After all, the doctor had said so. She wouldn't be convinced. So, I had the whole of the rest of the day to work on my dissertation and part of the next morning, because she wouldn't let me in there until after the doctor had been and given the thumbs up. I ran into the room and with the reels of tape spinning.

You see Bill, Golden started off a *totally* conventional painter; turning out Scottish landscapes, rooks and seagulls dropping down behind horses plowing brown fields; hedges, and trees with moss on one side; cottages with smoking chimneys and churches with steeples poking into a cloudy sky. Total crap! Only fit for jigsaw puzzles. Whole picture greens and browns and boring detail. And his jokey little logo in the corner, big A with a G sheltering under it like some cattle brand; talk about swank.

Then, one day, the guy turns left instead of right and walks by mistake into a major show of the Delauneys. Both of them; nearly thirty canvases. Blows his mind. All these rainbow-coloured circles; those stretched Eiffel Towers; again and again and again, each time different. Goes crazy. There he is, in wet, cold grey Edinburgh, selling his frigging awful paintings for shit-silly prices, because even sillier people actually *like* the boring sort of garbage he paints, beautifully drawn, with a vanishing point you could stick a thumb tack into; so goddam golden obvious.[12]

Must have been more to it I guess, but seems he simply got up next morning and left for France.

Money not a problem for the guy. His 'jigsaw puzzles' sell all over the British Empire, even America for Heaven's sake. Just feels he can't *do* them anymore. All he wants is to be a soul mate of Sonia; some sort of rub-off of Robert. Starts off in Paris. Rents an atelier; haunts the galleries and the dealers. Takes a few months, but soon knows more about his idols than they knew about each other; and they were brother and sister for chrissake!

Back home, dealer and wife both going nuts; money wells threatening to dry up. Been used to it by the bucketful. Golden was well off, capital-wise, but now he isn't turning out a couple of oil paintings a month for a market that could take a dozen. Dealer pissed off. Never put Golden under contract. Been such a regular supplier; dealer had such a nice business going never gotten round to it.

Golden's frustrated too. Has real skill. Can draw, and handle his tools. But there's some sort of block between his eyes and his hands when it comes to putting *new* images on canvas. *His* Eiffel Towers almost seem to have moss growing on one side! Heart bleeds for him but, tell you, this guy's persistent. Year or some after, rents a room and studio from some old girl who runs a shop on the ground floor selling art materials and chinoiserie, you know what I mean; brushes and black ink for calligraphy and these wooden signature stamps; they were all the rage. Turns out the old girl had actually *known* both of them, Sonia and Robert. Then, out of the blue, the old girl's daughter comes home to stay. Her much older husband just died. She and Golden take one hard and a couple of soft looks at each other and, within a week, they're upstairs together. That's Gay Paree for you! Seems to have been the golden trigger.

What the old girl tells him about how *they* painted, being in love again, wanting to do something for Ghislaine, the daughter; wanting to show her what he really has inside him that's just bursting to come out onto canvas, sends him off on some sort of painting frenzy. In scarcely more than a month, five weeks at the very outside, Golden has turned out an almost unbelievable fifty canvases.[13]

I'd actually seen them; the whole Golden Month, in Fort Lauderdale, month or two before that cruise. Blew me away, Bill. Just seeing what one man could do and how he was frigging born again as an artist, in just thirty or forty days. Can you just imagine what it feels like? Liked it so much I bought the book.[14] First four or five are real peculiar but, because you can work back to them from what comes later, you begin to make out ideas, motifs, colour schemes, shapes, juxtaposition and all that. Know what I mean?

Maybe just a few days into his binge, something glorious happens. Prison bars melt in the warm sunlight and the guy walks out into the landscape – but it's on another planet. Know early Mondrian; or the *young* Rothko? No, well I sometimes wonder if Golden's paintings look like how Mondrian might have developed if he hadn't gotten that studio looking out on a frigging railroad siding.[15]

Poor bastard didn't so much stop as nearly *die* of exhaustion. The two women had him hospitalised. When he could take anything in, Ghislaine tells him he simply has to rest; moves him away from the studio to a friend's house, in Argenteuil, just north of Paris.

Turns out, while he's off convalescing, the mother meets up with one of her boy friends. Don't get me wrong, I mean they were both in their late seventies. Tells him all about poor, inspired Monsieur Golden, who's just collapsed from overwork. 'Show me', says the old guy, out of politeness, but, when he's allowed into the atelier, nearly has a stroke.

Next to no time, rumours about the 'Golden Month' running like wild-fire. Galleries start sniffing around. Ghislaine and her mother fight them all off, saying he'll make his mind up when he's good and well. Nobody knows where he is. Just adds to the excitement. One of the newspapers with an Arts page runs an interview with the old guy who milks it for all it's worth and the story gets syndicated. This is where Mrs Golden comes back into the story.

Dealer sees stories about 'a new goldmine' and tries to stake his claim. Like everyone else, he's sent packing; feels pretty sore. Back home he goes and straight round to see abandoned wife. Doesn't take long to persuade her the allowance Golden's been paying is a damn sight less generous than she's truly entitled to, for all the pain and embarrassment he's caused her, and so on. And when she hears what some people are saying his new paintings could fetch, she takes the boat train and hires a Parisian private eye.

Way this guy works, Golden's tracked down in forty-eight hours and, pretty soon after, she's on his doorstep. Timing's perfect, or she might have had to scratch her rival's eyes out. Seems Ghislaine and her mother had gone to a family funeral up in Roubaix. Golden's well enough by now and he's either careless or just plain bored enough to answer the doorbell. Wife barges her way right in. Doesn't just ask; *demands* he ship the paintings back home.

Idea of parting with even one of them is a total no-no. In his mind, it's one complete piece of work, his new oeuvre, Opus 1 of his new artistic life. Downright refuses to hear of it.

So she says her 'Paris lawyer' is already drawing up papers. She'll have the whole lot seized until her claim is heard; might take five years, just to come to court. He'll have to choose – give her half now or all of them later; much, much later. But Golden's just as good at lying; well, I guess, not so good. His lie was financially dumb. Tells her she's too late. Already made an outright gift to the Orangerie because that was where he'd been 'reborn as an artist'.

But she believes him; storms off. She's scarcely out the door when he begins to like his own idea. So, *his* lawyer gets instructions. Acts *tout de suite*. Gallery Director has it splashed over the newspapers. Ghislaine and her mother see it at the railway station setting off back to Paris.

Wish I'd been there. Flaming row; old woman says such wicked things about Golden even her daughter is shocked. So shocked, throws her mother out, of her own house, and jumps into Golden's arms. Next morning they've vanished; just plain disappeared; huge hullabaloo. French police accused of total incompetence. Old woman even accused by one newspaper of double murder. Gallery moves like a greased frog. Golden Month goes on show and nobody, just nobody with any sort of reputation, can admit to not having been to see it.[16]

Now, here's this guy, Sauteret the local realtor, telling me the studio was where Golden disappeared to. Leastways, that's what I *thought* he was telling me. You bet some doubts began to creep in. 'Now hold on, mister,' I said. 'You may not know much about this but if the guy who owned this is who I think he is then I need some frigging proof.'[17] This gets Margot upset. Tells me that, as an artist, should be asking if the place *suits* me; not whose ghost haunts it.

'Okay, Margot. I know *that* but, hell, if somebody suddenly offered me the chance to live in the *original* Rembrandt's studio, don't you think I'd be excited?'

. Despite it seemed to annoy her, I just badgered Sauteret for more information. Shifty bastard. All he'd tell me was they'd been approached by the lawyers, asked to find a tenant. Hadn't even known the property was on the market. Next day, Margot tells Sauteret we want to go back and look at the place on our own; see if it's just right for us. Drive out there; open up all the shutters this time. Some of the rooms haven't seen daylight in a long, long time.

On the way over, tell her all I know about Golden, how I'd flipped when I saw the Month in Florida. She listens and seems to lap it all up. On one point, it came back to me afterwards, actually seemed to correct me; I think it was about when he went to Paris; it reminded me how she'd done that on the cruise. Kept asking myself how in hell I'd stumbled on the answer to a mystery been puzzling the art world and several police forces for years, but Margot said just see it as a sign it was all meant to happen. So, wander up the overgrown garden with her and turn to look back at the house. 'I *want* to live here, Joe,' she says and kisses me. And that was it settled. Went back on her own into Arles to sign up and get some things delivered. Wanted us sleeping there that night!

Alleging he was feeling much better from talking, Rembrandt managed, at this point, to persuade his minders to take us into the gallery in Carmel which had this small, exclusive restaurant on the upper floor. We sat surrounded by unhappy Hoppers, some seeming so new the canvas still looked wet. We'd barely sat down, not even America's compulsory glass of ice water on the table nor any decision made on which dressing we wanted on the inescapable salad, when the mystery blonde came towards us. I'd even started to get up; you know, typical English good manners, when Joe said, 'Yeah, Bill, can you leave us just for a couple of minutes?' Talk about feeling robbed! Even so, it seemed to me that, this time, she and I exchanged something approaching meaningful glances. I'd be revealing my male chauvinism if I said what I told myself *her* glance meant but mine said, 'I think I could really fancy you, if I worked on it.' My glances can pack in an awful lot; it's the training in Art History.

I was returning from the Men's Room five minutes later, thankfully unmolested this time, when I saw the man who'd been coming out of the place that night, now wearing a *different* revolting plaid jacket and being forcibly ejected by two of the gallery staff. The blonde was on the pavement (correction: sidewalk) outside, talking to him and not looking at all happy. A ruffled Rembrandt mumbled something about being asked for more painting kits and that 'the guy hadn't taken kindly to being told it was "Malévich or nothing" '. [18] The joke wasn't *entirely* wasted on me but the incident seemed to have upset Joe … Then my own thoughts interrupted me. This must be Fancy Dress! Oh shit, was the blonde working for *him*?

There were no more outings.

Next day, Joe needed to rest but I was, in several senses, restless. He'd been on the edge of a major development in his story that, at last, seemed to be relevant. And that American blonde had really got her hooks into my imagination, even if I didn't fully realise it yet. I made up my mind to ask about her when next I saw Joe, some twenty-four hours later. He finally picked up his story pretty much where he'd left off.

Wasn't unhappy to be left alone for a while; chance to wander round and round, drink the place in. All these unanswered questions buzzing in my head. Walking through the rooms and all round the outside seemed to be the best way to think.

I mean, Bill, if Golden had gone off like that, what had he done for money? What had he done for the rest of his life? What had he *painted*? Was he still alive somewhere? No, figured that probably wasn't likely. Couldn't remember when he was born exactly but he'd have to be damned old.[19] But so what! Think about Picasso.

No answers, of course, but, by the time Margot gets back, I think I'm keener on staying than she is. Not old enough to know this, Bill, but when you get to my age you'll look back on one period of your life and say, 'Christ, I was happy then.' Slept there that night; place barely habitable. She'd brought two of these inflatable mattresses, bottled water, all kinds of things; not giving you a shopping list. Point was we took possession! After supper out in the yard, she led me up to the studio, made love to me like she had only just discovered how great it was. Almost maniacal the energy she had. Tell you, I slept that night.

Next morning, woke and, just to begin with, panicked. She's nowhere around and the car is gone. Found a note. '*Eat breakfast and set up your studio. Back soon. Love, M.*'

She gets back in a couple of hours; guy in a camionette rolls up behind her, begins emptying out gas cylinders.

'Did you miss me?' she asks.

Funny thing, I hadn't; totally absorbed in setting out the studio. Even found an old easel propped against the wall, right where Golden must have left it.

'You bet I missed you,' I said.

Tells me to close my eyes and in comes everything an artist could need; few more things besides, *three* sizes of palette knife, a gallon of turpentine; and a couple of stretched, primed canvases. Talk about hint. Trouble is, not ready to be creative yet. Didn't really want to paint any more reproductions but, just for her sake, knocked off an 'original' Matisse and a somewhat so-so Cézanne. Margot took them away. Next day, bright and early, she brings me more canvases. Doesn't say anything but there's a curious air about her; like a slow burning fuse.

Maybe ten days or so on, that black square high up in the corner of the studio, the way into the loft space, crosses my line of sight again; always been vaguely aware of it, somehow. Finally, get curious. Knew a ladder's around somewheres. Thought about Golden while I looked for it.

More I thought more I felt he was a *total* artist; way he handled his paint, way his style developed; incredible in such a short time. Exciting. Baffling. Hell, you'd easily believe it took the guy thirty years, not some thirty forty frigging days. Must all have been fermenting inside him that long. But who in hell knows? Who'll ever know?

Saddest part of all was, in the last three four of his paintings, just a hint Golden's gotten some new vision, just beginning to develop.[20] Jee-zus! What he might have done. Unfinished Symphony. Found the ladder.

Even with a torch, for a moment or so, can't see a thing. Crouching in the entrance, remembered developing my own photographs as a kid; slowly, out of nothing, faint shadows form then become sharp. As my eyes get used to the dark, nearly fall out of the loft. Place is stacked to the rafters with canvases. Just for a moment, thought I'd found a stash of never-before-seen Goldens but, soon as I got my hands on them, realised they were blank – you got that, Bill – stretched and primed, ready to paint, but not a mark on them, just layers of dust. Felt an awful pain. Wasn't the disappointment of *not* making the discovery of the century[21] but a pain, rage even, for Golden. Seemed he's only had this one frigging month. Should have had the whole goddam calendar. Turning to get out of the loft, almost kill myself, making the *real* discovery.

Trip over something. Torch goes sailing and hits the studio floor. Hands clawing at the rafters. Bang my head. Just manage to hold on. When I calm down a bit, see my foot has snagged on a small pile of sketchbooks, tied up with picture cord.

Drag them to the loft entrance. I'm looking to see the ladder when Margot rushes in.

'What are you doing up *there*? Joe, are you crazy?'

Took a few moments more to struggle down the ladder with the books and then I take a knife to the cord.

Brace yourself, Bill. Begin to open the first notebook with Margot. Nothing on the first page. Nothing on the second. The third page blank. Fourth likewise. Fifth, and so on. Don't dare miss a page but from front cover to back there isn't a single frigging mark. *I'm* pretty disappointed, but Margot is out-and-out *angry*. Seems to feel Golden *ought* to have left some sort of record. Seems so goddam sure he *would* have done.

'Only looked through one book, Margot,' I said. 'Let's take the rest down to the kitchen table. Open a bottle of wine, at least be in a decent mood if we find nothing at all.'

And that's what we do. Get through plenty wine, but our mood doesn't get any the better. Drinking about a bottle a book. End of it all? Six bottles empty and so are the sketchbooks. Turn to the last page of the last book. Completely blank. Drop it on the floor – or maybe it just fell out of my hand.

I'm paralytic; Margot out of her mind. Not a nice person when she's smashed. Begins calling Golden all kinds of mean bastard, saying he must have done *some* sketches. Have to tear the place apart! Accuses me of not looking hard enough. Says if I couldn't love her then, leastways, could show some frigging gratitude, after all she was doing for me. Calls me a frigging little forger; chanted it again and again.

Finally threw up all over the table and passed out. Ugly sight. Helped her into the bathroom, undressed her, cleaned her up as best I could and shoved us both into bed; missed out on most of the next day.

Whenever it was, get myself up and have a bath. No frigging shower! Knowing what needs doing, put on denims. Kitchen looks one hundred and ten percent disgusting. Chairs overturned; empty bottles; day-old spew all across the table, chairs, floor and even some of the sketchbooks. Start to pick them up. One was folded open. Last one we'd looked at. Reached the final page and had to admit defeat. Picked it up and began to fold it shut. Know what spiral binders are like. Only seems to work if you keep on turning the pages one way. Try to go back and you get the feeling it's resisting. Turn over the final blank page instead – and there, thin as onion skin, is a letter head from an art dealer in Arles; handwritten bill for '12 Cahiers'.

Forgot about the stinking kitchen. Felt a bit wobbly. Haven't eaten since God knows when but I scramble up the stairs to the studio; grab the foot of the ladder. Black square at the top looks even more solid than ever. Gripping the sides of the ladder so tightly in a couple of steps get splinters in my hands. Hold onto the rungs instead and keep on going. Push my head into the darkness.

Of course, torch already smashed on the studio floor so can't see a thing. Make myself pause, trying to see into the gloom. All I can make out is the mass of stacked canvases. Decide to paw my way forward. Had a hazy recollection loft was floored over the joists. Inch forward. Up there, crawling on hands and knees in near total darkness, my mind catches up with my intuition. We'd found half-a-dozen sketchbooks but looked now like Golden actually bought a dozen. Where were the rest?

Left side of my brain tells me not to be a goddam fool. If the canvases are blank, or at least seem to be; if the first six sketchbooks are blank then, supposing any more even *existed*, every page will be virgin. I was too old to go chasing snow white virgins in a coal black attic. Put my hand forward – and go down into the void.

Didn't fall this time but wrench my back grabbing at joists, rafters, anything. Seems the boards only go about four feet in either direction. Canvases actually resting across the joists. Turn to try and get out.

Hands hurt. Head aches. Whole body weary. As I turn, sort of *contre-jour* effect, I just catch the outline of a shape, right of the opening, back from it a foot or so. Still on all fours, shuffle over and reach out. It's *another* bundle of notebooks.

Feel like one helluva clever guy. Found the clue, done the math. Now here's the school prize. Put my hand out to haul them towards me and they just disappear. Been beyond the area of flooring, balanced across a single joist. Just touching them tipped them over.

They drop like a stone; right *through* the thin ceiling; land with an almighty smack on the studio floor. Reckoned I'd better get down out of there. Margot would have heard the noise and be on her way to investigate. But when I get back down, no sign of her.

Bundle, still in its cord, sitting four-square on the floor in a pile of dust and plaster. Hole in the ceiling looks like torn canvas. Told myself I needed a drink first but when I make it down to the kitchen and see the stinking mess there, decide on coffee instead. Skip the details but, with Margot still out cold, came over the compassionate husband; cleared the place up, after a fashion. Made coffee for two and took it to the bedroom. She looks awful but she's still alive.

Reckoned she'll feel more like facing things washed and dressed than in a robe and with sleep in her eyes, so I fix a bath for us both and help her into it. So it's a fairly clean kind of thick-headed, furry-tongued couple climbing up to the studio some time later. Asks me why I'm taking her back there. Simply say, 'Trust me.' That's enough to start her trembling again. When she sees the dusty bundle, then the hole in the ceiling, nearly collapses.

Hunkering down on the floor, we cut the cord. Then a moment of real hesitation that seems to go on forever. First sketchbook slid off the pile onto the floor between us. Turn back the cover. Jee-zuz H. Christ.

Only a sketch. Hints of colour. Tiny notes in pencil here and there, all over the page. Casual glance tells nothing, but my eye is tuned in. Can see, straight away, this is an artist's study. Work to be put on canvas; cartoon with all the detail he'd need. He'd seen it first in his mind's eye, like remembering a dream then got it down on paper, so it couldn't escape.

Margot gasped in my ear. 'So he *did*. I was so sure.' She croaked, 'Turn the page.'

Maybe those guys opening up the Pharaoh's tomb had the same sort of feeling. For me? Like landing on another planet. Planet Golden. Only managed half a dozen pages. Had to frigging stop. Not only is every page a painting waiting to be born but, seeing the *Golden Month* so clear in my mind, just know these are the next steps. This is what should come *after* that first glorious burst of creation. And here I am, inside the mind of a *real* artist.

'Margot,' I said, 'don't give a shit what's in the rest of these books. I've just got to paint. Hold the ladder still, going to bring down a canvas.'

And Margot looked like a woman in love.

---

1   I *was* going to go through all of this to strike out the clichés but, as they say, life's too short!

2   Actually, let me confess as I re-read all this, none of this 'writer's block' stuff was true. The fact was I had been completely side-tracked by a passionate affair with, sad to say, a sociologist at Birkbeck College, to the extent that I had completely neglected my research and hadn't made any effort to get started on my doctoral thesis. Now that she wanted to concentrate on her finals rather than her climax, I might have more time for my master plan. I really was in deep shit but didn't want to admit it, least of all to myself.

3   *See* Ernst Gombrich, *Art and Illusion*, 1960.

4   Of course it wasn't casual, any more than his *liaison* with her was casual, but I didn't know that at the time. I really was *naïf* then (and now?).

5   'Shifty.' At the time, I had to look it up. Not any more.

6   Now *that* made me sit up. Everyone wanted to know what had become of him but nobody then had the answer which is why he was then said to have died in 19?? I don't want to say too much at this point because it should all become much clearer – well, a little clearer.

7   Bertrand Dhellemmes, 'La Maison Illustrée', *Connaissance des Arts*, Vol XXV, Issue 7. Exquisitely photographed; the man's a genius.

8   More likely it was the combination of a convenient legacy from an aunt, the price of a Laker flight and the sudden renewal of interest from a certain lady sociologist threatening to stop my work in its tracks? Let's face it; autobiographers tend to write their stories in order to portray themselves more favourably. Why should I try to buck the trend?

9   I've had to edit the transcript, of course, but the original tapes are in the safe deposit at the Yorkshire Penny Bank, as I still call it, in Harrogate.

10 Joe was right. Giorgio Vasari (1511-1578), who was a painter himself and a biographer of artists, says Michelangelo would sometimes make a copy of a drawing he'd borrowed then 'smoke' it so that it looked like the original or even *more* like the original, if you like. Then the crafty artist would return the copy and keep the original. At this point, I didn't think I had seen any original 'originals' in the Illustrated House, but I clearly needed to take a closer look.

11 In retrospect, should I have begun to wonder at this point, and to revise my view that *I* had persuaded Joe to let *me* conduct these interviews?

12 This was NEW. Joe, I love you. 'Get well soon.' Can I get you grapes, chocolates, pep pills, anything? Just KEEP GOING.

13 The famous 'Golden Month' that I had been studying in Paris. So far as I knew, from all the sources I had seen in France, the Delaunay connection had never been mentioned before. Joe seemed so sure of all of this but my referees were going to need evidence, examples, convincing argument. Now this I could really get my teeth into. My notebooks were filling up with ideas.

14 Lefebvre, D. (1937), *Le mois doré d'Alexander Golden*, Flammarion, Paris. Biggest problem is the quality of the reproductions, half of which are in black and white and the colour quality is vile. Now, my own views on what had been written there were being seriously challenged by all I was hearing.

15 This, of course, is where that idea came from in my thesis; not plagiarism please – call it research!

16 Now, up to this point, allowing for his clearly knowing the story in detail and for it having gained something in the telling – was I *really* the first person Joe had practised it on – he could have learned most of this from the newspaper and magazine accounts of the period. I had some of them in my various files and folders. It was true Golden had disappeared, 'missing, presumed dead' with his mistress. I had even seen one press cutting suggesting a suicide pact.

17 Took the words out of my mouth. Yes, I was hooked again and now it was getting serious. This was not just dissertation material; this was serialisation rights in *The Sunday Times* and a documentary on television. But there had to be PROOF!

18 'White on White' would be a typical Malévich canvas. Joe was maybe ruffled but not robbed of his wry sense of humour.

19 b.1880. See p.3 – and don't just think about Picasso. Intriguingly, his old friend and rival Matisse, who lived to a ripe old age, also began painting fairly conventionally and then took to Impressionism after seeing, of all things, the work of an Australian painter. But you can look that one up for yourself. I have a private and personal *thing* about Australians that has no part in this narrative, or even this footnote.

20 Bells began to ring. My own mental image of the pictures, at this stage, was not so powerful that I could run each one past my mind's eye like some psychic slide show on my mental laptop but the final painting was quite clear.

What was Joe talking about precisely? I had seen the Golden Month as being self-contained but evolving from start to finish. But finish? I was glad I was using a tape recorder because my mind was certainly wandering – though not for long.

21   It felt like that for me, though. Bugger it. Had Joe been leading me on?

2

By this point (can you just imagine!), he had my total attention but then the hovering nurse insisted on a break. The following day, Joe said he was feeling better but, frustratingly, didn't want to talk. Instead, he'd like to do some painting. I expected him to disappear into a studio. But, as I sat in the shallower end of the pool under a straw hat, thinking about my thesis, as one does in such circumstances, he emerged pushing a trolley loaded with paints, brushes, and so on, and squared up to the white space at the other end of the pool. What I watched, spellbound, had all the air of a conjuring trick. Without so much as a preliminary sketch, he began to apply colour in large bold patches and, as I sat there, damp with anticipation, a water lily began to grow out of the wall. It floated on the surface of a limpid pool with other flowers and foliage around it and reflected in it. I felt like some time traveller who'd arrived in Giverny – and sat in the pond – just as Monet set to work.

My mood changed about an hour before the salad, crusty baguette and glass of white wine I was coming to expect as my due. That was when 'she' unexpectedly emerged from the changing cubicle and walked towards me wearing one of the briefest bikinis I'd ever seen.

'I brought papers for Joe to sign but I don't want to interrupt him while he's working.'

'Thoughtful,' I said, very conscious that I was staring.

'Service,' she said. 'Service with a smile,' also very much aware I was staring.

But the smile did seem to be directed at me and I lapped it up like cream. Absolutely nothing more was said and she slipped into the water, swimming only part way up the pool so as not to get too near Joe. Was this display for Joe's benefit? If so, she was being very careful not to interrupt him. Was it for me? I was vain enough to hope so and as my young eyes tried to see through what little still covered her body I had time to wonder at this. My love life, once the acne cleared up, had so far been rather more wham bam than pursue and woo. I quite fancied the idea of being 'in love' but I didn't think I would ever experience *that* state of bliss. Lust was more my thing.

Later, in her more business-like clothes, she sat at the poolside table with Joe and I was introduced at last, but with no additional explanation, to Anna Glover. There was indeed a piece of paper for him to sign although he grumbled it was something she could have dealt with herself. What was Fancy Dress squeezing out of Joe, I speculated?

Joe went off for his obligatory rest and the front woman for Fancy Dress went off with her signed paper but I found it hard to work and impossible to get Anna G out of my mind until my next session got under way. So perhaps I ought to say a few more things about her. She figures prominently enough in the story after all. She was clearly someone cast from one of the moulds kept for making Californians. The trouble is almost anything I say will confuse the picture.

Anna was almost as tall as me. She was blonde, with straight hair, parted on one side and the longer side strands were tucked behind an ear that had her golden tan, toning with her sleek hair. Her forehead had no trace of worries, not even a crease between the eyebrows. The eyebrows were slightly darker than her hair and a perfect matching, mirror-image pair. The cheekbones swelled just enough to transform her face from featureless into fascinating. The nose, marking the centreline, was just the right length, straight as a die and didn't tilt up or down at the tip. There was a soft furrow on the upper lip like a sandy ripple on a sunny beach. The lips were warm, red and round and parted to reveal orthodontically perfect, shiny white teeth and blush pink gums. All that said, she was no raving beauty; no *Vogue* front cover. But there *was* something: I hate to use the expression but a certain *je ne sais quoi*. I hate to use it, not because it's a cliché but because I can't explain it or justify it in terms of her appearance alone. Whatever it was, and some part of it might have been the sound of her voice, the turn of her phrase, the tilt of her head, the backward glance as she left; whatever it was, when she had gone I was feeling different, not happier because the feeling came with minuses as well as pluses, but, well, just different. Hell, has it never happened to you?

I could go on and on and on but you get the message. This, I tried to joke with myself, was what Art History was all about or, if it wasn't, this would do instead. But I was wary; more than a bit suspicious of her, if truth be told. After all, I'd last seen her in the company of Joe's sworn enemy, who clearly wanted to chisel something out of him and who had been threatened with death. Anna might well be a little chiseller too, and I remembered 'Birkbeck' and *made* myself think of my thesis.

Don't know if I'm getting across to you, Bill. No ordinary experience. Only way I can explain is tell you what happened. Went up that ladder without touching the sides. Pulled a couple of the canvases off the stack; lowered them down to Margot. Might even have jumped down to the floor. Just can't remember; in such a frenzy to start.

Put the sketchbook up on my small easel at eye level. First canvas in front of me. Flexed the palette knife, put a brush behind my right ear, poured a stiff turps and squared up to it. Squirted little worms of colour onto the palette, cut into them and squashed them together; creating the tints and shades I wanted. What began to appear on the canvas was like seeing the face of God!

Margot could have tossed grenades into the studio for all the notice I took of her. Told me later, worked non-stop for six hours, with a look so intense she just crept away and got my bed ready.

End of that six hours, knew it was finished. Knew I'd created something wonderful. Was it original? Good question, stupid question. If an artist's inspired, does that mean what he paints can't truly be called original? Hell, nobody creates in a vacuum. Everyone's exposed to influences. Same influences for hundreds, or millions, of people. But genuine, five-star original artists shake up the kaleidoscope and produce something nobody's ever seen before. Truly believe I did create something original, Bill. But *Golden* was the starting point.

Put it another way. Composer finds a fragment of someone's lost manuscript, writes the whole symphony. Original? Depends whose name he puts on the score.

Next day, smell of coffee woke me. She brought a tray into the bedroom. Could hear the bath running. All came flooding back. More or less jumped out of bed; sank the whole beaker of coffee, wolfed down bread and apricot jam; in and out the bath in two minutes. Almost without speaking to each other, up there in the studio, another canvas clamped in the easel, palette full of rainbow spaghetti, second page of the sketchbook open and ready. State of bliss.

Don't *think* Margot put Benzedrine in the coffee. I was running on pure inspiration. Not so many clues on the second page but, God, I just *knew* what the guy intended. End of the day, Bill, no way of proving if it *was* what Golden would have done but this was *my* shake of his kaleidoscope. Margot didn't interrupt. Came in at odd moments, putting coffee or soup on the windowsill. No idea if I ever touched them. My eyes were telling me clearly what I was seeing. The other parts of my brain pretty well shut down, conserving energy. Had to rework one whole area but, by that evening, finished another painting.[1] 'After Golden', perhaps, like it says in the saleroom catalogues, but this was one *original* work of art.

That evening, more relaxed. Experienced painter, don't forget. Getting near total satisfaction; physically, from sticking the paint to the canvas and the smell of fresh paint in my nostrils; emotionally, just from placing the colours *I'd* chosen, or he'd guided me to choose, in all the right places, then, best of all, simply changing my mind when I saw a better place. Or painting a more satisfying shape. Took a swift look at the third page of the sketchbook; propped it up, ready for the morning. Already working out what the pair of us, Golden and his golden boy, Joe Rembrandt, wanted to do next. Went for a stroll after dark. Remember fireflies, like low-flying stars. Boy was I happy and did I have energy. Worked some of it off in bed, I'm telling you.[2]

Imagine. Up early, bursting with energy, enthusiasm, up for the challenge in front of me, new challenge every morning – but just what I'd trained all my life to be able to handle. Sure there were problems, setbacks, frustration, the whole bit. But it was *so* good.

I was a craftsman, you bet, but getting lessons, masterclasses even, from someone else, someone with something important to teach me. Golden's mind kept sending us both off in new directions. Got to recognise the signs; pencil notes about colours, maybe a few experiments or thumbnail sketches on the opposite page.

Worked my way, almost religiously, through that notebook; one page at a time. Treated it like the Bible. Read a fresh chapter of Revelations in the evening, slept on it and wrote my commentary the next day. Or maybe it was like reading a good detective story and resisting the temptation to turn to the back of the book.[3]

Way I was working felt so good, so well paced. Getting such satisfaction from it I was astounded. Suddenly, it's five or six weeks later. Look around and see nearly thirty canvases propped against the wall. Been so obsessed with each new painting, pretty well forgotten the previous ones. Been forgetting about Margot too; just the commissary keeping me supplied. Paint, turpentine, brushes, food, sex. Almost a routine. Realised it just a tad before she did, glad to say, and suggested we take a break for a couple of days.

Funny thing; *she* was reluctant. Afraid I'd stop painting, although she couldn't quite bring herself to say so. Past half way in that first sketchbook. Taken a month and a half. *My* golden month and a half. Maybe she was getting superstitious. But I'd no plans to disappear! Tired? Sure. But not exhausted like Golden. Fit as a frigging fiddle!

Took our little holiday. Three days sitting looking at Mont St Victoire — then straight back to the studio. As we get there, the little camionette just happens to roll up, with more gallon jars of turps; big, fat tubes of paint; quivers full of brushes.

Looked at Margot. 'Is this is a production line you're organising?'

Made her cross. Said again I didn't appreciate all she did for me and that sent me on another little guilt trip. Took another day off to tell her, and show her, how much I loved her. Then back to business. Ten days later, turned to the last page in the book, ready to study it and think about it.

There was no frigging sketch.

Instead, Golden had covered the page in spidery writing. Damned difficult to read; didn't have glasses then. But what I made out was, after a *week* – goddam it only took him a week, he must be lying – he'd filled one sketchbook and couldn't make his mind up. Start painting, or go on sketching and developing his ideas? Final sentence, if you can call it that, says he'll talk to Ghislaine 'when I'm feeling better'. So what was wrong with him this time? No clue in the sketchbook. And I'd *promised* Margot I wouldn't open the next book until we were ready to do it together.

The hell with that; just couldn't wait.

First page absolutely grabbed me by the balls. Golden had introduced a completely new theme. Till then, it'd been what you'd loosely call expressionist cityscapes.[4] Now, here was something almost completely abstract; patterns and colours that spoke to me of total control over design and execution; almost, but not quite, a complete break. You know what I mean; sort of shift in gear, like from early to late Rothko.[5] Higher speed, fewer revs. But, colour-wise, and the way the forms related to each other, unmistakably Golden.

Simply had to set up the next canvas and begin to paint.

Less to go on this time; design seemed clear enough but the colour hints more sparse; like bare chord structures. Had to improvise more; tried out new riffs. Collected a 'tone row' of different colours on my palette knife; drawing it across the canvas in a dozen different ways, Colours either blending, with a rainbow fringe or running up, down, across the picture, keeping their own identity. Once I'd started, of course, varied and combined these till I had the images just the way I, or he – what the hell, *we* – wanted. Now I was spending as much time scraping paint off as putting it on.

Now who was painting this canvas? Golden's sketch and inspiration, yes okay, but this was my skill and technique, interpreting, bringing it to life; turning telegrams into encyclopaedias. Been painting for three hours before I realised it was late afternoon and no sign of Margot; not like her to be away all that long.

Couple of hours later, just beginning to get dark, she got back. Both had news to tell but she got in first. Said she'd discovered a little gallery in Arles; branch in Provence of a major dealer in Paris.[6]

Had a *superb* range of work and the man who ran it was *really* charming and *very* clever. They'd had such a *long* chat about all *kinds* of modern art, and things. Finally, she had just dropped a *hint* to him that there might be something worth his seeing out at her little farmhouse and fixed up for him to come out to visit with us, when he got back from a trip up to Paris. Wasn't just mad; I was frigging furious.

'Shouldn't have done that without asking me first,' yelled at her. 'This is *my* work. *I'll* decide when it's ready to be seen. Besides, just started on the second book, can't be disturbed.'

That got *her* going. What did I mean 'second book'? Hadn't I promised she would be there when I opened it? May be my work, but it was her 'bloody farmhouse' and she was my 'goddam wife'. Anyway, what did I mean, 'just got started'?

Took her upstairs and parked her in front of the easel. She was nearly poleaxed.

'I never saw that before!'

'Hell no, you didn't. I only painted it this morning.'

'I mean this is a completely *new* Golden.'

'Fuck Golden. This is *me*. *I* painted this. *I* created it. It's *my* work.'

Just shook her head, said quietly, 'It's Golden's; even if he hasn't signed it.'

Swore at Margot and walked out of the house.

Walked up the hill behind the house; bright moonlight; could see my way through the olive trees. Just as well. Never really been right up there before. Made my way to the top, turned and looked back. Sky a blue and black Van Gogh. Night sounds. Earth cooling off after another hot day. Just like me. Very peaceful. Got to thinking, and getting mad with myself for being a selfish artist. Who else did I know ever had it *this* good? Just that, well, time, for the inspired, is in such frigging short supply. Had to use it *all,* had to get on with my life's work. So busy being an amateur philosopher didn't hear Margot climbing the hill. Then she stood in front of me.

'Joe, I'm sorry. I'm wrapped up in this too. You just can't know what it all means to me. I was unkind. Please forgive me.'

Sucker for an apology. Reached out and pulled her down.

'Careful. Mind the bottle.'

Could smell the wine under my nose as she passed it over. Took turns to drink. Reckon we only had a couple of mouthfuls each before I was all for making love.

'No, Joe, please,' she said. 'I think I'm pregnant.'

Lay out there for a couple of hours before we crept back, pretty stiff, to bed.

In the morning, like a man possessed! I was going to work to *create* something; something for my *family*! Me, a father! Margot was going to have a baby; our baby, my baby, wonderful.

Over the next month or more, worked slow but sure through the second sketchbook. Plugged myself into the juice just looking at the next page in the early evening and letting it charge my batteries overnight. In the morning, I was Rembrandt the high-powered robot. Could stand in front of the easel, work five six hours at a stretch. Then the batteries ran down. Didn't always finish a canvas every day now. In fact, it got like three, even four, days for each one. Having to put more of *myself* into every picture. Seemed to bug Margot just a tad, but she was keeping a tighter hold on her temper. And she kept putting off the guy from the gallery. As for me, just *knew* when a painting was finished and, for that matter, when it wasn't. Went at my own pace, but I never stopped.

Well, that's not strictly true. Did try to stop in the middle of the day for the first couple of days after Margot told me she was pregnant. But what with her saying to stop fussing and she wasn't sick and my urge to paint, that didn't last. Then, finally, we had that visit from the dealer. Sonofabitch!

Margot warned me he was due next day. Had to get the studio arranged she said, fold up the empty easel, put it to one side and all. Tidy up, for Chrissake. To begin with, grudged the time but, as I got to arranging the canvases round the atelier, could see they *were* a body of work. Not just individual paintings. Easy for me to put them in the right order but Margot set about numbering them on the back, and giving them titles. Not really titles; simply called them 'Golden Book 1, Number 1' and so on. Used typical blue and white gummed labels and French style of handwriting and numbering; you know, ones and sevens, fours and nines hard to tell apart till you get your eye in.

So anyway; up rolls this art dealer in a big car.

At first, didn't like him. At second, I still didn't like him. Hell, he was handsome, younger than me, probably same age as Margot, and she was all over him. I took him upstairs. Saw my friends round the wall waiting to greet us. First six hung on the wall, rest stacked in order. Smiled at them then forced myself to turn round holding the smile for him. Didn't expect to turn round and see Margot more or less holding him up.

Gets a little difficult this bit; all pretty emotional. I rush to grab him; not for his sake but to take him off Margot. He struggles; not because he doesn't need supporting but because I'm *in the way*. He wants to look at the paintings. And Margot is trying to pull me off *him*. Got to the start of the guided tour, but he just waves us away and sort of floats past the paintings on the wall. Lets me leaf through the other canvases while he leans on the only chair. Over and over again, all he says is 'Mon Dieu, mon Dieu, mon Dieu.' Finally turns to us and says, 'Cognac; then champagne!' Sits at the kitchen table, very quiet for a while, and then it all comes out in a rush.

'You are looking at something quite beyond price; a veritable fortune. This is an *unbelievable* discovery. How did you keep them so fresh, so pristine? You haven't been doing anything to them? That would be sacrilege.'

Jumped up, knocked over my chair, swinging the empty champagne bottle at him.

'You bastard! *I* painted these. Not frigging Golden.'

This time, he really did fall off his chair but, looking back, probably fright more than shock. Thought I was going to kill him. I should have done. Margot wrapped herself round me, hollering, 'Joe, Joe. Isn't that just what we needed to hear?'

Truth is, don't know what I 'needed' to hear. Me. One-time failed artist; only known talent copying other painters' work; a frigging little forger like she'd said. Even now, deep inside, knew something like that could be happening here too. But after all I'd been through, wanted to call myself a *real* painter. And here was this jerk who wouldn't accept it. Shrugged her off and walked out of the room saying, 'Bring the dickhead upstairs.'

And up they came. I took his hand. Seemed scared; maybe thought

I was going to break his fingers; which was not a bad idea. Just pressed one of them against the corner of a painting and as he felt the skin on the soft paint yield he turned to me with a look of complete incredulity; then a flash of cunning.

'Show me,' he said. 'Show me now!'

And I did.

Clean canvas on the easel. Paint-charged palette. He sat down on the one chair. Brought out a packet of those fat Boyars, wrapped in maize paper. Didn't offer *me* one. By the end of the masterclass, there were thirty butts on the floor and he was convinced.

'We are looking at a fortune here, provided...' Didn't like the way he looked at me, the way he talked, or the expression on Margot's face.

'Wonderful,' she said.

All I could say was, 'I need another drink.'

Bill Maguire, open-mouthed art historian, was in need of one too! Here was a collection of gilt-edged; no, I mean solid gold paintings, executed by someone called Rembrandt but *apparently* looking like the work of Alexander Golden and good enough to knock the chaussettes off a Parisian art dealer. Fortunately, for both of us, it was almost time for Joe to rest. Unexpectedly, the doctor arrived, bringing, I now believe, the results of tests. I was banned from Rembrandt's bedroom and used the time to work on my dissertation although I wondered if it was all going to be overtaken by events or revelations. Phoned Laker and said I had no idea when I would be ready to fly back. They warned me I had only a little time before my bargain-price return coupon expired. Just at that moment, I didn't care.

There was a break of twenty-four hours before Joe and I got back to it.

Telling you about that s.o.b. looking at *my* paintings and saying that, provided I was prepared to deny I'd painted them, they were worth a cool fortune.

Hardest part wasn't the suggestion some dead artist's pictures were worth more than mine. Happens all the time, for Chrissake. No. Working on these canvases, for sure I'd known I was being inspired by Golden. But that was the word – *inspired*. Wasn't the dear departed Golden turning white space into colour and form. It was *me*. Me! Okay, so I started out as just a frigging little forger, getting inside the mind of another artist. Imitating his brush strokes, his palette, the whole way he worked. Skill like any other but, don't get me wrong, it *is* a skill. Maybe I had originality years back, in high school, but that seam was worked out, somehow. Now, I seemed to have a *talent* again. Didn't take kindly to the idea of burying it. What was making me sick to the stomach was realising Margot didn't, couldn't, wouldn't even *try*, to see my point of view. Dealer-shmealer wasn't trying to change her mind either.

That evening, they wrung out of me a promise not to say anything to anyone – for the moment anyways. The dealer? You need a name? Robert Strauss. He pronounced it 'Stroes', like toes; got real mad when I called him 'Strouse', like louse, but he sure was one goddam cockroach.

Talked to Margot, ignored me. As a tactic, seemed to be working. She was sweet to me but made it frigging clear she wanted me to go along with it; just get in there and create money with my palette knife. But I wasn't Andy Arsehole painting two-dollar bills.

So, swearing to keep my trap shut, for now anyway, told them to leave me alone to get on with my work. That shut them up pretty damn quick. If the sight of a new batch of Golden's paintings made them greedy, remembering I was the goose, laying Golden's eggs, made them step back a pace. Ordered them out of my nest, saying I was broody, and shut the door.

Looking round, saw all I really needed – all I really wanted. Sketchbooks, paint, brushes, palette knives, turpentine and rags, plus a full pack of Boyars he'd left – and a clean white canvas. Thought 'Rembrandt, the *younger*, in his studio'. Set to and painted.

Painted all that day. Margot brought me food like before, just when I stepped back to look where I'd gotten to. Gave me the energy to get going again. Worked right through the night. Couldn't stop. Too fascinated the way things were developing.

What seemed to run in my mind, all this time, were images of running water; what you could see reflected on it, see floating in it, see looking through it. Running water like a series of distorting mirrors, or lenses that transformed shapes and colours, on and below the surface, on the river bed. To anyone else, completely abstract, but I was being carried *along* this river, the Golden River but on Rembrandt's raft, paddling with my brushes, steering with my palette knife. Seeing visions no one had seen before me. Reflections from the sky and the river bank, debris from upstream memory storms, the river bed, fish and weeds, a total other world.

Around dawn, walked outside and looked up at the sky; positively psychedelic. Sat on the doorstep, rested my head back against the wood and fell asleep. Boy, did I dream! Must have been around the middle of the morning when I woke up and crept back up to the studio. Margot and Strauss already there, with their mouths open.

Heard him say, 'Whatever you're feeding him on, it's about the right dose. How many canvases are there?'

Margot said, 'Thirty-eight, so far.'

He simply breathed, 'Millions of dollars.'

Golden River carried me slowly along for the next couple of months. Spending a week or more on each canvas now. Would take the sketchbook out to the table under the olive tree behind the house; study it for an hour, sometimes two or three, then make my own pencil sketches; try out some colours and shapes on paper using gouache. That alone could take me a whole day. Had near total recall of everything I did, every brush stroke and movement of the pencil; frame by frame. Meant I had all this to draw on working on the canvas itself. Work absorbed me ninety-nine per cent. But still that one percent of my mind was spinning round and around, trying to figure what was going to happen next.

By some kind of unspoken (to me) arrangement, Strauss came about once a week, usually in the early evening. Was tired then, wanting a rest and a drink. Took it outside and let him and Margot gawp at the paintings. She kept on numbering them, using these old-fashioned gum labels. He kept on counting them like he was scared one might be missing. But they were all there; all my children.

About three months on, realised I was coming to the end of the second sketchbook; three four more sketches, and as many blank pages.

Thought I'd get some more canvases down. Gave myself a shock. Loft that had been stacked to the rafters now almost empty. Only four canvases and that trunk; like they'd been synchronised!

Made me feel even more anxious to get the remaining blank spaces filled in. Carried a couple of them over to the top of the ladder. Made my way down with one at a time. Awkward. Each one had to be manoeuvred through the loft doorway while I stood on the ladder then slid down the ladder as I held it above me, stepping backwards down to the studio. Fetched two down and went back to back up for the third time. Wasn't heavy work but tricky. Grabbed the last two canvases, yanked them across to the hole in the wall and clambered onto the ladder. Tugging and cursing but still feeling they were precious and didn't want to damage them. Used both hands and slid them through the opening together. Lent back to get them through, onto the top of the ladder and, all at once, could feel, in slow motion, I was losing my balance. Made a frantic grab for the ladder with one hand. Swung round in an arc. Heels cannoned off the wall. Splinters in my hand hurt so much I let go.

Hit the ground with a colossal thump, completely winded. Landed on my back alongside the wall, congratulating myself I was still alive. But my outstretched foot had pushed the base of the ladder away from the wall. Next thing, it was sliding away across the floor at one end – and sliding down the wall at the other. Couldn't get out of the way. Struck me smack across the shins.

I was yelling, and the ladder had made a noise like a railroad car. Margot and Strauss came running. He yanked the ladder off my legs while she knelt beside me saying, 'Not again.'

'I don't make a damned habit of this, Margot. Get a doctor.'

Think Strauss would have liked to drag me out of the studio before anyone came. But even he had a thin streak of decency. While Margot drove to the village for the nearest phone he systematically turned every canvas to face the wall – then he got me an aspirin!

Shock wore off pretty soon but not the pain. Despite the aspirin I'd swallowed, it was hurting like hell when Margot came back with the doctor. Had run into him in the village. He'd yelled at one of the yokels to call an ambulance and come straight over. Strapped both my ankles and gave me a shot. By the time the ambulance crew were lifting me onto their stretcher, pain was down to a dull ache. Margot held my unbloody hand. Doc gave me another shot in case of tetanus. Felt like passing out when I suddenly remembered.

Whispered to Margot, 'How's the baby?'

Caught her off guard, she glanced at Strauss; after all it was meant to be a secret.

'Fine, Joe. Just fine. Thanks for asking.'

Then I passed out. Verdict was compound fracture of both legs. I'd not be on my feet for some time.

To begin with, too much out of sorts to even appreciate the pretty young nuns in the hospital but, soon as I did begin to take notice of them, Margot wrapped me like a basket of eggs and drove us both up to Scotland. She really didn't care for the place either, she said; happier in Hampstead, in her element in France but she rated Scottish doctoring above French. And the cottage was handy to hide in. Always looked after her appearance. Happy in a romantic way being pregnant. Happy in a 'fulfilled woman' way. But she hadn't come to terms with looking more and more like a sack of potatoes.

Local doctor was someone else from Morningside, like her lawyer, except he'd gone native. Been in Edinburgh but, after some sort of breakdown, he'd taken up life as the local medic. Persuaded Margot the nurse she'd hired for me could look after her too. Didn't so much say as imply that Margot could afford it.

Month or three after the accident, it was coming home to me I'd been interrupted; been in the middle of becoming an artist and fallen off a ladder. Set about trying to tell Margot I wanted to *do* something; not just admire the view or the nurse. Besides, loose ends needed tying up. Where were my paintings and what in hell's name was Strauss up to? Got both answers. The s.o.b. turned up. Say 'turned up' but Margot'd known he was coming; just hadn't gotten round to telling *me*.

Next day, was nursing some medicinal malt after my compulsory short walk, when the pair of them came in together. Give him his due; seemed pleased to see me; genuinely concerned for my health. Great act! Margot, who'd been just *too* damned nice to him in Arles (leastways I thought so, in the odd moments when I was even noticing anything except painting), seemed like she didn't find him so attractive now. Relationship more, what'll I say, business-like. So there he was. Maybe didn't help matters first thing I said was, 'Where the hell are my paintings?'

'Monsieur, you will find absolutely everything where you left it. Even the ladder is still on the floor. However, I have personally taken the precaution of putting locks on all the doors and shutters. And here are your keys.'

Producing them with a flourish they flew out of his hand and landed on the floor. Neither Margot nor I was physically capable of diving after them. So he had to scrabble and put them in my hand. By this time, Margot had sailed over.

'*I'll* look after these, Joe.'

For a week, Strauss tried to be Monsieur Nice Guy. Came with me for my walk; paused 'to look at the view' before I had to ask him to. Then he took Margot round and about, driving her the two or three miles from the cottage to the village and back; gone for hours sometimes. Maybe wanted to see the main road, just to reassure himself he could get away. He wouldn't stay with us, although we had two bedrooms. He stayed at the local inn, in their one bedroom that Margot and I had used when there was a leak in the cottage roof.

Could at least talk painting with him. After all, I damn well knew something about painting, and so did he. So, okay, the guy was a shit, but a damned clever shit. Understood painting as art, not frigging interior decoration, like most of them here in Carmel. Hell, watched a woman in the gallery here choose a painting with a piece of fabric in her hand. Held it up in front of each painting until she found the one that 'matched best'. Hot damn, would you buy books to suit the colour of your drapes?

Doctor had his hands full with the pair of us. My legs mending but still pretty weak; needed a stick most of the time, inside as well as out, stone floors and steps all uneven. Getting bored and better about the same rate, and Margot getting more obviously pregnant. Looking in the mirror did nothing for her mood.

Cunning old doctor in the habit of coming in every day; timing it so he could stay for lunch. No, that's unfair. Nice guy and, in the end, owe him a favour. Was Strauss who clearly needed a break – from being a nice guy, I figured. I suggested he go back, check up on everything in Arles and bring me back some brushes and paints. Only too glad, but Margot reluctant for some reason. Couldn't figure her out. Probably she didn't trust him out of her sight, or leastways out of the country. He was gone another month. Our last good month. Not golden, maybe, but it glowed. Beginning to feel safe without my stick and, with Strauss out of the way, subject of the paintings tended not to come up too often. Able to fuss over Margot like I wanted to.

Then he came back.

That first evening, all sat round the table at dinner. Seen almost nothing of either of them since he arrived in the morning. Said he'd been resting from his 'voyage'. Took pity. Poured a couple of shots of Lagavulin. Loosened his tongue. Began to talk, not so much to me as to Margot, about what should be done.

'The *new* Goldens are in excellent order. I have managed to hang eleven of them in the atelier and I have compiled a simple catalogue. With every canvas the same size, I do not need to repeat the dimensions. How do you think they should be framed?'

About to say something like, 'Get round to that when I'm good and ready,' when Margot answered. As I listened to what she was saying, realised she was describing glass and frames exactly like the Orangerie. Apart from the fact someone had tinted each frame to 'complement' the picture, which was sacrilege, just don't like glass for *oil* paintings.[7] Okay, you need to protect pastel and it's probably fine for gouache but the surface of an oil painting, the texture, the craters and volcanoes, the highlights and shadows – you've simply got to be able to get your eyes right into it all. Started laying out my opinions; Margot listened for while then she blew up.

'Joe, listen here. These paintings are not yours to *experiment* with. They're *Golden's* and they need to be treated like Golden's. You can't risk people *touching* paintings that are worth a million dollars.'

Christ, was I thunderstruck. These were my paintings. Said so: loud and clear.

Margot's face drained of all colour. Strauss looked even more like a horse's ass. They both let me have it.

Strauss took aim first. Perfectly simple. Admired my 'homage to Golden', 'artistic *tour de force*'; might even be worth something to a gallery. A painter, of all crazy things called Rembrandt, who *copied* Golden's style then went off a bit in his own direction. He might even visit it one day; if it was raining.

That left me speechless, so he had the chance to fire his second barrel.

Said I was only thinking about myself and not my wife and mother-to-be. Here was a wonderful opportunity, not only to repay her support and loyalty but a risk-free chance 'to make us all extremely rich'.

'And just who the fucking hell is *us*?'

That's all I gasped out before Margot pulled *her* first trigger, aiming real low.

'Joe, us is us; the *three* of us. Robert has all the right connections, and the credibility to give the paintings provenance. I've already agreed he should be our dealer. This is how I want it to be; for you, me, and the child.'

Damn, that wounded me. Couldn't find the right words without seeming to strike my own child. Probably couldn't have spoken anyway. Rigid with anger, disbelief.

'And Joe; Golden has to be respected here. This is *his* legacy. You're just the medium. I think God meant us to meet and we can't demean His gift by denying Golden, and not giving him the honour *he's* due.'

Tell you, these two people across the table from me were crazy; clean out of their skulls. Never *heard* such a mixture of greed and self-delusion. But what to do? She was my wife, my pregnant wife. And he so badly wanted a share of the loot reckoned he might even be dangerous. Poured another large shot of Lagavulin. Margot pushed a glass across the table to me. Didn't ask her if she really ought to be having it. Just tipped it in there. Pushed the glass back over. Downed my own in one swallow. Numbed the pain.

Jeez-us H! Wasn't arguing where inspiration came from. Inspiration is inspiration; just has to come from somewhere. Okay, Joe

Rembrandt's a master craftsman; forging – if that's what you want to call it – other painters' work. Standing in front of a canvas painting a Picasso, I *am* Picasso. But this was so, so different. The friggers just didn't seem to cotton on to it. Working on these particular paintings in that studio, in the same studio where Golden only managed sketches, I hadn't become Golden; I'd *become* Rembrandt, *Joe* Rembrandt, the *American* artist. And these two wanted to deny it all; wanted to take it *all* away from me. Wasn't even going to be a frigging footnote. Hell no. Couple of things might slow them up.

'Listen! What about the age of the canvas? Freshness of the paint?'

Came right back at me. Margot asked where I'd found the canvases; and who'd put them there. Who else would have gone to that bother? Golden, of course. Strauss simply mocked me. *His* firm would authenticate them. Paintings would be behind glass and, anyway, he'd dry and cure the paint, encourage a bit of craquelure. I knew he was right, knew just how damned easy it would be. Clincher, of course, was the art world would simply *want* to believe the pictures were Golden's. Wouldn't even *want* to consider they might not be genuine.

Reached the point couldn't say any more. Not talking to rational people; sitting opposite a couple of greedy zealots. Margot broke the spell, saying she was going to bed. Strauss whacked too, and groggy from the amount of single malt we'd gotten through. Acting 'mine host' told him not to drive; sleep it off in the spare room. Even so, still seething inside and carried another bottle of Scotch upstairs, twisted off the stopper, threw it in the bin. Brought up a couple of glasses from the kitchen and poured a couple of nightcaps – size extra-large.

Sitting side by side on the bed, neither of us spoke. She didn't seem sleepy; something *really* troubling her. Kidded myself it was conscience. I *was* kidding myself. After another nightcap, she got up, went over to the window seat. Wet and windy outside; nothing to see. Think I was beginning to drop off to sleep when she spoke.

'Joe,' she said, real quiet, 'you're one through-and-through selfish bastard.'

Maybe have been, maybe was, maybe still am, but no one who said they loved me had ever called me that before.

'Christ, Margot, if I *didn't* love you, I'd want to give you such a smack across the mouth for that.'

She looked round at me like a zombie, tears flooding down her face. Nearly paralysed with all I'd drunk but struggled to get up and go over to her.

'No!' she said. 'Stay there; and listen to me.

'These paintings are *mine* and my child's. They're our inheritance and you're *not* going to take them away from us. Don't look so shocked. What did you *think* was happening? Meeting up with you on that cruise was no coincidence. I was *looking* for you, or at least someone like you – and then someone like Strauss.'

My head was an exploding bomb. Simply put the bottle to my mouth and swallowed. What in the hell was I hearing? And seeing? Front of her robe was spilled open. Under her nightgown, swear I saw her belly move as our drunken baby danced in her womb. What was this crazy, frigging woman telling me?

'How do you think we finished up in Arles, Joe? Do you suppose I just *happened* to go into that estate agent's? You'd passed all the tests and I knew you could do it.'

Pain in my head was someone dynamiting away what was blocking the path to the truth. Truth I didn't want to hear.

'Do what, Margot? Jesus Christ, speak English.'

'English,' she says. 'That's some joke. I speak perfect English. But my natural mother spoke French.'

'Your mother? Who the frigging hell's your mother and what's she got to do with all this?'

Margot heaved her glass across the room at me. Hit the stone wall with a crash. Reckon it might have killed me if she'd reached her target.

'My mother's name was Ghislaine.'

And at this point, Joe burst into tears. I was aghast and after hopping from one foot to the other for a moment and handing him a Kleenex I had the presence of mind to ring for the nurse. In she came – but with the blonde in tow. *Her* look seemed to ask what in hell had *I* been doing?

1   And Joe's account *is* credible. After all, Gainsborough used to work at just such a furious pace, painting portraits.
2   Why did I immediately think about Anna Glover? Remember, I told myself, you have a deadline!
3   If this sketchbook exists, it would be a mega-discovery. There are so many questions I want to ask but, as I see him struggling to get the words out, I take the calculated risk of letting him talk to get the story finished and trade it off against what seems, at this point, the unlikely but not impossible event of his dropping off the perch unexpectedly. Another question, of course, was what had he done with everything. And another thing, I don't claim to know it all but, living and working in the art world, I had never heard of this Rembrandt, his work or his talents before they had been mentioned, obliquely, by an elderly Frenchwoman.
4   A wonderful clue that helped my own analysis of the original Golden Month. I was able to identify the dome of Sacre Coeur, but usually inverted, as a recurring motif and speculate about some others. The comparison with Robert Delaunay could hardly have been more opportune but some of the circles allowed me to drag Sonia in too. Gold dust!
5   Academically, I think 'early' and 'late' are overstating it but if you compare Rothko's 'Slow Swirl by the Edge of the Sea' (1944) MOMA, New York, with 'Number 18' (c. 1947-8) National Gallery of Art, Washington DC, you might get a feeling for what Joe was trying to say.
6   Aha! Is this where it's all going to come together? Of course some people resent footnotes at times like these. They either tell you what you know, plonkingly pointing out the obvious, or, probably worse, they spoil the enjoyment of working something out for oneself. But this is an art historian speaking and, if there's anything you learn in the academic world then it's the value of stating the obvious (a) just in case the peer reviewer hasn't got the message, or (b) to exchange the Freemason's handshake with him, or her nowadays, making clear you both know the same publicly known fact. Even more valuable in exams!
7   Hear, hear! I made a similar observation in my dissertation and have since had the satisfaction of seeing that the Orangerie's Goldens have been reframed in plain wood *without* glass.

3

Much of the Art History I had learned came from books. However, there is inevitably a practical and physical side. One has to stand in front of paintings, visiting galleries, occasionally being allowed, with gloved hands, to touch them. I had never read a book about sex, or relationships between men and women, if one discounts Henry Miller. Being something of an academic, that may help to explain why I had, so far, failed the practical. My very sensual sociologist had made the initial running and given me some master/mistress classes but I began, all too soon, to feel that I was simply one of her fashion accessories. With her strident left-wing attitudes there came the need to demonstrate liberation from male domination and it soon seemed to me I wasn't much more than her randy, right-wing handbag, carried around to impress and annoy her fellow revolutionaries. All of this may (or may not) help to explain why I was, at one and the same time, physically very aware and yet mentally rather wary of Anna Glover.

She was, I guessed, in her mid-twenties, about five foot nine or a shade less allowing for her high heels. I've told you already how she looked. I could add a little to that. Her well-rounded bust was shown off in a white silk blouse through which the contours could be seen if she stood at right-angles to the light. Today, her pencil skirt in a grey worsted pin-stripe stopped just below the knee and wrapped round slim hips but plump buns. The visible parts of her legs were shrink-wrapped in gauzy, glassy nylon and slid into plain but elegant black shoes with a buckle. We met up as I stood and watched her approach the whole length of the pool.

'Seen enough?' The tone was polite but challenging; her eyebrows were rising in reproof. Why lie, I thought.

'No! But I'll try to make it less obvious.'

That brought a hint of a smile but I was still on my guard, suspicious of her.

'You told me a few things last time about yourself.'

I nodded and wondered if I might insist on a few in exchange.

'I'm happy to say they all check out.'

'Check out?'

'Yes, and on behalf of Mr Rembrandt, I apologise for the fact that we had to do this but he told me he wanted to establish your *bona fides*. He's been giving you rather a lot of personal information. More than he has ever told me, I may say.'

Aha! That's given something away, I thought. And who *is* this woman; a private detective?

'We've been talking mainly about the history of painting, Miss Glover. That's what I'm especially interested in.'

'So I understand. And you can call me Anna. This is California, not foggy London town.'

That was a better sign. Keep going Bill, but stay on your guard.

'And since we might just have offended you by our inquisitiveness, Bill, be my guest for dinner tonight – representing Mr Rembrandt, of course. If that's okay, I'll come by to pick you up around seven.'

I tried to accept with studied nonchalance but, never having studied nonchalance, I made a complete hash of it.

'Rather!'

She snorted.

'You're just a B movie Englishman from Central Casting; but I like it.'

Over dinner, I finally learned that she worked in the Carmel branch-office of Rembrandt's lawyers, and had done so more or less since graduation. She'd been hired by Joe's long-time lawyer in San Francisco, an elderly German immigrant with old-world charm concealing a mind like a steel trap. Seems there was no connection with Fancy Dress after all. Pity! I love a conspiracy. Although she was supposed to be responsible for Joe's affairs, she admitted she had very little to do for him as his finances were entirely looked after by the San Francisco office and all she had on her plate was the gallery he owned in Carmel and making sure his property was well maintained.

To be frank, she seemed to know very little about Joe. On a personal note, I learned she didn't like her immediate boss in Carmel who was the son-in-law of Joe's lawyer; that both her parents were dead – her father had been a builder, her mother a housewife – and that she had a lively mind, a sense of humour and a zest for life; which can't all be bad.

Since it is my favourite subject, it can be assumed I told her about myself and since you know all that matters I can just add that, looking back on the evening with mild surprise, I came to the conclusion I'd ever enjoyed myself quite so much in any woman's company; sitting drinking her in but trying to do so a sip at a time.

My feelings were a puzzle as well as a surprise to me. My two previous relationships had been fairly basic. Would they or wouldn't they – in the first case she wouldn't because, in those days, mainly one didn't; the second you know about. I don't know if I'd ever even thought about 'love'. Concupiscence I could write the chapter on. Now here I was, looking at Anna and aware that I was imaging enjoying all kinds of simple things, like a stroll round an art gallery (my scene that I would share with her), or along the beach together (more her scene, perhaps). Was this a sign of a more mature Maguire?

She talked business only once.

'You do realise that everything Joe has told you is in the strictest confidence.'

'Anna, he never made any such condition but, if it helps, I am only interested in what he has to tell me about one particular painter.'

'It helps.'

Some of the time, we didn't speak but still seemed to be exchanging messages. What I *told* myself she was saying was, 'Bill, I think I could get fond of you, but don't let's rush this.' By the coffee stage, I was really wondering if I could be falling in love with her, not just the wine and my hormones talking, and more than thirty-three-and-a-third per cent convinced I could persuade her, convince her – but never compel her, of course; women's lib and all that – to love me back.

How else was I to interpret the way she was beginning to look at me?

She drove me back to the illustrated house and, as we said good night, she leant across her wide automobile. I became quite frantic with anticipation. Lightly but lingeringly she patted my hand and I had to settle for that. But, once she had driven off, I put the patted hand to my jealous lips. Maybe I should have bitten my hand off.

Next morning, Joe was ready to talk again.

Don't know how long it was before either of us said another word. Seemed like hours. Made damn sure I had my tartan carpet slippers on before I picked my way over the broken glass. Put the eiderdown round her. Didn't seem likely she'd want to climb into bed with me. Took it without saying anything, but the tears kind of dried up.

Heart was pounding and my chest hurting almost as much as my head and my legs, but that didn't stop me pouring another shot. When she stretched out her hand, I passed over my glass and drank from the bottle. Then, because I still loved her, brought my chair over and sat beside her. She nodded to her glass and seemed to make up her mind about something. And that was when she spilled the beans; not every bean, I guess, but a significant can full.

Said she was sorry I hadn't broken my neck instead of my legs because now she had to spell it out for me plain and simple. Told me her mother and Golden had skedaddled up to Roubaix and then he'd made a secret visit to his lawyer in London and moved funds to Switzerland before coming back for her. They skulked around in out-of-the-way places while he grew a beard. He was still pretty tired out. She cut his hair short and dyed her own. Then they ventured out and pretty soon found a farmhouse to rent. Just as well because Ghislaine was pregnant and getting damned tired too. That farmhouse, *the* farmhouse, was where Margot was born. God dammit, I was married to Golden's daughter. They don't tell stories like that any more; not even in books. But if she was introducing me to my father-in-law, it was some sad and sick old man I was meeting.

Told me her father was depressed as hell. By the time she was old enough, say three four, to be a real Daddy's girl, he didn't want to play. Spent most of his time making little colour sketches and tearing them up. Even tried painting straight onto canvas but that didn't work either and all that went on the bonfire along with the torn-up sketchbooks. The guy had a real 'painter's block' or whatever the hell you call it. Trouble was, he felt like some plugged volcano; inside all white-hot, molten mass of ideas but head and hands solid rock. Been allowed just the one eruption and nothing more; then some fault line slipped.

Then one day Margot got bitten by a snake. Maybe she'd been asleep in the grass and put her hand on it when she woke up. Something like that I guess, but she hollered like a stuck pig and Ghislaine and Golden panicked. Ghislaine shoved her on the cross bar of their one bicycle and pedalled off to the village with Golden loping behind with Margot thinking they were running away from him so hollering some more.

By the time the village pharmacist has done the necessary and called the doctor, Golden gets to the village in a state of collapse and so father and daughter both finish up in hospital. Margot's out next day but he needs a couple of weeks under sedation while they listen to his heart. Funny thing, seems to have started him dreaming – in colour. End of a couple of weeks he's yelling to get out and get his hands on his sketchbooks again. Seems like he's dreamt his way back to where he was before he collapsed in his Paris studio.

On the way home, they stop off at his regular store and Ghislaine cleans the guy out of sketchbooks. And while she's in the store, Golden is telling Margot he's going to paint lots of pictures and they're all for *her*. Next couple of weeks, Golden is singing like a lark as he sketches and yells at Ghislaine to get canvases organised. Boy does he want canvas; enough for the *Cutty Sark*. Ghislaine and Margot have to travel back into Arles and bully the shop into getting them stretched and primed. Shop makes a fuss, wants money up front for such a big order. Why does she want so many at one time? Is she having fifty painters over for a party? This is Arles but even Van Gogh wasn't that crazy. But she insists; it's what Golden wants.

Four five days later, up rolls a camionette with two guys and Golden drives them bananas forming a human chain to pass them up to the studio then on up into the loft. They drive off convinced he's crazier than Van Gogh. Then Golden almost drives Ghislaine nuts because now he wants paint, great fat tubes of it. Says he's only a few sketches to do and he'll be getting down to the serious business. Ghislaine puts Margot in her best dress and they ride the bike into the village and take the bus to Arles. On the way home, they have to walk back from the village because of the parcels slung over the handlebars, the crossbar and in the saddle-bags. Ghislaine is telling Margot she'll have to be real mousey-quiet for weeks and weeks to let Golden get on with his painting but Ghislaine's the silent one as they get back to the farmhouse; bushed with pushing the loaded bicycle. So it's Margot who rushes in, calling out for Daddy and stomping up to the studio.

Throws open the door but it bounces right back; something behind it. Shoves it open again, runs in – and falls over Golden. He's on the floor and Margot gets down on her knees to wake him up. But he won't wake and he's cold. Margot screams and Ghislaine comes on the double and soon she's screaming too.

Long and short of it is Golden gets buried in the local churchyard but under the name he'd been calling himself, Alexander Orr, and Ghislaine is broke because all the money is in his name and they aren't married. She's at her wit's end; keeps crying about all the lovely pictures he was just going to paint and how that would have made them so much money. And Margot's remembering he'd said they were for her – and she wants her pictures as much as she wants her Daddy. Margot may have gone on talking but, pretty much at that point I passed out; but not before thinking, 'Fuck you, Margot. They're *mine*. Mine and Golden's maybe – but he's dead.' Maybe I even said it. Not sure.

Assuming all this happened more or less as Joe, or for that matter Margot, had told it, this could just about explain why there was no record of where Golden had lived and, it now seemed, died, after he and his mistress left Paris in a hurry. It would explain how the paintings, the original Golden Month, now belonged to the Orangerie – if the transaction had gone through legally, and that might be worth checking on, if only for what the research might give me in extra pages for my dissertation.

Anyway, it did look as if there were no more Goldens, my secret hope, but that there might be some twentieth-century Rembrandts. If I could unearth these, it would just about guarantee my career, never mind my doctorate. I would need permission from Rembrandt, of course, to go and look for them and I really ought to be escorted. Joe couldn't do that. What about his legal representative? That thought sprang to mind because Anna had left a message for me while I had been listening to her client. Enigmatically, she said she accepted my invitation to dinner, which I hadn't issued, and that, since I didn't have a car, she would pick me up around seven. The message added that my suggestion of the new sea-food restaurant along the coast, that I knew nothing about, was brilliant. Suddenly, from thinking myself the hunter, I was prey to a certain anxiety. I knew, only too well, what sort of a person I was and how readily I could be deflected from the narrow path of dedicated scholarship. But since I was who I was, I decided to schedule an early evening shower and a second shave, and put on clean underpants. At the back of my mind, there was even the nagging thought that I didn't have an 'eraser'.

Then I sat down and asked myself a straight question. Could I possibly be falling in love with Anna? The answer wasn't all that simple. Who couldn't like, be fond of, want to be close to such a friendly, not unattractive all-American girl? But did I even know what love was and did I have the time or the temperament to consider these questions *before* I completed my thesis? On that inconclusive note, I went through to the warm patio beside the pool and waited for the planned afternoon session with Joe.

Next morning, mother and father of all hangovers; sticky, bristly, smelly; aching in every bone in my thick head. No sign of Margot and, right then, wasn't looking. Everything hurt, especially thinking. Slid into a bath making a vow not to come back to Scotland a third time. Even if they offered me the frigging throne. Got my outside looking clean, but inside felt and smelt filthy. Cleaning my teeth didn't help. Breath like a sewer.

Guess about an hour from the time I woke I tottered down one flight into the dining room. Saw the coffee percolator and toaster on the side table and homed in on them. Mistake really. Scottish white bread is concrete crust, top and bottom, wet cement in between, but burning the surface makes it almost edible. Come to think of it, wasn't so keen on the coffee either. Scottish coffee's either stewed in its own juice till it's bitter as shit or simply isn't coffee at all; just warm, peaty water. But that morning I poured the coffee, buttered the toast, and ate.

Began to think about Margot. Nothing very pleasant. I was married to Golden's daughter, for fuck's sake! Until last night, I'd *loved* her. Maybe still did; but I didn't *like* her! Part of me could feel her pain. Rest of me didn't. Kept thinking about my work over these past months. How I felt, through and through and through these paintings were magnificent, original and *mine*.

And then I heard a car start up. Hobbled over and looked out. Saw Strauss in the driver's seat, beside Margot. Cursed and swore. Figured straight away she was running off to get ahead of me; planning to put the paintings out of my reach. Probably going to work too. Took only five minutes to get to the main road; a couple of hours to the airport. Even if I phoned ahead, what could I say to make them stop her? She'd get on a plane and be in the south of France the same day. Probably never see her, certainly never see my paintings again.

Conned! Used! Robbed! Ditched!

I stumbled out onto the gravel to yell after the car, already out of sight round the first of five hundred bends. Grabbed a handful of gravel and flung it after them. Before I got back as far as the door, it started to rain, Scottish rain; heavy, cold lead shot. Jee-zus, I was wet. Made it inside and slammed the door. Gust of air blew a letter off the hall table. Heard it fall; then saw it lying there. On the cover, 'JOE'.

She must have been up hours before me, if she ever went to bed. Three pages of it; spelling it all out.

Said *she* was Golden's daughter and I was a louse! Clever louse sure, one who could forge paintings, but who would ever believe me if I claimed I'd painted *her father's* work. They'd call me a greedy American gigolo. Now I'd served my purpose: I was history. She'd buy me off if she had to but she didn't propose to waste much time or money on that. She'd be getting Pinstripe on the job pretty damn quick. More trouble I made, less I'd finish up with. Shit! If this woman wasn't mad, like psychotic mad, was sure as hell mad at me.

But what had I *done*? Only one colossal, frigging favour. And I hadn't been *hired* to do the job; I'd volunteered! Loved her, loved my work, and been *inspired* to do it. Even felt, just like her goddam father, I was doing it for *her*. I'd have shared it with her; totally. Besides, the crazy bitch didn't seem to *need* the dough.

All too much for me at that moment. Maybe there wasn't another plane until Monday but went upstairs to pack anyway. Don't know if I planned to walk but wanted to be ready to go; get to Arles, speak to Margot, beg for another chance; agree to anything, absolutely anything, if only … Then the phone rang.

Of course, in a bloody cottage up a stinking glen beside a freezing loch in frigging Scotland, there's only one phone in the whole house, in the hall, down the stairs, and I'd just recovered from two broken legs. Made it in one piece all the way down to the last two steps then tripped and fell. Banged my head on the table and my flailing hand knocked the handset off the hook. Lying on the floor, grabbed at it, pulling the whole thing off the table. Crashed to the floor beside my head but at least I got the phone to my ear. Yelled down the line, 'Margot! Is that you?'

Wasn't. Voice at the other end, man's voice, said, 'Stay there, Mr Rembrandt. I'll be right over. And pack yourself an overnight bag.'

Stay there! Where in the hell else would I go? Jesus. In any case, already packed. Sat in the cold hall, bag ready, Burberry on and belted, waterproof hat pulled down. Nothing to do but listen out for the car. No one was going to *walk* to the cottage in that hellish downpour. It was the doctor's car scrunched and squelched on the gravel. He dashed for the door and I yanked it open. One look at him told me *real* trouble was coming.

'Mr Rembrandt, do you have a drink in the house?'

Too taken aback to speak. Just steered him into the kitchen, opened the last Lagavulin.

'Pour *yourself* a dram, man,' he said.

Poured two shots. His was over his throat before mine was at my lips. Took the hint and had a good swallow. He took a deep breath and looked me in the eye.

'Right,' he said. 'I'm most terribly sorry to tell you this – but there's just been a dreadful accident; involving your wife and the other person in the car. I'm very much afraid he's dead. Killed outright. And I must be honest, Mr Rembrandt, I can't hold out too much hope for your wife.'

Grabbed the doctor by the lapels and yelled at him. The Scotch gave him the burst of energy to tell me the rest.

Coming round the last bend to the main road in the heavy rain and probably much too fast, car had met the milk truck turning into the farm. Car driver had pulled the steering wheel over the 'wrong way' and cannoned off the truck across the ditch and head first into a tree. People at the bus stop had been down there clawing at the wreck within seconds. Could have taken their time as far as Strauss was concerned. By coincidence, doctor himself had been driving along the road. Even had a medical colleague with him, down for a fishing trip. They'd spotted a spark of life in Margot and gotten her out of the car up to the farmhouse. Left his friend in charge waiting for an ambulance but, to be blunt, wasn't sure we'd get back there while she was still alive. Wanted me to come at once.

Had to lean on him to get as far as the car and he had to lift my legs in before he slammed the door. I'd nothing left inside. Like another dead man. Set off, with the doctor peering through the windshield. Raining so hard he only got short bursts of vision and not too clear at that. Thank Christ it was daylight.

Talked to me as he drove. Didn't take it all in.

'I've called the ambulance. There's one in Selkirk. We'll have to get her to hospital immediately. They'll take her to Peel, or maybe up to the Royal. At all costs, we must try to save the child.'

Took me to the farmhouse. Allowed a quick peep at Margot but she was being guarded by the other doctor. Ghastly colour. Then the local 'bobby' steered me into another room. All the junk they'd hauled out of the car was piled there, including Strauss, under a sheet. He turned back the corner.

Not even sure I *did* recognise the bloody mess, but I nodded. Head came round the door. Doctor said, 'Ten more minutes. Get your stuff together and wait at the door. I need to get your wife ready.'

Turned to pick up my bag and saw it sitting beside Strauss's camera bag. Guy had a real swell camera. Hasselbad. Saying to myself he'd not need this for a while, slung it over my shoulder and found Margot's handbag underneath. Picked that up too and opened it. On top of everything else, her passport and her keys; could recognise *them* better than I'd recognised Strauss. Put them in my pocket, slung the handbag away and walked out the door. In the ambulance, came slowly out of shock and began to sober up.

The other doctor travelled, not our medic. Did nothing all the way except look at his watch and shake his head. The paramedic gave me the odd pat on the shoulder. Slow but sure, beginning to realise my life had totally changed.

Jee-zus! Just imagine. Happy, expectant father, married to lovely woman; so supportive. Become what I'd always wanted to be; practising artist with a place in the sun. All coming together. Then, with no warning signs I'd been smart enough to see, all gone totally wrong.

Margot had told me things. Said things! Couldn't imagine even living under the same roof with her again. Now she'd gone and got herself nearly killed. And, with her, my own, my only child; someone – crazy thought came into my head and wouldn't go away – someone I'd have taught to paint. Shook my head violently, trying to shake out that image. Who in their right mind would wish that fate on anyone?

Doctor told me that, because of the pregnancy, they were heading straight for the Royal. In the driving rain, took nearly two hours to get up to Edinburgh. Convinced by then I'd lost wife and child. No more comforting looks from the paramedic. Margot taken away immediately. Almost forgot about me, then the organisation got into gear. Parked me in a room. Told me to stay put. Brought me what they called tea. Undrinkable. Fell asleep in the chair.

Seemed only minutes before the door opened. In came two of them. One fresh faced, in an operating gown, almost seemed to be smiling. Other was the doctor whose fishing trip had been loused up. Was it still morning?

'Good afternoon, Mr Rembrandt,' said Fresh Face. 'Well, you're a father.' I started to grin.

Then Fisherman looked straight at me. 'And a widower.'

Explanations in spades but all too confusing. Took me to see Margot first. Cleaned up, looking peaceful and lovely. Blotted out all that had happened back in the bedroom. Bent down and kissed her then burst into tears. Sad faces and strong, friendly arms steered me into another part of the hospital.

In a ward like it had no patients; just clear plastic boxes, tubes, cylinders and dials; led me up to one box. Sweet young nurse beamed up at me.

'Here you are, Mr Rembrandt. Here's your daughter. She's not very well at the moment but, don't you worry at all, we'll do our very, very best to help her pull through.' And there was a tiny, pink, skinned rabbit with all kinds of things hooked up to her. Couldn't get in to touch; and even if I could, she looked too fragile.

Felt all kinds of emotion. Love. Anger. Self-pity for sure. Came over the rich American.

'I want the best medical treatment money can buy.'

Fresh Face gave me a 'look' and said that was already happening but, this being Scotland, there'd be no bill for it. Patronising, socialist sonofabitch. They prised my fingers from the incubator and steered me out of the room.

'It could be a couple of weeks, or even a month, before we can be confident she *will* survive but we'll keep trying,' said Fresh Face. 'Do you have somewhere to stay in Edinburgh?'

Took a taxi to the Caledonian. In my pocket papers they'd pressed on me with sympathetic looks. Guessed they were to do with Margot and my daughter. Got room service to send up some of their cooking whisky – had enough single malt for now – and cried myself to sleep.

What a hell of a story! The direct relevance to Golden, never mind the thesis on which my future life and happiness depended, seemed tenuous. But I was so moved by what Joe had told me that I could hardly say a thing. I switched off the Uher, stood up and patted Joe's hand. He looked up and nodded. 'See you later,' he said. I just nodded back and left him to rest.

But I didn't rest. I went back to my room and, while I showered and shaved, I treated my inner eye to Golden images and thoughts of 'buried' treasure. Time would probably prevent me from doing anything before finishing my thesis – that deadline seemed to come two days closer every twenty-four hours – and, in any case, this was too good to waste on a dissertation – but afterwards … here was material for my first book, fame and fortune. I decided, prudently (sneakily?) to say nothing about all this to Anna. Otherwise, the next thing he'd reveal was that the place near Arles had been struck by lightning, or destroyed by an earthquake.[1]

Anna was prompt and I reckon I might not even have mentioned our mutual friend if she hadn't, point blank, asked what he was talking about. I can hardly have been convincing when I hummed and hawed and said it was all fairly technical but we were still talking about a little-known painter we both admired and thought was due for a revival.

'All that time talking about one guy? How much did he paint that there's so much to say?'

The mood of what she surely intended as a romantic dinner was more than a little cool at the outset. The sparkle and fizz that had been her style up until then was almost entirely gone. She knew perfectly well I was keeping things from her and that meant I was failing the key test of any blossoming relationship: willingness to exchange confidences and secrets. Was there something else, on her side? I couldn't say. What a sensible art historian with a deadline should have done was accept the situation, think positively about the freedom that gave him to concentrate on his make-or-break deadline and study the menu, trying hard not to be appalled by the stated prices or that even more expensive phrase, 'at market price'. Instead, sitting beside a young woman who had, after all, demanded a date with me, I began to talk some more about myself, my childhood and then the experiences in France that turned me on to Modern Art. And because I betrayed some confidences about these experiences, and told a few stories against myself, her mood seemed to lift. If I was holding back about Joe, maybe it was in the same way as she would protect client confidence. She began to smile and look at me over her ruinously expensive sea food timbale and costly Chardonnay. And Anna Glover had a beautiful smile.

'I've never been to Europe,' she said – and I read all kinds of subliminal messages into that matter-of-fact statement.

'I hope you'll plug that gap in your education soon.'

'Let's drink to that.'

In the car park afterwards, we stood in the darkness, listening, with Hollywood symbolism, to the ocean crashing on the rocky shore a hundred feet below, my arm round her shoulder, hers round my waist – and then she turned. It was a long and gentle; a more loving kiss than I had ever known.

'Now I'd better get you back to your studies, *Doctor* Maguire.'

My sleep was filled with very pleasant dreams.

Next morning, Joe was up, dressed and sitting by the pool before I came through and I dashed back for the tape recorder. Just as well because he began talking almost before I sat down.

Woke up pretty confused. Took me more than a few moments to remember where I was and what in hell I was doing. Then it came back. Slam bang!

Been a talented artist; rich and loving wife about to give birth to our first, our *only* child. Got myself up and ready to visit my only living relative and the remains of my previous.

Peering into the tiny mirror in the chilly bathroom, shaving, remembered the last time I'd been in Edinburgh. Pinstripe brought those documents with him; scarcely gave me enough time to take them in before he had my signature witnessed. My basic needs would be taken care of but, if Margot died first – it seemed almost a joke then – I'd still have to earn a living. Okay, could still do that I reckoned, and my initial capital, my instant, bankable reputation was still sitting in a farmhouse in Arles. Or was it?

Sudden panic. Margot and Strauss might have had the paintings removed already. And, legally, whose paintings were they? They were *mine* surely; I'd painted them. But were they mine now she was dead? Maybe they belonged to my daughter? Pinstripe seemed to have every angle covered. Even so, hadn't been thinking of having a family then; far less a family funeral. In my mind's eye, remembered some words in the agreement; made me sick to my stomach. Didn't say anything about any frigging paintings; just 'all Margot Orr's possessions'.

Pinstripe had spelled it out. Money *and* possessions – and possessions included paintings, right? Hellfire! Even after her death, Margot was going to rob me. Damned if I'd let her. But where were they? What could Pinstripe and his friends do? Could I stop them? Hadn't the least idea.

First things first; get over to the hospital and see that scrap of humanity I'd created. Yes, Margot, you carried her but *I* created her. And you were clinically dead before she was born. Have to find out about giving Margot a proper send off, the best she can afford. Best get in touch with Pinstripe; he'll handle that kind of thing. Me, I need time to think. Hangover I'd woken with yesterday never really gone away. Now, I'm getting angry and upset again, pain drilling into my head. Remembered aspirin in my bag and opened it up. Grabbed the bottle and swallowed a couple. Saw a clean shirt and a quiet tie that went with my other jacket. Hung them up and began to transfer things from the pockets of the jacket I'd been wearing all day before. Very first thing I put my hand on was that poisonous farewell note.

Stared at it for a moment or two then screwed it up tight and tossed it into the big O. Finished moving over my pocket book and some coins then got dressed. Began putting the rest of my gear into the huge wardrobe; more like a family vault than a piece of furniture. Picked up Strauss's camera bag. I guess I'd stolen it but, what the hell, he wasn't going to miss it and, in all probability, I was going to have to go on thieving; starting with stealing my own paintings back.

On an impulse, I rescued the screwed up letter from the waste basket. No point letting the chambermaid see what kind of an asshole my wife thought I was – not that I had any plans involving the chambermaid. Shoved it in Strauss's camera bag, shut the wardrobe, and left the room. Picking up that letter was the smartest thing.

On the way to the hospital, my head began to clear a little. Started to think about some of the questions that needed answering; questions other people were going to ask me. Margot had been killed in an automobile accident. Where had she been going? Why had *Strauss* been with her, not me? Why had he been driving, and way too fast? Reasonable questions for someone, anyone, to ask. But now they'd ask *me* for the answers; not Margot.

Was I going to tell them we'd had a flaming row and she'd walked out on me; that she'd been going to Arles to run off with my paintings, saying they were hers; hers, or her father's? Her father! Lying in that churchyard (she says). What kind of a story was that? Maybe Margot had gone mad. Hey, was this anything to do with her mystery 'illness'; the one she was supposed to be convalescing from on the cruise? Didn't matter much; secret died with her; and that's when it hit me!

The secret; the goddamn secret; the precious, frigging secret. Apart from me, who knew *anything* about the paintings? Only Strauss and Margot. And they both died yesterday. Now, all I had to do was make damned sure it stayed *my* secret, my story – and only mine. Gotten that far in my thoughts when the taxi stopped. Came back to the present and remembered I was going to visit my daughter.

Made me put on a gown this time and took me into the ward with the plastic boxes. All pretty solemn and I caught the mood. Been looking forward to this but now I'm feeling scared. There she is; still tiny, naked, and vulnerable but, thank God, alive.

'Would you like to touch her?'

The nurse gently takes my wrist and puts my hand into a hole in the side of the box with a kind of sleeve. She puts my hand on the baby's arm and said, 'If you press *very* gently on her wrist, you'll feel her pulse'.

Tell you, can *still* feel it. My own child's heart beat.

Think I understand now why the nurse did all this. If my child was going to die, at least I'd gotten to know her a little. She and I had a bond. Felt so good about it. Turned to thank her, but Fresh Face loomed up at my side, asking if we could have a 'little talk'.

Told me it was still pretty much touch and go because she was premature and been delivered just after her mother died. Possible oxygen starvation and all that. Better not to build up my hopes. Even if she pulled through, might be months, years even, before they could be sure she hadn't been damaged. Damaged? He spelt it out: brain damaged. What a thought. Going to need a great deal of looking after. Looking at me, into my fifties, a widower; I could tell he wasn't sure if I could handle all this.

'You take care of the next few weeks, Doc, and I'll take care of the rest,' I told him. Should have gone to see about Margot but I'd near enough forgotten about her. Climbed into another taxi. Funerals can always wait.

Back in the hotel, nearly pulled the curtains down trying to get some light into the room, even with hundred watt light bulbs burning somewhere up there, near the ceiling. Took a chair into the window bay, pulled the pad of hotel notepaper onto my knee, and took out my fountain pen. Thoughts still pretty confused so maybe ought to write down what I wanted; or needed; or felt. Anything to get back in control of myself. Picked up my pen.

Dear Margot,

You selfish bitch! Now look what you've done; not just to you and Strauss but, dammit, to me and the baby. What you ought to have done right at the beginning was turn over one helluva lot of money to me, your husband, so I could look after our child, bring her up in America, the best place in the world, and be free to paint what the hell I want and keep it or burn it, as the mood takes me. After all, that's what your damn father did.

Yours

Joe

Felt better; for a few minutes. But it was like one of these cures that, pretty soon, leaves you feeling worse.

Looked at the page. It was way, way too late now to change Margot's mind. Screwed the page into a ball and threw it in the basket. Then, suddenly, I reached into the basket and fetched it out again. Big idea!

Put that second piece of crumpled paper into the camera bag, grabbed my coat and went out into Princes Street. Dead and alive place on a Sunday; nothing open. Had to walk all the way to the railroad station to find some action. Bought a writing pad; same kind Margot always used. Basildon Bond; pale blue paper, matching envelopes; and a pen with a nib like Margot's. Ink the colour she liked. Took a taxi back to the hotel. Legs hurting like hell. Told the desk I wasn't taking any calls, except from the hospital. Went back up to my room and locked the door, had some of the cooking whisky, sat down at the writing desk, filled the pen, and wrote my name a dozen times to get the ink flowing; then opened up the pad of blue writing paper.

Spread out the crumpled page that told me just exactly what she thought of me; copied out a few of her nastier remarks. And when I say copied, I mean *copied*. Not just the words but the writing; every twist and turn. In about an hour, I'd written and rewritten the letter three times. Artistically speaking could see it had gotten better each time.

At that point, tore everything I'd written into shreds and pushed the pieces down the pan. That wasn't easy. In the end, had to roll up my sleeve and push the remaining scraps round the bend to stop them bobbing back up again. Dried my hands, wiped my face, refreshed my glass, sat back down again, and picked up the pen.

Dear Joe, as Margot had really meant to say,

I'm so sorry we rowed last night. Please try to forgive me, and put it down to the way this pregnancy is making me feel. I said some really wicked things, none of which were fair or true. Sorry, sorry, sorry!!!

You are a loving husband and I know you are going to be a wonderful father. It wasn't kind of me to insult you the way I did. But I'm going to make up for all that and straight away. Just you wait and see.

Listen Joe, I think we need a breathing space. Just a few days, but please, please don't be anxious. Strauss has to go back to Paris and he'll look after me on the way there. Then I'll go on down to Arles and wait there for you. Give me about a week to myself to do some good hard thinking and then follow me.

I miss you already, darling Joe. I'm looking forward to our new and better life. If that seems mysterious, you'll understand soon enough. Just post the other letter to my lawyer, please. I haven't any stamps. I'll see you in about a week. Send me a telegram, then fly down to Nice and I'll meet you there.

All my love, always

Margot
X X X X

Read it over few times. So good I began to cry, and a teardrop fell onto my damn near perfect letter. Got so cross with myself, after all the work I'd done, I tore it in half and crumpled it up. Then I had a big laugh, smoothed it out and put the two pieces in the pocket of my other jacket. What I'd subconsciously done, like an old pro, was add 'authenticity'.

Then it was back to the drawing board. Took another sheet of paper and began again. This time, signed and dated the day before. 'Margot' took a different tone with Pinstripe.

Over the past few months, she told him, *I've not been behaving very well. I realise now it is just the effects of my pregnancy but I <u>have</u> caused Joe real pain and mental anguish calling him wicked things, like my 'poor relation' and worse. I even told him that the pictures he has been painting belonged to me, not him, because I paid for the paints and the canvas. What an insult that must have been to a real artist like Joe!*

I am telling you this because I need a confessor. You've known me long enough to realise this is not my normal behaviour. I need to change all this. I love Joe and he and I need to be a proper couple now that my baby — I mean <u>our</u> baby — is on the way. I want to change my will straightaway so that Joe becomes my sole heir. If anything were to happen to me, he must have *the means to bring up our child properly. I do not want you to argue with me. I know I am changing <u>everything</u> but this is how it must be <u>from now on</u>. I will sort out our day-to-day finances with Joe myself but, as far as I am concerned, he and I are going to be an ordinary husband and wife from now on.*

Yours sincerely,

Margot G Rembrandt

Had to look in her passport to see how she signed her name. Her given names were Margot Ghislaine, born in France, naturalised British subject, family name Orr.

Looking at what 'Margot' just wrote, I had to agree anyone calling me a frigging little forger wasn't too wide of the mark. Like my paintings, gotten inside the mind of my subject. Mind you, didn't have any illusions. Margot was dead and it was too late now to waltz off with her money – if there really was any. No, just a bargaining chip. When it came to the in-fighting, wanted to screw more out of Pinstripe on the sympathy vote, make damn sure that father and daughter were plenty okay.

Most satisfying moment was reading Margot's original letter for the last time then tearing it into little pieces and burning them in the big glass ashtray.

Finishing touch was to address an envelope to Pinstripe, put Margot's new letter in it, seal it down and go out and buy a stamp from the vending machine in the hotel lobby like I'd been following her instructions, just before I got that phone call in the cottage. Plan was to find her letter in my pocket, like I'd forgotten it. Put the stamp on the letter; and then I nearly blew it. Letterbox right beside the vending machine and, not thinking, began pushing Pinstripe's letter in. Then my mind goes into reverse. Jerk my hand back so fast I drop the letter and have to scramble for it on the carpet. Stand up and look round with 'this guy's a crook' written all over my forehead, but nobody seemed to notice. Shoved the letter back in my pocket and went right out to hail a cab. Wanted to visit my daughter again and whisper to *her* what I was up to.

Little Pinkie is still alive but she's gone yellow. They tell me about the jaundice before I see her. Makes me all the more anxious; determined to see she's given the right start in life. Fresh Face taking a well-earned break but the nurse says whichever way it goes it's a whole month before Pinkie's out of intensive care. Then maybe another month or two before she can leave hospital. Nobody says the big 'if' word; don't have to. Helps me make up my mind. One more time, don't go to see about Margot. Decide I'll dump all that on Pinstripe; after all she's *his* frigging client.

Back at the hotel get one great big fright; huge policeman waiting. Boy, do I feel waves of guilt. Of course, he's sympathy itself. Sorry to bother me 'at a time like this' but people in charge of the fatal accident inquiry and the Procurator Fiscal, whoever he is, been on to his sergeant to make sure I come in to make a statement so 'matters can be cleared up quickly'. Wants me to turn round and go back out again. Ask him to come up to my room saying I reckon I might have something there they probably need. Go up together and, making sure he's watching me, open the wardrobe and fish the crumpled, tear-stained and torn letter out of my other jacket.

At the police station, shown into a grubby little office with olive green paint, blue tobacco-smoke air and piles of off-white paper. Police Sergeant spreads a form out in front of him, picks up a pen. Would I mind telling him if I knew where the late Mrs Rembrandt and the late Mr Strauss (which it pleased me he rhymed with louse) had been going, the morning of the fatal accident, and why? Drag out the silence till he's beginning to look real suspicious. Then just nod and pull out the letter with a sigh that should have won an Oscar and hand it over.

Slow reader. Remember wondering if he was memorising it; or maybe saying to himself, 'This guy's up to something.' Felt my ears burning. Then he looks up.

'I'd say this goes a long way to explain matters, Sir. I'm very sorry. I shall have to keep this for the present, I'm afraid.'

Agreed to have it photostatted for me. Had me complete a short statement and sign it. Then only too willing to have me driven back to the hotel. That all limbered me up now; ready for the lawyer now.

His long, solemn face makes him look more like a mortician. He's heard the news, how I don't know, and tries hard to look sympathetic. Comes round the front of his desk, grips my hand and pats my back. Even pours out two pretty mean shots of sweet sherry before settling down, rubbing his hands, and asking for all the gory details.

Take him through it, moment by moment, and he drinks in every word. Manage to keep off mentioning the letters till the very end. First of all, tell him about my tiny scrap of a daughter, lying defenceless in hospital, how much I was sure Margot would have loved and cared for her. Explain what the doctor has said about how long it could be; all of that.

Begin to tell him about the row the night before the crash; how I blame myself for this; worried that it had been the real cause. He protests sympathetically. How could I have known? That's when I give him Exhibit 'A'. Soon as he reads it, looks real solemn and asks what I've done with the letter Margot wanted me to put in the mail. Slip it out of my pocket and hand it over. He flips it over and seems to nod with approval that it's still sealed. Before he even had time to open and read it though, tell him I have a real bad headache; ask him if he'd mind if I just went back to the hotel to lie down. Said I was thinking of going down to Arles for a few days, 'Where Margot and I were so happy, just to think about her there; before coming back for the funeral.'

Agrees with all this, saying 'No haste, nothing need be rushed,' and all that stuff. I'm across the road and walking along the sidewalk when I hear him hollering after me. Break into a sweat, and very nearly broke into a run. Grab the railings to steady myself and wait till he dodges the traffic and crosses over. Hadn't expected him to spot the goddam fake and come after me quite so quickly.

'I'm so sorry, Mr Rembrandt, but have you been to the Registrar?'

Pinstripe explains. The hospital authorities would have given me the papers. Reach inside my jacket and fish them out. Didn't tell him, I hadn't even looked at them.

'Mr Rembrandt,' he says, 'I'm afraid both events need to be registered and, normally, this would fall to you as the relative. However, in these trying circumstances, I can undertake the duty for you if you will be so kind as to instruct me.' Told him I so instructed. Then he asks me one question I'm not ready for.

'And what Christian names have you chosen?'

Had absolutely totally no idea. Told Pinstripe we hadn't chosen any. Assured me I had a few days before I had to make my mind up. He even tries a feeble joke that, nowadays, people can always change their names if they don't like them.

'Anyway,' he says, 'we shall have to meet again very soon.'

Think; that's true! Just as soon as you read that letter, you're going to come after me and give me a real hard time but, for my daughter's sake, I'll be ready for you. Shook hands and I went on back to the hotel.

Half expected him to phone before I'd even gotten back there. No messages, so when Pinstripe didn't phone within the hour, I decided to get out of town, out of the country. Mean to say, hadn't had any hand in the accident or Margot's death, had I? But what would *you* think if you were a lawyer and had gotten a letter from a client written just before she died saying she wanted to totally change her will? Frigging suspicious, that's what. Asked the hotel to get me on the next flight.

Plan was get back to the farmhouse, see how Strauss had left things. Make calls on one or two people in Arles. Try and get some answers. Then back to Brigadoon to see Margot decently cremated.

Late next afternoon, rolling into Arles in my hire car, stop at a red light; see a photo shop, pull over and go in there with the spools of film I'd found in Strauss's camera bag. Hadn't realised just how many there were. Then hit the road to the farmhouse.

Nothing had changed. Stray cats came running up but it was just curiosity; didn't look hungry. Opened the kitchen door; real mess; obvious Strauss hadn't bothered to clear up. That could wait; just had to go see. Absolutely, totally *not* prepared for what greeted me.

Somehow or other, Strauss had managed to hang about two-thirds of the paintings round the studio walls in two rows, grouping them and in the right order. Rest neatly stacked in the corner. They were all there. Never really *seen* my own work arranged like this. Dumbstruck.

Forget false modesty, Bill; they looked frigging fantastic.

Must have spent a couple of hours, just wandering round and round gazing. Wasn't the first to see this exhibition but – the Golden curse, or whatever it was – everyone else who'd ever seen it was dead! Cold, stone dead, and the secret of my paintings was *my* secret; no one else's, till I chose to share it.

When my eyes were burned out, left the room and went downstairs to clear up. Took me a while. By the time it was finished, completely whacked. Hauled myself off to bed. Didn't sleep much. Couldn't seem to pee very well. Pain in my groin. Kept dreaming about my daughter. Cursed the fact we'd never put a phone in.

In the morning felt like shit but had to begin the research. First, the realtor. Gave him the *Readers' Digest* version. Wanted to get hold of the owners, explain the new circumstances. Ask them if they'd sell me the farmhouse. He was sympathetic but instructions he'd gotten from the lawyers were crystal clear. Didn't want any contact. Already said too much! Apologised, but 'bound by the ethics of his profession'. A realtor with ethics? Jeez, I'd heard everything now.

Felt he might be open to reason, folding reason, like most men. Told him determined to buy, money no object, *whoever had to get some*. Catching my drift, remembered an errand for his assistant and once he'd gone, pulled a file and slid it towards me and left me alone with a folder marked, in big letters, *'Propriété Golden'*.

Very little in it, but enough. The next clue. A letter from McFunny-Farm & Jockstrap, WS, lawyers in Edinburgh, just along the street from Pinstripe's hang-out in Heriot Row. Written in French, but it seemed like it was true the discovery of the farmhouse had been a set-up. Copied down some details and was out the door before the realtor came back.

Planning to follow up the lead; visit the lawyer. Couldn't even guess what he'd tell me. Like as not nothing. Can't squeeze lawyers' balls same way as realtors'; leastways not in my experience. Meant leaving the farmhouse, so had to make it secure. Bought some groceries; picked up the prints at the photo shop; shoved them into the camera bag and drove back.

Wasn't looking forward to hauling all these frigging canvases back up the ladder again but I wanted to make damn sure no one else knew about them till I was good and ready. Couldn't cart them off, could I? That would need a truck and where could they go? Hampstead? Heather Cottage? Okay, isolated, but I never ever wanted to go there again. That just left the loft.

Not sure how long it would take me. Ate some bread and cheese, drank a couple of glasses of my shopping and got started. Meant clearing away some stacked canvases and – goddam carefully this time – propping the ladder up against the wall, under the black hole. Took a deep breath, began to climb, holding onto the ladder with one hand, single canvas in the other.

Made three more trips. Ran the torchlight all round. Empty. Lugged the first four from the front right in back of the loft.

Planned to hoist them up there, in reverse order. Gave me another chance to look at each one and remind myself how I painted them; not just that physical act of creation, the way living paint moves under the knife, but the *smell* of linseed and turpentine – like the smell of sex! Can't explain this to anyone, but even some of the most trivial thoughts in my mind as I applied a particular brush stroke came flooding back just looking at it again on the canvas. Like looking inside my skull. Kept going for another ten canvases before collapsing onto the bed.

Early next morning, made coffee and drove into Arles to a small hotel. Booked a room for a week, managed a good pee at last, had a passable shower and fixed up to get some laundry done. Then bought some painkillers, small saw, bag of nails, some two-by-four, sheet of ply, and set off back to finish hiding my life's work.

Hauled up another thirty paintings. Kept going on aspirin and adrenalin. As each one went up the ladder and into the dark, silently said 'Au revoir'. Not goodbye; but I sure as hell didn't know when I'd see them again. Meantime, no one else would; especially not anyone sent by Pinstripe to take inventory.

Before calling it a day, measured up the rectangle and found that I'd wasted my money on the saw and the two-by-four. Ply fitted more or less exactly. Going to need a can of whitewash but that could wait. Feeling quite light-headed. Got back into Arles; made a call to

Edinburgh. No change; meaning no improvement but nothing worse.

Reckoned another day should do it. Only four paintings and some blank canvases left in the studio. First thing was getting the pictures sealed in. Don't know if you've tried handling a board up a ladder nailing it into place, with only two hands. Don't recommend it. Life threatening! Needed a break before I painted it. Don't look at me like that, Bill. Of course I should have thought of painting it first, but I wasn't going to take it down again!

Warm outside. Sat on the back step and leant against the wall. Fell fast asleep. Next thing I know, someone's shaking me. Panicked – maybe been dreaming – and struck out. Came to my senses to see I'm assaulting the local postman. What with my French and his dignity, explanations don't come easy. Get him calmed down, pour two fingers of cognac and shake him by the hand. All smiles and he's climbing back on his bike to set off when he comes out with one word I *do* know.

'Merde,' he says and grabs at his pouch. Pulls out little blue envelope and thrusts it at me. A telegram! If the postman hadn't caught hold of me, might have fallen on the ground. Message can only have come from Edinburgh. No one else knows where I am. Just knew it *had* to be bad news. That's what telegrams are for. My daughter must have died!

Postman sat me down again on the kitchen step. Must have read it anyway. Already knew it was something terrible. Took a deep breath, put my thumb into the corner, thinking we hadn't even chosen a name for her. All too late now. Cheap buff paper poked out of the blue envelope like broken bone. Unfolded it. Block caps in a French fist:

'DAUGHTER WELL STOP IN LIGHT OF CIRCUMSTANCES WHICH CANNOT ELABORATE IMPERATIVE YOU RETURN EDINBURGH FORTHWITH.'

Let out a yell of relief. Jumped up and hugged a very confused postman. Then felt wary. Was Pinstripe acting the clever bastard? What in the hell did 'in light of circumstances' mean? Had he taken the letter to the police? Were they trying to lure me back? Couldn't just ignore it, but what to do? Even thought of sneaking back, seeing my daughter then flying off to the States without telling anyone. Could they get me *there* for what I'd done? Whole point had been to squeeze out some extra dough. Margot maybe wasn't rich as Croesus, but now she's dead as mutton and doesn't need her loot. Me, I'm running on vapour, and not a red cent to come if I skipped. Besides, wasn't doing it for me.

Maybe ought to have replied but I let the postman go. Still had things to do. Reckoned once the board was up there a few weeks, no one who didn't out-and-out *know* there was a loft up there would ever notice. And only one person alive has any idea what's up there.[2]

Made a bonfire of the remaining blank canvases and all the empty sketchbooks. Seemed longer then but reckon only took a couple of minutes to get them going. Primed canvas burns pretty quick. Poked about in the flames and propped the stretchers so they crowded over the hottest part. Had to go on tearing paper, feeding it into the bonfire; there was so much of it. Bits of canvas, like burning bats, lifted into the air. Stayed up there till only thing left were the metal spirals then stumbled back down to the farmhouse. Hard to see anything; been staring into the flames so hard. In the kitchen, looked at my watch. Saw my hands and arms were filthy. Washed them in the kitchen sink and, in the mirror above it, saw my face was black too. Stripped to the waist, washed, then put my clothes on again and went out to the car. Turned it round to put the headlights on the door, collected up the empty can of whitewash, brush, all that stuff. Put them in a carton and stowed everything in the trunk. Finally, picked up the camera bag, put it on the front seat, turned the key in the farmhouse door and drove carefully back into Arles.

Next morning, drove around till I spotted a builder's skip and dropped my rubbish in it. Went back to the realtor. How far in advance had the rent been paid? Expected him to look it up but he just waved his hands about looking confused. Mumbled something like 'situation was not normal'. Instructions were to let the property to a Madame Rembrandt who would bring a letter of authority. Paid for looking after the property but there was no rent. He'd just received another payment. 'Perhaps this is confidential information but …'

Spur of the moment, asked why, when we first met, he mentioned the name Golden? Bastard looked *real* guilty. 'Madame asked me to do so. She said it would be a pleasant surprise for you.'

Walked round to the PTT. Sent a 'returning shortly' telegram to Pinstripe. Checked out and bought a plane ticket. Knew where I was heading; Just couldn't figure what I'd do when I got there.

Comfort break and, I had a couple of things to think about. It wasn't that they were mutually incompatible, just that I could see great difficulty in coping with both at the same time. One was Anna. I could see how, physically, our relationship was likely to end – now there's a Freudian slip – I meant end *up*. Getting into bed with Anna ought to be the beginning of a relationship but I was really scared it might mean the end of my thesis, my career and all of that. I could just hear the 'Honey, it's cold outside' line that she would come out with. And if I was getting a bedful of wonderful sex what might I not agree to in a weak, or do I mean a limp moment? But I had other, equally self-centred, equally selfish thoughts.

Joe had already given me so much to consider in regard to Golden's own paintings and, between sessions, I was completely reappraising what I'd originally thought about them. I seemed to have enough now for a *couple* of theses, plus a monograph, not to mention a *catalogue raisonné*. All of this would need my getting back to London and then over to France: there were several years of very satisfying work in prospect. If there really was a complete set of Golden Rembrandts lying asleep in an attic in Arles, it would be the making of anyone's career, never mind the artist's – and never mind *anyone*; I'm talking *me*. But why, for God's sake, was he telling me all this – a professional art historian for whom academic principles were transmuting alchemically into something of a flexible philosophy – if he didn't expect me to hightail it for France as soon as I could decently get away? Straight after the funeral, perhaps; skipping the ham tea, or whatever they have in California.

How could I have seen what was coming?

Monday afternoon, back in Edinburgh and, straight from the

airport, went round to the address in the realtor's files. Elegant street, every front door up two three steps. Brass plates polished. Looking at my reflection, wondered if any doorman would let me in. Door opened smoothly enough. Stepped into a silent hallway. New carpet. Place spoke money; much more than Pinstripe had ever put on display. Lawyers, in my experience, starting from that guy with the broken jaw, don't spend on carpet without some client's paying; and this outfit must have some rich clients.

Smooth lady looked up; didn't even speak, just arched an eyebrow. Told her my name, that my late wife, Margot, rented a property in France they were responsible for. Asked to see whoever looked after this. Miss Aloof held open door of a small room and waved me in. Sometimes wonder if they were watching me through some one-way mirror, waiting till I got up to go; thirty minutes seemed like a couple of hours. Getting real tired of the way the leather sofa creaked every time every way I moved. Long enough! Stood up, said out loud, 'the hell with this; I didn't have to come here.' Perfect timing.

'Even so, Mr Rembrandt, I'm glad you did.' Tall guy stood in the doorway, mohair suit, limp hair, damp handshake, and no trace of Scottish accent saying, 'I should very much welcome a talk with you.'

Apologised for keeping me waiting. Impressed the hell out of me producing a *drinkable* cup of coffee. Said he'd been consulting files and calling a retired partner before he was ready to talk with me, since my visit was 'unannounced, if not, altogether, unexpected'.

Began to have uneasy feelings. Had come to get answers, but now *he* was asking the questions. First off, how come this visit? None of the partners had ever been in touch. Didn't need to protect the realtor but said he'd been called away for a moment and a glance in the file had let me see their name. Things didn't tie up. Wanted some answers. Damp Hand made some remark about the realtor's 'regrettable breach of professional etiquette'. Wasted on me.

'However, now that you are here, Mr Rembrandt, what, might one ask, is the specific point of your visit to this office?'

Pompous prick was irritating the hell out of me; maybe that's why I remember every word he said. Or is it because of what he said; who knows? Pitched right in to him. Too damn much my late wife hadn't told me. Wanted to find out how come I'd been kept in the dark. Looked at me for a moment and repeated my words, 'Late wife? And who was your wife, Mr Rembrandt?'

'What the hell is this? You're asking me who my *wife* is, I mean was?'

'I do assure you, this is important.'

'My wife was Margot Orr. We got married last year in Scotland. Her maiden name was Golden.'

And he began to shake his head.

'Her *maiden* name was Moreau; that of her natural mother. Her father's name was, indeed, Golden. But her parents were never married. Our client has been at great pains to establish this.'

'Your client? What in hell's name are we talking about here? *Who's* your frigging client then? Not my wife?'

'My firm represents Mrs Euphemia Golden who is the legal owner of the farmhouse near Arles where you have been living.'

'Mrs Golden? You mean *not* Margot's mother?'

Again, the guy shook his head. 'No, I am referring to the widow of the late Alexander Golden.'

'Jesus. What's going on here? We're going round in circles?'

'Mr Rembrandt, satisfy me as to your identity and I shall give you a great deal of information which, in all the circumstances, I think you deserve to hear.'

Damp Hand leafs through my passport; hands it back. Says, 'I believe you are indeed Joseph Rembrandt.' Now pay attention, young Bill. From now on in, it gets complicated.

Takes me through into his office, sits me in a comfortable armchair and parks himself opposite, flips open the humidor.

'*Romeo y Julieta*? I don't believe they're available in America at present.'

Still had no idea where all this is going? Even so, haven't had a decent Havana in a long time. Lit it with real care and got a blue-grey haze building round my head in just a couple of minutes.

'Spit it out then, damn it. Like your cigar, but I don't like games.'

You'll never believe what he told me. Seems the first Mrs Golden was the *only* Mrs G, and she was tough as old boots. Had to be. Still alive and into her late nineties. Been moved only last year into a nursing home. Pretty deaf but could still see and could still bite. Still refused to sell the house she'd lived in for seventy years. 'Where would I go when I'm better,' she'd asked. Got some spirit. After all, she's the one that stormed over to France to demand her rights. Well, she lost that round. At first, she'd been the wealthy one in the marriage – family money – until the first and only Alexander Golden started producing saleable paintings. She was the one who owned the big house and garden and insisted on a painting shack in the garden so there was no mess in the house. But Damp Hand's uncle had told him she'd followed him down the garden, yakking on all the time he painted and insisting on cleaning his brushes, sometimes even before he could get the paint onto the canvas.

Anyways, when the sun broke through the green and brown mists in front of his eyes, looking at all those Delaunays, guess maybe the chance to paint in peace was at least part of the reason he split. Anyways, Golden's gone, his wife's abandoned and pretty sore; not just pissed off at being ditched but mad about the money.

Then, around ten years later, up on her doorstep turns this younger woman, French, not bad looking and towing a kid behind her. Saying she's the second Mrs Golden and, unlike Euphemia, she's given Golden an heir. But there's no birth certificate, no wedding certificate either, or she's lost them; no proof. And another funny thing; she's saying Alexander has disappeared again. Not a thing about being dead, being called Orr or anything else.

Instead of getting out her usual ten-foot pole, the first Mrs Golden listens to the whole story, and all the time she's looking at the kid. Can *see* the resemblance; it's his kid all right, and she finds herself wishing it was hers. They say money talks, Bill. Never a truer word. All against the advice of her lawyer, Damp Hand's uncle, she puts it to the flat-broke Ghislaine that, in return for cash down and an annual sum, Euphemia gets a share in Margot and total ownership of the farmhouse.

The Mrs G share is supposed to be eight weeks a year in Scotland, then when the kid's eight she's to go school in Edinburgh. Looking around at the wealth dripping off the walls mostly painted by their mutual 'husband', and she didn't even have the cab fare back to the station, seems Ghislaine said yes. Trouble was – well there were two troubles. First off, Margot actually seemed to like it better in Edinburgh than with Ghislaine's relatives in Roubaix and, second of all, the war came along while Margot was over visiting Scotland and they didn't even hear from Ghislaine until that was all over. Then they get a letter from a *notaire* in Roubaix saying he represents M and Mme Mondicourt and asking for the back pay due to Mme Mondicourt, formerly Moreau, plus return of her daughter for six years to make up for the time lost during the war.

But Mrs Golden and her lawyers dig the dirt on the Mondicourts; find out she's married her pimp and has a drink problem. What with the fact that Margot only ever talks about her father, never her mother, they figure a pretty modest sum would buy off the threat permanently. And they're damned right. What's more, though she's old enough to be Margot's grandmother, Euphemia adopts the kid and gets her British nationality. Another thing, she fixes up the painting shack as Margot's play house although the kid's already a teenager. And when young Damp Hand comes into the business, that's pretty much how things stand.

Margot's doing well at St George's, brilliant at French, keen on Art, plays lacrosse, all that frigging stuff, and when it's time to move on she says she wants to work in an art gallery. Her 'mother' makes her train at the local secretarial college first but she's soon working in a swanky private gallery that represents all the well-known Scottish artists post-war. She gets a miserable salary but Ma Golden gives her a generous allowance so she's doing all right. About that time, Damp Hand the nephew gets told to look after Margot's legal and financial affairs while the uncle sticks with Euphemia.

That's how he has to call on her one day and is shown down the garden to the shack where Margot's resting on a day bed, recovering from 'flu. Needs her signature on an income tax return or some such. Inside of that shack is a revelation. Every square inch covered with reproductions of the Golden Month, postcards and what looks like at least two copies of the Lefebvre book ripped up and pasted round the walls. And get this, on the table there's a book about van Meegeren. Damp Hand knows next to frigging nothing about painting but he's heard of van Meegeren because there was a question about copyright in his finals and that talented old forger's case had been a useful example to use in his answer. Then to cap it all, when he says something about what he calls 'this tribute to your late father', she spits tacks and shouts at him that 'Daddy's not dead' and that one day he's coming back 'to give her all his *new* paintings'. Bizarre.

Couple of months later, she announces to Euphemia that she's been offered a job at the gallery's new London space in Cork Street but Damp Hand happens to know she's actually moving in with the son of the gallery owner who's been packed off to open up the London market. It was when she was dumped by the son, and sacked by the owner, about a year later, that she had a long breakdown and spent another year in rehab. Relations with her Scottish mother were cool, perhaps, but Euphemia is forgiving and actually suggests the classic 'long sea voyage' to help her recover. Go figure; this is where I come in. One more thing, Margot changed her name a second time. She'd gone from Moreau to Golden and now she called herself Orr. Damp Hand had to explain that little joke to me. But he doesn't know what I think *I* know about the late Alexander, and I don't bother to explain that joke to him.

Seems that's the end of his story, then, out of the blue, Damp Hand tells me that he's heard that morning my daughter is doing well and asks if I've been to see her yet. Jeez, do I feel guilty about not going there first. Been planning to walk along the street to Pinstripe next but instead I ask him to call me a cab. But when I get up to walk across his office, never make it to the door. Jolt of pain like a massive kick in the balls knocks me down. Bang my head on the edge of his mahogany desk. Come to a day later, in another world.

Talk about a long day. I couldn't compare myself to Joe, who must have been through the wringer telling me all this, but I was in information overload. Somehow, I needed to relax and unwind. Nothing had been arranged between us but, on the evidence, as she might say, or judging by appearances as I might, it would be surprising if I didn't hear from her. On cue, Joe's man-about-the-house brought a phone out to the poolside where I was looking at my almost unintelligible notes and sinking a cool beer.

'Professor?'

'Counsellor!'

'Want to go to a party?'

And that was the evening taken care of. I had time for a shower, yet another shave and a thirty minute snooze before it was time to get out there, looking eager. I'd been told to wear jeans and a beach shirt. It was someone's birthday bash and after meeting a few others in a bar on Ocean we were joining the birthday boy for a barbecue on the sand. Already in the bar the evening began to go wrong. And it wasn't my fault.

I was being glad handed round the group of ten or so who were starting there and my English accent was doing me no harm at all with the girls. I hadn't time to notice if this was putting Anna's nose out of joint but that might have been the next situation to develop, the way one of the girls seemed to take a fancy to me straight away. I sloped off to the men's room to off-load some of the beer, lest peeing on the beach was frowned on in Carmel. And that was where I saw, for the first time in my life, a vending machine selling protective clothing. Furtively, I swapped a dollar for a packet of two. Back in the bar, there was a row going on. I could hear Anna's voice raised.

But it wasn't her and her 'rival'; it was her – and mine. A tall young Adonis, American-handsome with perfect teeth, wavy hair and a sun tan, was bawling at Anna, and she was yelling back. Their friends were shouting at them both to calm down but they were all grinning; this was sport. Then this Clark Kent look-alike spotted me. I was so obviously un-American. Straightaway, he broke out of the surrounding ring of spectators, came storming over, grabbed me and, before anyone else had time to react, ran me out of the bar. I remember thinking it was time to get out of Carmel too; it was getting too dangerous. On the sidewalk, he swung a wild punch at my head. I swayed back but it caught me on the chest and knocked me down. With a perfect sense of cinema, however, he managed to do this just as two of Carmel's finest (and thickest) pulled up alongside. Before those in the bar could intervene, we were being bundled into their patrol car and driven away.

Skip the details but, after fingerprinting, photographing, and emptying all our pockets and having the contents listed, we were put in separate cells. Not too many minutes later, I was told 'my lawyer' had arrived and wanted to see me. She was escorted into the cell. She waited until we were both locked in then she rushed over and threw her arms around me.

'Anna, can you get me out of here?'

She nodded. 'But I need to tell you something quickly.'

It didn't surprise me to hear that my assailant was her locally-based boy friend but I didn't like to hear that she had been in a 'relationship' with him and that he had seriously proposed marriage last Valentine's Day and been put on hold for six months. Handsome he was but intellectual he wasn't and that was where the problem lay. They'd been high school sweethearts and while he led the school to triumph after triumph on the sports field she had led the cheering from the touchline. After high school, however, her mind became more acute through exploring law from all the angles; his more obtuse through working in his parents' furniture store. Then, as the song puts it, 'Along came Bill.'

The up-side from this brief police-cell revelation was that she clearly preferred me to him. The downside was her equally clear assumption that, having won her from Adonis, I would be taking over his several rôles; boy friend certainly, lover most likely, and long-term partner presumptive. I liked her very much, would enjoy sharing a bed with her but I was still too green to get married, far less engaged. It was all happening too fast and too soon. Then she kissed me, with much more passion than the first time, and I slipped into rôle one without feeling any pain and looked forward to rôle two as soon as possible, suppressing fears about rôle three as too far into the future – beyond tomorrow – to be worried about now.

She banged on the cell door and we were escorted to the desk where I was administered a severe frown and then had the embarrassment of having my possessions restored in front of Anna. The desk sergeant intoned 'One two-pack rubbers' and got me to sign for them.

The beach party was obviously the place to avoid and I may have my first Mexican meal to blame for the fact that we did not finish up having protected sex that night. After eating red-hot iron filings through a wet facecloth, I pleaded to be driven back to Joe's where I dosed myself with Pepto-Bismol. Next morning, I could still feel the chillies on my breath and in my mouth and all through my tender alimentary canal.

As I ate a pink grapefruit, both halves, and several slices of toasted Wonderloaf, washed down with three full mugs of Folgers, I wondered nervously if I were engaged. My lawyer might well think so. Meantime, in the here and now, Joe seemed ready to explain what had happened to him. The Golden connection might seem tenuous but I was too wrapped up in Joe's own story to worry about that for the moment.

Have some vague recollections of people crowding round. Pain in my groin real terrible. Wanting to pee so damned much, wouldn't have given a damn about pissing all Damp Hand's Persian carpet but no way could I 'go'. Must have been an ambulance, then nurses and doctors.

Next thing I'm waking up in fits and starts, seeing someone looking half my age, no white coat but a bow tie and a big smile, peering into my face. Had a sparky first meeting.

'Ah there you are, Mr Rembrandt. Welcome to Cumlodden Clinic. I was wondering when you would be joining us. After all, it is *your* party. Good morning, my name is Mr Alexander Waugh.' He rhymed it with 'loch' and I didn't find out how to spell it for weeks; another frigging Alexander, Jeez.

'Don't I get to see a doctor?'

'I was one once, before I became a consultant surgeon. Mr Rembrandt, we need to talk.'

'Talk about what, for Chrissake. What's the matter with me? What've you done?'

Very simple, he says. I'd been ill for some time and should have complained about my symptoms sooner if I hadn't been too busy doing other things. It's cancer of the prostate and he'll need to start treatment straight off if I'm going to have a chance of recovery. Going to be no fun at all and he wants my signature on a consent form so he can wave it in front of me when I get sore and ask him to stop. Ask him if I have a choice.

'Certainly; I can put you in a quiet room at the back of the Clinic, and keep you sedated until you eventually expire, but that would be an expensive waste of my training and of a much needed bed. You *do* have a *chance* of life. I sincerely hope you'll take it.'

How long would all this take? Six months minimum, then another six for R and R.

Asked him 'So what are the odds for me, right now? Actually put his soft, pink hand on mine and looked me straight in the eye.

'Fifty-fifty, but I wouldn't suggest an excessively large stake.'

Began to like him.

Skip the next two three weeks except to say I got bulletins about Baby Rembrandt, mostly fair but never sunny. Then, one morning, after Waugh's visit, nurse asked if I felt well enough for visitors.

Wasn't conscious enough to guess who they might be. But round the curtain comes Pinstripe with someone else in tow. He starts off in his goddam round-the-houses way.

'We shall have to ask you to be so kind as to forgive this intrusion on your bed of pain.'

Cut him short.

'How did you track me down?'

Simple enough: he'd had a call from Damp Hand.

'In all the circumstances, Mr Rembrandt, I feel I have to obtain your instructions.'

'I'm going to tell *you* what to do?'

'Mr Rembrandt, I think you really ought to allow me a moment or two to tell you where you presently stand. I very much doubt that you can possibly be fully cognisant of your very much altered position.'

My "very much altered position" I told him is lying prone on a hospital bed, with my ass stuffed with cancer and chemicals and, what's more to the point, only limited means to keep myself and my baby daughter going. Didn't need him to come and tell me that. How *is* my daughter, anyway? Great deal! *We're* both in hospital and her mother's dead. Some family. Hadn't consciously seen someone purse their lips before.

Told him, 'What you can do for me, as my lawyer – Margot's lawyer anyway – is squeeze some money out of the system to see my daughter gets medical care, then a decent start in life. That'd be a real service. Never mind me. May not be here all that long anyhow.'

Reckon some of my pent up fear was coming out. Pinstripe just happened to be in the way. He managed not to flinch under fire, and when I paused to reload, he tried again.

'Mr Rembrandt, I rather think that we can do more for you than you presently realise. You will need to let us explain things in our own way as the matters are legally somewhat complex. But you must, I do assure you, be made aware of them immediately.'

My outburst left me feeling tired enough just to lie there and listen.

He'd been personally responsible for drawing up Margot's will, like he'd been responsible for the pre-nup under which I wouldn't inherit a red cent. Pinstripe concedes I might well have been entitled to a share even so; the law here in Haggis County being different, but when he says it doesn't matter now he starts to lose me.

'Whadya mean fella? Telling me she's left it to some cat and dog home?' Winced with pain, had to draw breath and that gave Pinstripe another chance.

'No, Mr Rembrandt. She has bequeathed her entire estate to you. Not only this but you need to be aware that, only last week, Mrs Euphemia Golden passed away and, since we have been advised by her own lawyers that her entire estate, which is substantial, was bequeathed to the late Mrs Rembrandt, it follows, since you are the only heir, that this estate comes to you as well. You will be able, after the appropriate duties have been paid, on both estates, to make your own, quite ample provisions for your daughter and yourself.'

Jee-zus Kee-rist! What had he just said? Was Pinstripe sitting there, briefcase on his knee, bowler hat smack in the middle of it, telling me he'd had a vision. That Margot had come down to him in a dream, telling him to take care of me after all? Life isn't like that. Maybe I was dead already and being tormented, just like I deserved.

'Mr Rembrandt, you will recall that you delivered a letter to me from your late wife.' Did I recall? Sweet Jesus I recalled! Thought to myself they're coming to arrest me; in my hospital bed. But the other man in black hovering there wasn't a detective. Some friend of Pinstripe's. Introduced as an advocate.

Pinstripe said he'd consulted him because, the way the letter was worded, it just might possibly be read as her latest and last will and he needed to be entirely sure of this in law. I went *very* silent.

'The letter expresses the intention that Mrs Rembrandt had formed of giving due and proper recognition to the fact of your marriage and to the loving way you had behaved towards her. She wished to have her entire estate bequeathed to you which, if the earlier provisions had not been made, would be the normal course as between spouses. Since Mrs Rembrandt's earlier will clearly did not bequeath her estate to you, what I had to establish, and what Mr Farquhar-McCutcheon here has given as his *unqualified* opinion, is that the wording of the letter can be read, quite unambiguously, as the last will and testament of the late Mrs Margot Rembrandt. We shall have to have this homologated by the Court of Session, of course, but we are in no doubt about the outcome. You, Mr Rembrandt, are your late wife's sole heir.'

Must have lain there in silence for couple of minutes – the advocate even consulted his watch – battling between wanting to know some more and the urge to laugh myself sick.

'But how can a letter be a will? Wills need lawyers, witnesses, and all? Leastways, they do where *I* come from.'

Smug glances between these two. The advocate got in first.

'We are talking here about *Scots* Law, Mr Rembrandt, and this document is a holograph will; that is to say, it is written, dated and *signed* entirely in the testatrix's own handwriting. Under Scots Law, such a will does not require to be witnessed in order to be legal. It was the wording of the letter that, in these circumstances, was crucial, given that it must have been written only a few hours before her death, but, having studied the wording with great care, my opinion is unqualified. The letter constitutes a holograph will and you are, in consequence, your late wife's sole heir.'

'And I need your instructions,' added Pinstripe.

'Look after my daughter, number one. Get her the best of

everything. Then come back and see me next week if I'm still here, number two. Need time to think.'

Meek as two lambs, they stood up, nodded politely and left. And there I was; a middle-aged father, a widower, a talented artist, accomplished forger, riddled with cancer and rich. Jee-zuz, was I frigging rich. Not such a bad day as it had started out.

Joe's doctor came by just at this point and as I backed out, the guy told me to give Joe until the afternoon as he was going to run some tests and then administer some injections. He actually walked with me to the door of Joe's room and said, in a quiet voice, that whatever it was we were talking about, it seemed to him I was doing Joe a lot of good, taking his mind off things. Flattered by that, I went to my own room and worked quite earnestly on my thesis – which took my *own* mind off things.

My testing time seemed likely to come that evening. We had agreed to go for a steak and then Anna thought it 'might be fun' to show me her small apartment on San Carlos Street. I knew what I didn't want to happen, but I knew what was almost certain to.

After my note writing, I had time for a couple of dozen lengths of the pool before the well-tossed Waldorf salad and snooze that seemed to have become the pattern for the visiting art historian. It was getting on for four when Joe sent word he'd like to see me. I wondered when I could get him back on the Golden track.

---

1   Maguire's Law: All inanimate objects are naturally vindictive, especially farmhouses.

2   But now it's two, Joe. And you're dying! Thoughts I ought to have been ashamed of were running through my head. How long had I got? More to the point, how long had Joe? How soon could I get there – to Arles, I mean – break the news, write the monograph, sell the serial rights, buy the villa (and a little apartment in Paris for study trips and giving a few lectures) and become the lover of Anna Glover? Cold mental shower!!!

4

'When you're down on your luck,' my fortune cookie said one time, 'think how you can help someone else.' Neat, huh? Needed something then; take my mind off my own problems. Of course the one thing, I mean one *person* mattered most was just a scrap of humanity in an oleo tub, somewhere else in Edinburgh. Still being given a daily bulletin and the news is good only because it isn't bad.

Me, I'm lying in a hospital bed, in a foreign country: at least the natives speak some kind of barely comprehensible English. Had money now but not health, so wasn't going to be much use to me. Depressing to admit it, but that's when I sent for Fancy Dress. Nearest thing to a friend, and once in New York he'd introduced me to that kid brother of his.

Kid brother was all-American; clean living, hard working, happily married, active in the community; all that. Didn't seem to have more than a cupful of the bullshit that oozed out of Fancy Dress by the quart. Only one thing stopped him posing for Norman Rockwell on the cover of *Saturday Evening Post*. Didn't seem able to have kids.

If I was going to die – more like *when* I died – wanted my daughter brought up in America, not elsewhere. I'd *seen* elsewhere! Call me prejudiced but as one *rich* American wanted my daughter to be another. Wanted to make damn sure she had a good start in life even if I wasn't around to see it. Made me feel good, and miserable at the same time. Hell, wanted to be around to see. What else point was there?

But even if I lived, what was a convalescent cancer victim doing, fifty-some years older than his daughter besides being a widower, even *thinking* about being a suitable parent when there was this couple, Kid brother and his wife, who might just be the ones to do it. Leastways, if I died, sure she'd be in good hands. Cabled Fancy Dress; Western Union.

Said I was sick, needed his help and could pay for it. Asked him and his brother to get the hell over here, Pan American. Reckon the smell of money brought him running. I'd just had surgery, so one ghastly sight greeted them. Fancy Dress was new into Polaroids. Only looked at one. Boris Karloff wasn't in it! In the spells they were allowed in, we talked. Leastways, Kid Brother and I talked. After half a day, Fancy Dress got bored. Went off exploring, and practising spending my money.

Kid Brother was everything I'd remembered but, straight off, said he had to get his wife to agree to any deal. Shows how often I did this; I should have thought myself. Told him, fetch her over. Put another three four days onto the whole deal. Had to put up with Pinstripe coming back to see me.

Told me just how much money I'd have in the bank, even after socialist taxes. If we went on living in the UK, or, more to the point, if I died there, the stash would all go to my daughter, but only after another bundle of tax, one helluva of a bundle of tax. Asked him to set things up to see she was taken care of, not ripped off, even if I only lasted a few weeks. By the time we'd gotten through, nurses were *hauling* him out of the room.

Next day, Kid Brother and his wife came round. 'Only two visitors at the bedside,' the sister said, which was great because I could send Fancy Dress off and speak to the pair of them. Was she lovely! California suntan. Great figure. Yes, I could still notice that. And sensible; almost too sensible. Real Doris Day.

Back home they'd already been talking about going for adoption. Even so, Doris seemed pretty wary about having the baby's father crowding them, trying to second guess every decision; like where she went to school, approving her friends, all that. Logical, from her point of view but, truth was, hadn't given this any thought. Realised I'd pretty well been assuming I'd live nearby, and keep dropping in – if I survived.

Okay, might not survive, and if I did, maybe not for long. So, agreed to that point – for now. If they adopted her legally, wouldn't live in the same town, wouldn't visit more than three four times a year; wouldn't *ever* tell her who I was. Part of me really resented all this, but my better side liked Kid Brother's wife more for being so practical and sensible. Wasn't all though!

Looks me in the eye and says, 'Frankly, Joe, the money's a problem. I mean, don't get me wrong. We're glad you're rich. Couldn't happen to a nicer guy and all that, but if you were us, would *you* adopt a Woolworth heiress? Look at it this way. If a kid has too much money and too many things, she's not like the other kids on the block. She's different, and they won't like her. And besides, what's she got to struggle for? Why should she work hard in grade school? It doesn't figure.

'And look at it from our point of view. We work pretty hard and we pay our bills, but there isn't much left over most months. We'd like to do better and have a chance to move up the ladder but we don't figure on doing it just because we're our daughter's hired help, getting a wage for looking after her. What kind of parenthood is that? I mean, we love you, Joe, for thinking about us this way, and we came because you asked us to and because we wanted to thank you but neither of us really want you to buy our help.'

And then of course, just as I'm getting tired and just one helluva frustrated listening to all this – not least because it made such goddam, all-American, good sense – she does the sweetest thing. Leans over the bed and kisses me on the forehead and her sweet-smelling, Doris Day figure presses against me for a second or two.

Said, 'While you're here, go round and see her. Tell me how she *really* is.'

Sure touched the right button. Made us all cry a bit. Said she'd be glad to and off they went. Day later, just when the treatment was making me want to die – not just fade away and die, but die, die, die right now – back come Kid Brother and Doris, this time with Pinstripe in tow. Kisses me again but can't appreciate it so much this time and they only have a few minutes visiting rights so straight to the point. My daughter is beautiful, getting stronger all the time, out of the incubator and Doris has held her in her own arms. More than I've done. She and her husband already head over heels in love with her. Struggling hard to be practical and sensible, act like Doris Day should, but, boy oh boy, does she *want* that baby! And there I am, sick as two parrots, ready to die and willing to give away a part of myself to someone who, week ago, was a total stranger.

'Talk to Pinstripe,' I tell her. 'Sort out a sensible deal.' Pass out even before they're shown out.

Pinstripe comes back a couple of weeks later; tells me they're ready to discharge my daughter pretty soon, so urgent now to make my mind up. He's looked into the background of Kid Brother and Doris, and gotten a glowing reference from a very reputable lawyer in 'Frisco. Looked at all the possible financial arrangements. Got suggestions to keep everyone happy.

In a nutshell, a trust or some such animal, enough for schooling right through college and beyond, Blue Cross, Blue Shield; all that stuff. Then, at twenty-seven, not a day sooner, she hits the jackpot; seriously rich. By that time, if she has the values her new parents plan to drill into her, might not go to her head as well as her pocket book. Odds were yours truly wouldn't be around to see what kind of mess we'd all made. Pinstripe brought a stenographer and typist along with him and had me make my own will on the spot – typed, signed and witnessed in the hospital. Left everything I owned, every frigging heritable and not forgetting every movable, to the heirs and successors of Kid Brother and Doris Day. Nothing handwritten this time! Pinstripe also reported he'd had Margot defrosted and then cremated with the late Mrs. Golden in a touching double ceremony.

The nice Bill Maguire, as distinct from the ambitious art historian and the lustful lawyer-lover, was much moved by all this. But, once again, I was getting restless. Was my willingness to stay on and listen to this fairy story outcome because I didn't want to miss any Golden nuggets, or, just as likely, because I couldn't get Anna out of my mind or my mind's eye? She called unexpectedly to cancel our date: a major legal project had come up that involved reading masses of documents against a deadline. I found myself pleading that we meet up; and soon.

Fortunately for him, and for my patience, when we talked in the early evening, Joe's hospital sequence drew to a close and, after paying a great deal of money for his own treatment – not being British born like his daughter – he made it back to America. So I can let him rest for a while and catch up on my own story.

Not long after I had slipped between lonely sheets that night, my bedside phone rang. I snatched it up.

'Bill?'

'Anna. I've been thinking about you!'

'I certainly hope so.'

'Not just thinking about you.'

'That's good.'

'When can we see each other again?'

'Bill, soon, I hope, but you got to tell me the truth.'

'Haven't I?'

'Possibly. But listen up. This isn't easy. I've told you I'm already in a relationship.'

'Anna?'

'And it's been getting serious. He keeps wanting for us to get married but I guess I'm not sure. Don't feel ready for it. And besides, it looks too much like he thinks it's a smart career move. He's been promised a partnership, in the family business. I think he simply figures it's time for a man like him to be married. His *mother* keeps saying so.'

'Are you trying to let me down gently?'

'I don't think so, Bill. I *think* I'm trying to ask you just how you really feel about me, because it would make a difference to feel sure you'd been telling me the truth.'

'The truth?'

Why did her question automatically make me *feel* guilty?

'Bill, not so long ago, I think I heard you say you loved me and nobody's ever said that to me like you just said it.'

I *think* I heard myself say that too. Why are lawyers so literal? I think I meant it, then.

'Anna, sweetheart, where are you? I'm coming round right now.'

'Stay put, Bill Maguire. Keep your distance. This is too important. If you really, truthfully love me, everything between us can be put on hold until I tell *him* the truth.'

'The truth, Anna?'

'The truth, the relevant part of the truth, and not much else besides. Okay?'

'Listen, Anna, this *is* getting very serious. Don't you think we ought to meet?'

'Dammit, you pompous Limey, why can't you just say, "I love you."'

And the phone slammed down. I tried to ring but first it was engaged and then it went into her answering machine. I hung up and lay down again, but sleep was out of the question. Had I failed again, liked I seemed to do any and every time someone offered me love – not love *without* strings but rather the love that binds, that commits, the excludes all other loves, that forces you to make your mind up when you, I mean me, hell you know what I mean...

Just as well I had the Uher with me because, if I'm honest, my mind was on other things and another person as I sat next day beside my host.

Eight hours time difference and all, maybe wasn't in the best shape. Even so, took a cab from the airport straight round to Kid Brother's address. Didn't expect what I saw: run-down, three-storey timber frame, needing *minimum* two coats of paint, building materials all over the yard and Kid Brother out front, loading two-by-fours in his pick-up. Pretty taken aback to see me.

'Hell, Joe. We knew you were coming back to California but I don't reckon Doris is going to be happy you just came right over without calling first. Anyhow, she's not in right now. She and the baby are visiting with her sister. Listen, you and me got to talk a little.'

Could feel real pains round my heart. What *was* all this?

'Doris is getting real anxious. She's afraid, after all you've promised, you're just going to crowd us and keep so close tabs we won't be able to change a diaper without you wanting a sniff. Know whose kid she really is but, *legally*, she's Doris's now, and mine too. Just don't want to feel you hovering there, across the street, watching the house, ready to send in a posse soon's you hear a baby crying. I mean, Hell, here you are *already*.'

'Dammit to hell, she's *my* daughter. Only natural? Haven't seen her for months. Probably won't even recognise her.' Thought of that kinda tightened the grip round my heart. Had to sit down on his porch.

'What you expect me to do? Write?'

'Joe! A phone call would have been enough. Doris is convinced you won't like this place. Says we ought to bring the baby to see you at your place, or in a hotel, or something. Like for us to move, for all our sakes, but I'm not taking in as much as I'd like right now. I haven't any spare dough.'

'For Chrissake. You need dough? I got dough. Lots of dough. Dough is all I got. You want a better house? I'll *give* you a better house. What's the problem?'

'The problem? Jeez, that *is* the problem! Doris don't want your dough and Doris don't want you hanging round here neither, looking down your nose how we're raising *our* daughter. Doris wants it her way! And I want it Doris's way – if I know what's good for me. Please! Go home Joe, and give us a call so we can fix to meet the way Doris wants it.'

Afraid I was going to be sick. Asked him to call me a cab and sat and shivered, even in glorious California sunshine. Totally defeated, climbed into the cab and left him to it.

'Don't tell her I came. Then neither of us is going to get it in the neck.'

Agreed to that, you bet. Stood in the road and waved me off. Thought to myself I'd paid good money to check them out and the report wasn't worth shit. Sure, swell couple, kind to their dog, go to church. But turns out the guy can't run a business, and Doris is paranoid. In her mind, I was planning to call round one day soon with the local sheriff and take her baby away. Damn good idea too, but not just for the moment. Hadn't the strength. Had to play this one long.

Back at my hotel, ate a *real* hamburger, 'hold the lettuce, heavy on the mayo, side order of dill pickle,' washed down with a Miller. Feeling like an American again, took a deep breath and made the call.

Doris answered. Pleasant but nervous. Said she was sure I ought to rest after flying over – after all, she and Kid Brother had been totally whacked. Maybe the weekend would be all right. They'd come by my hotel, just for an hour or so. Simplest to agree. Didn't want a fight; leastways, not yet. Wanted to see my daughter.

Turned up in a very clean car; saw the Hertz sticker. Doris in back with Little Pinkie. Right at the beginning, it was wonderful. Got to carry my baby from the car park, right through the lobby, all the way up in the elevator and even into my suite, Doris hovering at my elbow all the way. Felt just fantastic; like a new Dad should. Guess it showed too much. As soon as we reached the room, Doris grabbed her back.

Waiters, arriving on schedule, covered up the awkwardness. In no time at all, Doris was telling me all the wonderful things *her* daughter was doing, including starting to cut a tooth. Lapped up every word of it and, what's more, behaved myself real well.

Then I asked Kid Brother, 'How's business?'

Doris leapt in with the answer.

'Just fine, Joe. Fine and dandy. Couldn't be better. Could it?'

Gave her husband a desperate look and he read the signal like she'd held up an idiot board.

'Fine,' he mumbled. 'Booming.'

Then Doris was up and packing all the things she'd brought, getting dirty and clean diapers in the same bag.

'It's time we were going. We have things to do.'

Struggled not to explode; ask her what damn things she had to do that were so frigging important she had to take my daughter away when I hadn't seen her for months and, if I counted it up, hadn't seen for as long as this in all her life. Signals told me that if I made any kind of protest then Doris would make a disaster movie out of it. Just had to nod and say something about time marching on.

As she wound down the car window to say goodbye, I began to say, 'I'll see you …' Quick as a flash, she jumped in. 'Yes, maybe in April, sometime.' Then she wound up the window and gave Kid Brother his orders. Watched them drive off, and then tottered back into the hotel. This time it had to be a Scotch.

Next day, hired detectives.

Told them to find out all there was to know about Doris and Kid Brother. Don't ask how they did it but, pretty soon, I knew more about them than they did themselves. Kid Brother was a craftsman, but no organiser. Shouldn't be working for himself, but seemed Doris wasn't going to settle for anything less. In debt? Sure, not head over heels; but let's say well above their knees.

No chance, after signing all these papers, for a frontal attack. Anyway, Hell, didn't want that. I'd agreed to all this because I was dying. Survived so far, but that was bonus. My big fight postponed; Death had taken a rain check. Wanted my daughter brought up in America. That's in hand. Now, wanted for her to have a half-way decent life of it. Wouldn't accept 'charity', okay, but they had agreed to me covering education, and any medical bills. Seen a paediatrician already, quite a few times in fact. Any more absolutely *had* to be without their knowing. Might get a tad suspicious if dollar bills began to arrive in the mail. In the end, it was real simple.

Needed a lawyer and went to see the guy who had given Kid Brother such a good report. Ready to pick a fight with him over his judgement but, as it turned out, he was a real gentleman. Pre-war import from Austria, still a very slight accent and, surprise, surprise, could talk intelligently about modern art. Had me eating out of his hand within the first ten minutes. Turned out the firm managed a whole swathe of property. No time at all, Kid Brother's being hired regularly, paid well and, what's more, promptly. Funny thing, lawyer didn't have to keep on priming the pump. Pretty soon, when he began to *look* a bit more prosperous, other people offered him work so, behind the scenes, lawyer fixed things so the maintenance manager went to Kid Brother and told him he didn't want to lose him to anyone else so how's about some help with order systems, bookkeeping, all that stuff, plus guaranteed work for the next six months, and so on, and so on. Before he knew it, Kid Brother was their full-time subcontractor, pulling in good money.

Old lawyer enjoyed this bit; doing good by stealth. Seemed to have a soft spot for Kid Brother. Pretty much left them all to get on with it; moved out of town and rented a little house here in Carmel, sulked until April. Then I called.

Could almost swear she'd forgotten all about me; didn't even recognize my voice. For a moment, seemed totally confused, then she recovered, asked how I was feeling. Told her just fine and wasn't it about time for one of my 'occasional' visits. That sent her into a spin.

'Joe, could you wait a month or two? We're just about to move house and everything is all topsy-turvy. I want for you to see her in our *new* place. I'm sure you'll like it.'

Liked the idea of them moving to a better place; about time too. So, without really wanting to, agreed to call her again in a month; then put in a call to my gumshoe. Sure enough, no plans at all to move when I phoned but, very same day, Doris called a dozen realtors. In six weeks, she could tell me with a straight face they hadn't moved when they'd hoped to but it was all set for a couple of months time, give or take. Chatted a little bit about teething, first steps and all, but pretty forced. Had to hang up or I'd have yelled at her.

By now, what with weather, wealth, walking on the beach, and a decent diet, was beginning to feel more like the old Joe. On top of that, thinking it was time to fit in that visit to Arles. Sat out on the stoop and conjured up the sounds, smells, sights of the place, and asked myself just what I really wanted to do there.

Had a few quiet moments just remembering all the effort put into those canvases tucked up in the loft. *My* paintings; and now more than just possession; ownership, title, legality. Mine because I'd painted them. Mine because, even working from Golden's sketches, I'd left him far behind artistically. Might have suited me back then to let Margot feel they were Golden realisations but, for all her knowledge of art, she just couldn't see how little Golden had needed to hold my brush. I wasn't painting by numbers any more or inventing games for rich blue-rinses on cruise ships. This was Art with a capital A. And *I'd* done it. Alone. Solo. Me!

Painful admitting this now, but hadn't once noticed how damned obsessed she was. Thought her adoring looks were the way she felt about *me*. Damn fool. More I ran events through my mind's eye, more I saw I'd been conned. But so what? Been conned into painting some goddam wonderful paintings and, one day, whole world would know it. I knew a good con when I saw one.

Made me curious, for the first time in a year or more, nearer two, to look at the sketchbooks. Took them out, almost reverentially and put them on the veranda table. Picked up a glass, some olives and, as an afterthought, my new reading glasses. Latest indulgence. Hadn't needed those painting large canvases. Opened a bottle of wine; just happened to be 'Goldener Oktober'!

'You would have liked this,' said, raising a silent toast to the father-in-law I'd never met and, for a moment at least, wished he was there, to share the experience. After all that fussing, poured another drink and got down to turning the pages. Should have put them straight in the furnace.

And would you believe it, right on cue, in comes a tray of food for him (which he mostly sucks through a straw, poor Joe), and the nurse with a kidney dish full of syringes to take blood out and pump medicine in, bottles of horse pills and all the rest. You could tell something was coming but, the way Joe was telling – and most of the time, it seemed, enjoying telling – his story, he always made it dramatic and surprising. Anyway, I had plenty work to do. One, try to call Anna; two, call Laker and put them off again; three, swim then toy with an omelette; and, four, work on my dissertation. Since I carried out my tasks in order of priority, next to nothing was done to my dissertation except re-reading what I'd written and sleeping on it.

There was only the answering machine when I called Anna. It was good to hear her voice but I didn't dare leave more than a very bland, 'hoping to hear from you sometime' message in case someone else heard it. On an impulse, I rang the local office of the lawyers, Handschumacher's. A receptionist, who spoke too fast and with an accent like Manuel's, told me *Meez* Glover was out of town and might be away for several days. I could hardly ask if she'd gone off to end her other relationship so I left no message there.

Laker reminded me that my return ticket was at a special price and I had to return soon unless I was prepared to pay a surcharge. Flush with my own very small legacy and ready to flash my new Diners Card, I thought what-the-hell. So many clocks were ticking now. There was the count-down to my dissertation. That deadline was an immovable object. There was Joe's 'How to get rich and paint wonderful pictures' story that could come to an abrupt halt without notice, or just might go on for ever. Like Scheherazade, Joe might be keeping himself alive by telling me a thousand and one stories. And then, there was my new love interest. My youthful career had not so far been helped by my too-willing libido; that irresistible force. The wine was cool, soothing and soporific and I snoozed over my manuscript. I came too as Manuel gave me a gentle shake. Joe wanted me.

First few sketches fascinating; just as exciting as when I first looked and saw that economical, deliberate way Golden put colour on paper. Jewel-like clusters, special combinations he's clearly fond of. Getting a real buzz from the memories it all brought back. Wearing eyeglasses now, could see more *detail;* like the way he consistently puts one rich magenta *against* lighter tints and darker shades of it, subtle things hadn't quite been aware of before. Pencil notes in other parts of the sketch still the same. Hadn't needed glasses to know 'ChWh' meant 'Chinese White'. Finer details scattered across the page, how he'd seen his paintings building up; shapes, symbols, motifs, all working together and the way his colours emphasised this. Felt closer than ever to Golden in spirit, but real sad. Poor sucker missed *his* chance to get all these ideas down on canvas.

   Took my time. Treating each page like some illuminated manuscript. Why in hell hadn't I looked at them every day since I'd gotten hold of them? Talk about *addictive.* This was the Torah; the paintings were just Reb Rembrandt's commentary. Not only seeing much more detail, but getting to think how *differently* I'd paint each picture *now.* Wondering if I'd done it right, whatever the hell 'right' means. Would sure-as-hell do it other ways now, and getting to feel *should* have done! Totally frustrating to feel my paintings not so much wrong as just *not right* any more. Probably have to do them *all* again! Fell asleep drunk. Didn't dream at all. Woke up with a megawatt headache; throat like hot razor blades. Could hardly speak but called my doctor. Money croaks! He came right round and took one look.

   'Quit talking for a week, and take these pricey, pink pills.'

   Now I dreamt a lot – mostly about Margot. All the time, seemed like she was watching me. Saw her looking at me when we went to the farmhouse first time. Anxious look; would I like the place? Watching me when we started going through the sketchbooks; suspicious look, checking my reaction. Watching me as I painted each canvas; was it *right*? Overwhelming impression? I'd hardly been out of her sight for a second, and all to produce a loft full of paintings that cost her her life.

In daylight, dreams can seem crazy. Artistic paranoia; 'They're out to get me!' 'Rembrandt's work's *so* derivative,' quote/unquote. Dammit, that was the real problem. I knew I'd been inspired, but would the art world think so? Would I get the recognition? Would anyone even be interested?

Thinking about Golden made me go out and buy that book again. Wanted to study the Golden Month, see where that first burst of energy really got him; look at it with a new eye, one that had seen Golden's later ideas develop, knowing the agonies he'd endured, and *hadn't* survived, trying to flush a second genie out the bottle.

Looked at each one a long, long time. Only managed two three in a day; making notes, making sketches, ideas for development. Took me three whole weeks, working right through the book. Even read the Introduction. Seemed now like total crap.

Spent another whole week looking over my *own* sketches and notes, a real eerie feeling developing all the whiles; like I was beginning to become aware of something; like, every so often, I don't know, the Golden Month seemed to develop, shift up a gear somehow. Each group of six started to look more and more distinct. Each painting, like one side of a cube built round one set of original ideas; secret little ideas, motifs, icons, cross-references, all running in patterns. Each throw of the dice, each idea, curiously different but genetically linked. Sure there were echoes, colours, shapes from earlier cubes, but treated in a new way each time. Made thumbnail sketches all round the colour plates just to convince myself what I was seeing, like some development of a development.[1]

Could feel in my bones, never mind see, *years* of painting possibilities from the ideas in this one run of paintings. Had Golden given *me* the Midas touch? Everything I'd touched, since meeting Margot, had left me rich – and cursed. Just as well I was paying someone else to cook and clean. Might have starved, or gone crazy. Spent my waking hours looking, looking, looking and making sketches, notes; getting more and more convinced I'd cracked some kind of code.

All this time, been neglecting those farmhouse sketchbooks; been working on the Paris Golden. Could see something like *eight* groups of six paintings. If *I* were hanging them now, would put them in *separate* rooms. Then, Jeez-us, it hit me! End of the eighth series, two pictures left over! Like a frigging smack on the head when I looked at them again. Why hadn't I made the connection? Don't ask. Somehow, just never put the two series together. 49 and 50 must be part of the *next* group Golden had planned, and surely would have painted if he hadn't collapsed, been hauled off to hospital, then run away with Ghislaine.

But real pain of the smack was the totally blinding realisation – that meant the first four sketches in the Arles series *were actually numbers 51 to 54*.

All those farmhouse experiments hadn't been some crazed artist struggling after the perfection nobody can create. The poor frigging bastard had been desperately trying to make the reconnection, create a bridge *back* to where he'd been forced to break off. Time and again, failure. Then suddenly it happens, and he's off again, six at a time. Like some frigging series in math; the 'Golden series,' G cubed equals a vision of Paradise! Jeez, had I really cracked it? Could see how *my* first four paintings so neatly dovetailed in.

Was Margot right after all? Was I just some sort of artist-medium, letting the spirit of Golden express itself, like he'd always intended? Would need to see the canvases again, set them out round the walls of the studio, but the thought of going back there just turned me over. Couldn't face the physical effort yet, never mind the mental upset. That's when I remembered all those photos in the camera bag! Never once looked at them. Now they were going to save me a trip to France. Still in their envelopes in the bag at the bottom of the closet. Hauled them out. Began to deal out prints from an envelope.

What Strauss seemed to have done was take one photograph of a whole canvas, then several details. Seems like I'd started around halfway through. Put these prints in the middle of the table then, once they were all set out, looked quickly at the first photo in several packets till I spotted the ones that belonged immediately before or after. No rush. Took a couple of days just setting out and enjoying seven eight packets. Covered most of the paintings, working out from the middle. Hadn't looked at the beginning or end.

Listen, getting tired, Bill, but I want to tell you just one thing, because it all goes to hell in a moment. Hardest thing for me to come to terms with. Knew now, just knew for a fact that, if I could only get back there, *I could make these paintings go on forever.*

I was getting to recognise the signs. Joe seemed to like to build to a climax, some sort of cliff-hanger, and then send me off to stew for a while. However, this time, whatever was to come, I needed to get my notes down on paper very swiftly just to make sure I had understood what he'd been saying, even though I would still have to go back and verify, from the original Golden Month, whether I agreed with this new critical reading. I thought I knew them; but now, how could I be so sure? I certainly hadn't been aware of the subtle six-pack 'patterns' he said were there, *but neither had anyone else.* But when you're *not* looking for something you may miss it until, as seems to have happened with Joe, it casually smacks you in the eye.

I suppose the same could be said of my lady lawyer, about whom I could not stop thinking. With my earlier Birkbeck experience, I knew how easily I could be side-tracked, which is a crass thing to say about someone like Anna; but the last thing an average art historian with a dissertation to write against a deadline needed right then was falling in love. Trouble is, are the parties involved given any real choice; are the options spelt out?

I waved away the glass of wine with my Eggs Florentine and wolfed the lunchtime snack down before rushing back to my notebook. My academic mind had just had a dozen more thoughts, each mutually incompatible, which in academic terms is not necessarily a bad thing. What was a 'bad thing' was encountering the doctor coming out of Joe's room. Expecting my usual strokes, I began to purr but it wasn't such good news. Radiotherapy was due, even overdue, but Joe's tests were showing he wasn't really, of all crazy things in this mad world, fit enough for it. We could still talk but the sessions had to be no longer than an hour, with two hours of rest to follow and, just as soon as the tests showed positive, they would take him into the clinic for a couple of days. He might not be fit to talk for a whole week after that. Wondering what I would find, I walked into Joe's room. His translucent, bony hand beckoned me. He took hold of my hand and squeezed it feebly.

Listen Bill, listen. I simply got to tell you this. Next morning, got to the beginning of the series. Fantastic. Photographs totally confirmed what my memory been telling me. My first four so obviously continuation of Golden's final two. Images moved closer and closer to where Golden had left off. *That bastard Strauss must have seen it too!* No wonder he believed the way to squeeze extra bucks from the art market was saying *my* paintings were 'Golden's second month'. Then *another* thought struck me. Smack!

Like Golden, *I'd been interrupted.* When my legs got hit by the ladder, still had unpainted canvases and Golden sketches to work up. That sent me back for another look at the sketchbooks. Looking very carefully this time, glasses perched on my nose, could see the final four sketches *did* begin another series. Another series, but *weirdly* different! Hints of something real wild and crazy; like Wilhelm de Kooning maybe? With my glasses on, could make out some tiny, spidery writing in the corner of the last sketch,

I'm ill. Sick. Dying? All sketches, no paintings.
Can't stop! Chest pains!'

Look!²

You can understand it, can't you? Wanted to get back to work. Just a few sketches, then canvases to paint; just to finish that one series. Then; who knows? Another six; another sixty-six? Felt a crazy urge, a Golden glow. Wanted to get right back there; get on with the job. Picked up the last packet; began to lay out the prints. Knew they'd bring me to the end of *my* paintings. Dealt the prints out real slow; came to the very last one. It was something else, but *really* something else! Taken just to use up the spool? You bet I wasn't meant to see this one! Recognised the place at once; the bedroom of the inn in the village near that frigging cottage, and on the bed, naked, beautifully pregnant, fast asleep; Margot! Dressing table in shot, with hinged mirrors; angle of one mirror reflecting a side view of the photographer in profile, and naked as well, standing taking the picture. Strauss!

First thought: Margot was right; better I'd broken my neck. Leastways then might have been tucked up in the same Provencal cemetery, keeping Golden company. Instead, Margot finished up keeping Strauss company – before and after death. Just how long had *that* been going on? Jee-zus.

Felt such a blaze of jealousy, anger and disgust, I began tearing up the prints; one by one, piece by piece; in two, four, eight, then the next one, and the next, and the next. Threw them all into the fireplace; on the ashes of last night's fire. Took some time, so many to do, but just couldn't stop. Picked a few scraps off the floor and stuck the unshredded photograph of my wife and her frigging French lover on top of the pile, then tore up the film envelopes just to cover up my burning shame and anger. One flick of my Zippo and up she went. Saw the pile of negatives, fetched them over and tossed them, strip at a time, into the flames. Flared up and twisted in a kind of death agony. Not too different from how I was feeling. In five minutes, nothing but ash, nothing. And my heart was cold lead.[3]

Felt an overwhelming urge to run away, from where I was to anywhere – anywhere except Arles. Arles was spoiled, soiled, totally polluted. Needed to put distance between myself and anything to do with Margot, Golden included. Anything was better than just sitting there until … Until what? Didn't know any more. Put my things, precious few for a millionaire, into my car, wrote a note, left a hundred bucks for the help, and set off up US#1. Kept driving north for several days; Rembrandt on the road! Better than thinking. Finished up for absolutely no reason whatsoever on the ferry to Bainbridge Island, beyond Seattle and a dead end. Found a place to rent, bought a couple of six-packs and two fifths of Bourbon, moved in, and pretty soon passed out. Throwing up in the john, quite a few hours later, had the leisure to start thinking again.

First big thought was Margot. Only woman I'd ever really loved, unselfish love. Still did love the original Margot. Loathed the greedy bitch Margot, the crazy Margot so in love with her daddy but, oh boy, I loved Margot on the ship, Margot in Italy, Margot in France, Margot in love with me. Still loved *that* Margot. Always would. Shit, I missed her.

Next big thought was about little Pinkie. My daughter, as far as I knew. She'd probably have a better life with Kid Brother and Doris Day. Better to butt out of their lives, everybody's lives. Damned if I wanted to go back to Arles now. That was all shit-spoiled for me. One day, maybe, I'd start to paint again. Meantime, if I took my head out of the john, might just admire the view of Puget Sound.

---

1   Which, of course, is one of the key concepts I advanced in my dissertation – after all, once it had been pointed out to me, it was so blindingly obvious that I simply couldn't *avoid* mentioning it. What was wrong, however, and unscholarly, was giving Rembrandt no credit for this insight.

2   And, before my eyes, Rembrandt slipped an open artist's sketchbook out from under the bedcovers. But, *before he let me properly focus on it*, he seemed to change his mind, snapped it shut, and slid it away!

3   And mine too, for a different reason. Photographic evidence of the Rembrandt sequel to the Golden Month, especially considering the professional way it seemed to have been done, would 'stand up in court;' even if the original works were lost. I felt a guilty start when I found myself actually imagining that a credulous academic art world might even believe, on my assurance, they were Golden's, not Rembrandt's – and Rembrandt was dying, going off to where he couldn't contradict 'Professor' Maguire,' or 'his charming partner, seen here at a cocktail party given by his publisher!' I'm truly sorry Joe; I couldn't help myself thinking these things.

5

Dear God, Joe, is that it then? All these sessions, a stack of cassettes, pages of notes, rising anticipation – a major horde of modern art just waiting for *me*, Maguire the magician, to reveal to academe and the public – and now? Did I feel a slight rising sensation of scepticism? No photographs, a sketchbook which I hadn't really been allowed to see. It could be empty, as could the mythical loft in Arles. Joe, I've squandered a chunk of my legacy, and now it looks like I've consumed a valuable chunk of my time. Okay, I grant you this, credit where it's due, you've given me some extraordinary insights into Golden – but nothing else, and no *evidence* of anything else.

We took the compulsory break there and I was glad to escape from the emotional atmosphere in the sick room. Was that the end of the story? I'd be glad, in one sense, if it was but, for less than wholly honourable reasons, sorry if that was true.

Rembrandt's nurse, watch in hand, gave me a nod and told me Joe was on a higher dose of painkillers but had specifically asked not to be sedated *too* much, so he could go on talking to me – because there was something he wanted me to do. Now what? After all, some of us have a dissertation to write and a life to live – hopefully in France, and did I still remotely think of a permanent companion? The idea was not at all unpleasant. And maybe, in the long winter evenings, I could turn all this into a work of fiction. Who, these days, doesn't fancy himself as a bit of a writer?

Must have liked the view from my asylum window; stayed there long enough. Graduated over time from being chased by divorcées, then some wives, to wealthy widows. Lived quietly, frugally, sketching wildflowers, birds, not much else. Spent years up there, watching the

Washington rain fall. Then shit happened, several sorts, pretty much all at once.

Time for my once-a-year meeting to sign off on my income tax. Even that could have been done by mail, but old Handschumacher felt he ought to meet one of his big clients once a year, for public relations reasons and – surprise, surprise – because he had family in Seattle. Just before this, the local bank manager wrote me, asking for a meeting. What with my life being so ornery, my 'allowance' wasn't getting used up; had over $200,000 plus in my checking account; way too much. He wanted me to invest, and maybe even speculate a little, 'in order to supplement my pension'. If he'd known how much more there really was, stacked against the wall in California, he wouldn't have written; he'd have called round personally!

With no explanation, lawyer asked for this meeting to be at his cousin's offices, instead of our usual hotel lobby. Got me real jittery. Asked him straight out, was I broke, would I have to start earning my living again? Thought I was joking; told me my net worth. Could have bought a Picasso. No, what he wanted to talk about, and in private, was more serious. It was family!

Doris, poor woman, totally out to breakfast, lunch and supper too. Dementia, for Chrissake, pre-senile dementia and in someone much younger than me! Husband, next to useless: he and the child constantly rowing. She's scheduled to go off to school now but that meant no one around to look after Doris. Kid Brother in regular work but it's getting harder to finagle this. There are all kinds of problems.

First off, lawyer's afraid 'the daughter' will give up plans for school. Shame, because she's bright. Money paid out on her education been an investment. Enough still there for a damn good school. But Kid Brother has more or less gotten round to believing *he's* earned all this money. Been paid over the odds for the past twenty years. And now, Jeez, he's started to drink it!

Keeping him in work getting harder; and the girl's saying the family money ought to go on long term care for Doris, not law school. Just getting the low-down on all of this, when the flustered cousin comes in and hauls my lawyer out of the office. Comes back looking like death; which is appropriate. Few hours ago, Doris just wandered off and decided to WALK when it said DONT. All over.

That put things on hold, leastways until after the funeral. Told my lawyer, do something, anything; but get Kid Brother sobered up, kept in work and funds, and kept goddam separate from *her* funds. Wanted my – their – our …that girl to go to school; get a start in life; know how to handle money. No laughing matter. Small fortune coming her way down the turnpike, and Doris hadn't been wrong about some rich folks being stupid. Stayed pretty sane myself, sure, but then hadn't touched or used mine all that much. Might explain it.

Walked out to the sidewalk together with the lawyer. He was heading for the airport and me for the parking lot to pick up my new toy – yeah, that's right, the Edsel. Really think I bought it to annoy the pushy Boeing engineer on the lot next door to me. Where was I? Don't let me wander off the point here, because this is real important. Law offices just across the street from the Seattle Art Museum. Outside it, posters and banners about the current exhibition. Not reading the papers or being on any mailing list, known nothing about it. Tell you; jaw hit my chest. I'll never know how I crossed the street without being sent to join Doris – instead of going in to see the 'Golden Month'.

When I really became aware of my surroundings again, was standing in front of 49 and 50, and an attendant was patting my arm. Real sweet. Was I all right, did I need to sit down for a while? Took me into their first aid room, sat me in a chair; went off to get the nurse and bring me some coffee. Because, right there, in Seattle Art Museum, was having my first damn good sob in a long time. Cried for Margot, sobbed for my own parents (both of them), wept for Alexander Golden, shed a few tears for myself, and for the daughter I'd been denying myself all those years.

By the time the nurse came, was feeling much calmer. Sat and watched her drink my coffee! Explained; just had some bad news about a friend and, somehow, the raw emotion in the paintings had set me off. She wasn't on my wavelength: a nurse, not an art lover. No point in telling her Golden has more emotion in one brush stroke than Greta Garbo in a whole movie. Probably never heard of Garbo either. Asked her for a glass of water, drank it off and went back to the paintings.

This time, walked even more slowly round the whole series, just to remind myself, as if I needed it. Looking at the *real* paintings again, not reproductions, more than ever convinced. No doubt about it. Even if that wasn't the way they were hung in the gallery. In numerical order okay; no one played around with that convention – but, most times, the "sixes" were started in one room and completed in the next.

As for the final mini-series, it started here in Seattle but I knew *for certain* now I had finished it – and begun the next – all those years ago in Arles. Then just abandoned it, and shoved everything up in the loft.

Stayed in the gallery till it closed, walking round and round, and making the attendants more and more suspicious. Found my way back to the parking lot and drove down to the ferry. Really looked at Poulsbo that day, for the first time in God knows how many years. Sorry folks but, Jesus, was it ugly. Must have been asleep. Rip van Rembrandt. What I needed were paintings, images on the walls, colour, pattern, design. Christ, I'm an artist, not a frigging hermit. What was I doing here with my head up my ass? Should have been painting canvases, not picking frigging cabbages. In the bedroom, kicked one of my slippers and it shot under the bed. Wanting to kick it again, I don't know, reached after it – and put my hand on the camera bag.

Don't mind telling you, had another damn good weep. Almost a breakdown. Sobbed myself sick then fell asleep, damp and stinking on the bed. Hadn't drunk anything either, but woke in the morning with something like a hangover. Nothing in the house for it. Had such a healthy life style. Never ill. No aspirin; not even willow bark to chew! Made myself herb tea from a stale old packet someone had given me three Christmases before and walked to the window. Where was the view, the peace and quiet, the rural situation and all that shit the realtor handed me? Disappeared so gradually I'd never missed it until yesterday, until today, but not, God forbid, tomorrow.

Stripped off my stinking clothes, bundled up the bedding and rammed everything into plastic bags. Had the longest, soapiest shower of my life and put on my cleanest clothes. Tied the tops of the plastic bags real tight. Packed all that really mattered in a couple of suitcases.

Stowed them, and the camera bag, in the trunk of the Edsel. Put the plastic bags in the back seat. One last look around and then a letter and a check for the help (again!), locked the door and got into the car. Went round by the realtor to sling in the keys and the municipal tip to sling out the bags. Left Poulsbo and Bainbridge Island for good and felt quite rational about it. This time heading south, back to the light, back to sunshine; California, here I come – again.

Nice for you, Joe; the sunshine and yellow warmth of California. As for me, I think I am heading for the dirty-grey grottos of Bloomsbury. I am getting to be quite uninhibitedly fond of Joe. He's a gentle and gifted raconteur but, at whatever cost to short term relationships – or even to Joe himself, now I come to think about it – I must break out of here. I am in my comfort zone. My work on my thesis is dragging and its quality sagging. I really ought to go home to a chilly cubicle, a filing cabinet – but the comfort-loving Bill Maguire would rather be here in Carmel.

Now, finally, as I seem to be steeling myself to get out, Anna has called and we have spoken briefly. I even fibbed and said I had to go because Joe was calling me and the nurse was being strict about access, and all that sort of thing. We are going to meet the day after tomorrow for lunch as soon as she gets back into town. She's taking me to the 'Surf'n'Turf' place round the block from her office. She 'thinks' her afternoon will be free. Joe has already said I can borrow the Edsel whenever I like so I shall feel like some movie star – maybe I should run for Mayor – as I drive through beautiful downtown Carmel.

Even in that brief conversation, I could *feel* the gentle, sweet, insistent pressure. Anna thinks she is in love; she has cleared the decks and now she wants something which, being a capable Californian, she is going to get, unless I am completely mistaken. I know I am not *yet* in love with Anna but my fondness, and those other feelings of anticipation, desire and even jealousy of the ousted Adonis, combined with my typical masculine weakness in the face of temptation on a plate or a pillow, all looked like having their predictable effect. So I am saying to myself that, if I do finish up officially engaged to her, and a lot else besides, before or during or after the next twenty-four hours, I must take it seriously. This time, please, no running away. Unless, of course, she won't agree to let me finish my thesis. Two more pages of the thesis are drafted but I'm on no upswing: yet I have to keep this going.

The two hours are up, and Joe seems especially keen to have another session. Check the batteries, put in a new cassette, switch on, stand up and let's go and talk Golden.

Needed the slow drive south to get my thoughts together. Kept asking myself, 'Why am I doing this?' Finally reckoned it mostly had to do with growing older. Fit, yes; but not immortal. They call it remission, remember. So? So, needed the warmer climate. And I'd 'rediscovered' Golden. Knew now I'd been in some sort of denial for too many frigging years; deliberately shutting off my own innermost, most important creative urges. Because I'd been cheated; because everything felt corrupted by betrayal. What a waste! But now, after years of wearing blinkers, was seeing again. Been 'art dead', if you like, but now, coming alive again. And if I was alive, I had to paint. Crossing over into Oregon, it all came totally clear to me.

I really want to see my daughter. Maybe even tell her this time I love her.

Have to 'break the law' to do so but, what the hell, so sue me! Got deep pockets. Want to make sure she doesn't make some damn fool mistake, like quitting school. Doris can't be the excuse now, but who knows what her feelings are for Kid Brother. Don't care what it takes to fix. *She* has to get an education; unlike her father. And this time, I was going to *build* a place, in Carmel, with acres of wall to hang pictures on. Pulled into the next Howard Johnson and hit the phone.

Long before Carmel, I'd gotten the details of half a dozen lots for sale and Kid Brother, though he doesn't know it yet, is lined up to work, full-time, non-stop, on the dream house – just as soon as I know where it's to be. Choice not difficult. Three of the lots were together in a hollow on top of a hill; regular sun trap. Large and wide. Could build right in the middle and sink it below the line of sight of all the neighbours – that appealed to the architect. Appalled my accountant though when I bought all three lots at the asking price. Got my own sketch plans worked up. All done inside a month. Put the Edsel in the shop for overhaul, and to keep it out of sight. Too distinctive. Hired a car so ordinary could drive past and, thirty seconds later, be damned if you could remember seeing it. Drove up to San Francisco and cruised slowly past Kid Brother's house. Crazy thing to do. He'd probably not recognise me, even if he was sober, but couldn't count on that. I'd have a harder job recognising my daughter. Last time I'd seen her she weighed around thirty pounds. But she was *my* daughter, and she was Margot's, so surely!

Parked at the opposite sidewalk. Crowd of tall, slim, high school girls chattering down the street. Half a dozen of them but I would know my own daughter. Then one of them, but *not* the one I'd picked out as it happens, crossed the street and walked into the house. Not really like Margot, or me for that matter. Felt a bit of a chill wind at that. So much for certainty!

Lawyer had warned and double warned me. I'd signed all kinds of promises and as far as this young woman herself was concerned, she was Kid Brother and Doris's daughter. I'd promised not to speak to her or do anything crazy. Couldn't have anyway; so emotional could hardly breath, never mind speak. Only saw her for about a minute but, bar none, it was the happiest – and the bitterest – minute of my life. Know what? Made me want to get back down the road to Carmel and *paint*!

Going to have to struggle to reconnect – Hell, doesn't that sound like you-know-who but if I could just *complete* the second series then there could be a series three; with no frigging instruction manual this time, and no safety net. And series three would be *pure* Rembrandt. See what I'm getting at? Golden started it; then I'd been hooked. That fired *me* up and brought Golden back to life. Maybe I came alive in the process too, but then I was knocked sideways, or backwards; into suspended animation. Been off in some sort of hibernation. If I woke up now, could I still paint? And who would I paint like? Like young Joe Rembrandt? Grown-up Golden? Or Golden from beyond the grave? Maybe this time, *this time*, like the real frigging Joe Rembrandt.

Knew what else I had to do, and there was more than enough dough to do it. Sat in Handschumacher's office and told the old forty-niner to get the hell on with it. Kid Brother never felt a thing; in charge of building a house in a hollow up a hill, for some mad millionaire; with a bonus as big as Texas for getting it done on time. Had it all set up for him; all he had to do was insert tab A in slot A, tab B in slot B, and so on… . Didn't always get *that* right. Jesus, was he arrogant. Been kept in work all these years; felt fireproof. Someone watching over him, like in the song. Never ever had the least idea how or why, but it made him cocky, more and more difficult to manage, especially now he was a lush. Had a friend introduce him to AA. That helped; sometimes.

Hid up in a penthouse with a north light on Ocean. Wore dark glasses and a hat if I went out, but didn't need to try too hard. Kid Brother lived in a trailer on the site and ate all his meals in a diner on US#1. Weekends, he went home to San Francisco to get lightly fried on Fisherman's Wharf. That's when I'd go up to the lot, see how it had progressed. Most of the time, getting along just fine, but every now and then, had to get things changed around. Sometimes I just wanted things done differently but most times it was Kid Brother, screwing up. No telling him! Had to be told the "mad millionaire" had changed his mind again.

He and his daughter getting along real fine now, mostly because they didn't see too much of each other. And because, out of the blue, she'd won a cash prize in some essay competition Handschumacher suddenly heard about and persuaded her to enter. Had myself a quiet smile.

I'd asked for wall space. First idea was space to *hang* pictures but, sitting in Carmel Library looking at some of those *quattrocento* frescos I remembered painting, got this terrific urge to put my own paintings straight onto the walls themselves.

Bided my time, until the house was finished, before marking off twelve-inch squares on the wall and getting out a stick of charcoal. Sometimes think if Manuel had known my doctor's phone number he'd have called him over when he saw what I started on one morning.

Been working up the Golden-Rembrandt iconography in my own sketchbook. Yeah, great word! Found it in an art book. Anyhow, wasn't coming right. Hoped if I took that first wall, by the pool, where the

Monet is now, spread myself across it, might be able to work things out King-size before painting a smaller canvas; opposite of working *up* a sketch, more like working down. Seemed like a good idea when I thought of it.

Enjoyed it at first; like an exercise routine, getting the muscles warmed up, co-ordination between mind and hand, and all of that stuff. Kind of indulged myself to begin with; novelty and, same time, familiarity. Then stepped back and took a look. It was crap. Totally devoid of meaning. Maybe the scale was wrong, or maybe hadn't been concentrating like I used to. Who knows? Took a bucket of whitewash and went right over it three times.

Tried again. Marked out two blocks, about the size of actual canvases. On the left, ideas I had for the next painting of the second series. Worked for several hours; had a pause for thought. Didn't look at all bad; not right, but not too bad. Began to paint the second rectangle.[1]

Wanted this to be a natural progression, the logical development. Wasn't half way into it before I could see; making no progress; just repetition. So, out came the whitewash. Most satisfying part of the whole exercise! Had a break for half a day before I tried again.

This time, took one image. Can't give it a name; sort of a colour worm. Wasn't a thing, just an idea, really? Reckon this turned out better but when I covered it all over in its white overcoat and tried to make an actual painting, it just wouldn't work. So depressed, nearly jumped into my own pool. Spent the next two days purging the wall with gallons of whitewash.

Thought maybe I needed to work my way back from where I started out as a painter, all these years ago. Picked another part of the house and asked myself, 'How would Chagall have gone about it, if he'd been given this wall instead of the Paris Opera House ceiling?' That got me going; really motoring.

Old skills and God-given flair. Soon there's a sham Chagall jumping out at me. His *dealer* would have bought it; and I should know. Pleased with myself, but not one hundred per cent. After all, this was just an exercise to keep me *warm*; keep me interested, and get my painting muscles back into trim. Wasn't creating new, what you'd call original, paintings. Left the Chagall there for the moment and chose another stretch of wall. Won't talk you through it all but, several months, well more than two years later, came to a sudden halt. House looking splendid, especially the Douanier Rousseau bathroom. That French photographer came by. In a weak moment, I let him in. But really, Bill, Getty could have moved in here without needing to swing round by the auction rooms first – but none of his collection would have been an original Golden or a modern-day Rembrandt. Hell, I was sick of it and I was ready to quit. And that's when Kid Brother's liver finally gave up the ghost.

Just before he died, got my lawyers to offer her a job. Getting straight 'A's, going to graduate top of her class, for sure. Planning to open an office in Carmel anyways, so they gave her the chance. Had to keep her at arm's length from my personal affairs, leastways while Kid Brother was alive, and afterwards didn't know what to do; so just did nothing and kind of let things drift. Wanted to talk to her so much, so very much; but that was another thing just couldn't get started with.

Handschumacher, funny old guy, seemed more cut up about Kid Brother than about Doris, so he was no help. Reckon that's why I started talking to you, Bill, and why I asked her to check you out. Told her some crazy story about being worried you were connected somehow with Fancy Dress. Wasn't true, of course, but I needed something. You two needed to be on speaking terms.

And that's when I knew.
And Rembrandt knew that I knew.
I laid down my pencil; switched off the Uher.
'Does *she* know yet?'
He shook his head.
I closed my eyes and uttered a silent curse.

Another thought struck me.
'How old is she, Joe?'
'Twenty-five – just.'
There was a silence. He hardly breathed. Then he put one hand on mine.

'Someone's got to tell her. I can't do it. I don't want my lawyer to do it. Please.'

'I can't do a thing like *that*, Joe! Don't ask me.'

'In return for all I've told you? *Please.*'

This was the payment due.

I hesitated, then nodded, and he relaxed.

'Thanks Bill.'

That night extra nursing staff moved in, wheeling cylinders of oxygen; and the doctor, with a long face, forbad me access until further notice. I never spoke with Joe again.

So, there I was, trapped by a foolish, emotional promise to tell the truth.

The truth. What's that?

A promise. Was it binding?

And did I owe it to Joe, anyway?

What about Anna?

And what about *me*?

If she had been *there*, I don't know what on earth I would have said. Instead, next morning, when I called round on the half-chance she was already back in Carmel, I was shown into the office of the local partner, Gerry Abramowitz. He waved me into a shiny plastic chair and asked how he could be of service to someone from 'your wonderful country'. Yuk.

I checked that he *was* Anna's boss; asked, insulting to a lawyer now I come to think of it, if I could talk to him in confidence; took a deep breath and dived in (not 'dove' for God's sake!) pretty well head first.

'I'm staying up at Joe Rembrandt's house. Been talking with him quite a bit, about painting and artists and, well, to get to the point, he's pretty much been telling me the story of his life; he just couldn't seem to stop. I reckon the story could have gone on for some time to come but, last night, he had some sort of crisis and the doctor says he has to rest for a week or so. The point is, I'm listening to this story which is fascinating but, at the same time, he's introduced me to Miss Glover, Anna.'

Abramowitz leered.

'Now, what he told me yesterday, at least what he didn't deny, is that Anna is really *his* daughter and, to get to the point, he's expecting me to break this news to her. And that just makes me feel like nothing on earth. I mean, how could anyone do this to me? I'm a total stranger. Besides, where's the proof? It would be a terrible thing to say to her if it really wasn't true.'

Abramowitz got up and came round his desk and parked himself on the corner, looking down at me.

'How come you think Anna is Joe's daughter?'

'It's only his word for it but the core of it is the Glovers took Anna in when her natural mother died.'

Abramowitz shook his head, smirking at me.

'If he's told you that much, guess I can spill a can or two of the real beans, but you gotta keep this under your hat, okay? Yeah, you're right; Anna's almost certainly his daughter. Joe says she is; not to me you understand but to my father-in-law, and, of course, lawyer to lawyer, Nathan told me the basic facts when I opened up this office. I reckon she could look a bit like him; and a bit like her too, although I've only seen photos.'

'Her! You mean Margot?'

'Now who in the fuck's Margot? This one I don't know and I thought I knew them all. No, I mean Gilly. Gilly Glover who walked under a truck a few years back because her husband, Robert Glover III, the boozing building contractor from Berkeley, wasn't sober enough at the time to remember to lock the back door so she wandered out onto the highway.'

I was realising now I'd never had traceable identities for the people in Joe's story. He'd used his own labels; Damp Hand, Pinstripe, Fancy Dress and so on. He'd called the couple who adopted his daughter Doris Day and Kid Brother and, until I sat in that chair, I had never heard their real names.

'Got to admit, Joe was never one to talk much to *me,* but my father-in-law knew him from way back. We all assumed the kid was his wild oats and Gilly was where he sowed them. Well that's what wealthy sons from rich families did; still do for that matter. Other people do it too but it never hits the newspapers.'

'*What* rich family?' I asked, and silently switched on my tape recorder. Abramowitz grinned at me, settled himself comfortably in the chair beside me, unbuttoned his waistcoat (which he called his vest!) and took a satisfied breath. He planned to enjoy this.

'I thought you said Joe's been telling you his life story. Maybe he didn't go back that far. So okay then; we're talking about the Rembrandts of Rembrandt Steel in Bethlehem, Pennsylvania. It doesn't exist now, of course. Joe's pretty savvy old man sold the business to a bunch of suckers in early 1929 and sat out the recession on top of a pile of cash – then bought up the bits of America Joe Kennedy didn't get to first.' And before my very ears, Abramowitz demolished almost every wall, every gable and buttress, every pediment and soffit, every balcony and verandah, and most of the view from the complex structure Joe had built for me over the previous weeks. About all that could be seen from beneath the debris was Joe's ability to draw and paint, and even that was subverted in the cause of a lecherous lifestyle, described in jealous detail.

As Abramowitz described him, Joe was the idle, no-good, only son of a wealthy, establishment family who winged his way across America from one love-nest to the next. He would shoot the line that he was an illustrator for an advertising agency handling their lingerie account and charming pretty women into posing for him.

'That gets them interested and, like a charm, they mosey on back to his studio and pose for him in the raw; then perhaps they don't feel like saying no when Joe strips off too and shows them his paintbrush. I mean, if I had that talent, would I be a lawyer? I might need one, though!'

And in that instant there was no world cruise, no rich young Scottish bride, mother and heiress, no farmhouse in Provence, no broken legs, and no stash of canvases, no Scottish cottage, nothing to substantiate the string of lightning sketches Joe had flashed past me with the speed of a ciné-film and the skill of a conjurer. I was the Golden Ass and the new Golden hoard was a fiction, a myth – except for that one inescapable thing, the one thing I could now see *with my own eyes*. There *was* a deeper artistic scheme to the Golden Month than anyone else had ever realised. Whatever else was fiction,

I owed Joe that one blinding insight, an insight that would gain me my doctorate and set me up in the job I wanted. But did I owe Joe so much for all this that I had to sign away my liberty to satisfy him? As I pondered, Abramowitz went on and on, his story getting cruder by the minute.

'What it amounts to, this time round, is either he forgets to buy a six-pack of rubbers, or maybe he even feels like a seventh screw and, surprise-surprise, Gilly winds up pregnant, at just the wrong time.'

It was the wrong time because, in this version of the 'Life of Joe', his widowed mother had just threatened to cut him out of her will if he misbehaved again; and a pregnant girl-friend, as opposed to wife, constituted 'again', not least because this was one girl-friend of Joe's his mother happened to know too; her and her family. Joe used his money to bribe a friend and Gilly to get married, for the sake of the child and Joe took himself off up to the Pacific North-West and made his own fortune in real estate, nothing excessive but just enough to keep him in funds until he collected his eventual inheritance.

And now, here is Joe, sick, apparently for the second time and it isn't looking good. We're into death-bed confessions and Joe seems to want to tidy his own life up at the expense of buggering up two others. What did he want; absolution? But he just can't stop pretending; he can't stop fantasising and he seems to think everything will be all right if someone else gently breaks the truth – wrapped up in a lie – to Anna. And that someone has to get his pay-off.

'Way I figure it, Joe's betting on her falling for a handsome, David Niven guy like you, and just hoping your British tact can break it to her gently and, who in hell knows, the way she's talking about you, it just might be working. You look a lot better to me than the guy she's been dating, some jock whose parents own a furniture store. Well, good luck to you, if you're the lucky fella. I reckon if that's the price of becoming Joe's son-in-law it's worth paying and to qualify for the big prize seems all you who have to do is tell her she's *his* daughter. Hell, *I'd* do it – for my usual fee. Maybe afterwards, it won't seem so difficult. You're sitting in the catbird seat, fella. Could be a real story-book ending.'

'*A story-book ending!*' That got to me. Mills & Boon? Cock & Bull more like. I'd been set up. I'd been *conned*, and I'd seen too many B movies not to know the consequences. Before I got badly burned I needed to untwist the strands of Joe's fairy tale and shake out all the lies and embellishments.

If it *was* a fairy tale then just touching it would destroy all the magic. In fact, that was already happening. It was already too late. In five foul-mouthed minutes, Gerry Abramowitz had completely demolished my dream scheme.

Academic glory – Arles – Anna. *Arseholes!* Apart from Anna, it was all an illusion; a clever con, the last fling of a fatally-wounded fantasist. Abramowitz had brought events up to the present day but by a completely different route, one devoid of any attractive scenery. Gone were the romantic nights on the cruise ship and the dramatic events in Scotland. Margot was already fading from view. Pinstripe and Damp Hand were legal fictions. Strauss never took these photographs. Unpleasant creep though he was, Abramowitz was the reality. It had to be so. Why else would Rembrandt's own lawyer sit in front of me and tell me all of this if his wasn't the *real* Rembrandt story, the whole story – and my version simply another of Joe's feculent forgeries? And why, oh why, was he doing it?

My chest felt tight. My heart was beating way too fast and my temples throbbed. I'd been taken in by that extremely rare version of the Cinderella story; the one in which Buttons gets the girl and the fairytale *golden* future; that bloody word again! Now I knew it was alchemy, fool's gold. However attractive Anna was, even on such short acquaintance – and let's not beat about the bush, for reasons we neither of us could fathom, Anna Glover and I were becoming increasingly and powerfully attracted to each other; maybe she more to me than me to her but who's counting – there was no way I was going to let myself be picked out, or even picked up in some bar, sold some specially written romantic fiction, then be expected to tell Anna this was the real story and then live out the rest of my life knowing, as I would now, that I'd *lied to her*. After all, if Abramowitz knew the truth then surely *she knew the truth*. Or did she? Just think about it, if I went ahead and told her a complete lie and *then she found me out!* Ye Gods, was I frustrated and angry.

No! Joe's dirty work was a job for the lawyers. Not Abramowitz, I hope, who'd not only told me, but had so clearly relished telling me, the sordid details. No, his father-in-law should do it; the long time senior partner in San Francisco, the one who seemed to know all the facts, and might very well not have shared every last detail with his unattractive son-in-law. Then, as a rich young heiress, she could go out and find a suitable partner. I couldn't see *now* how that could ever be me. Bugger and shit! It's just not fair, and there's no logic. From not wanting it, now I felt like I was being robbed, not just of the gold but the girl; and it could all have been scripted so differently.

Let's say I'd never called in there and never seen Abramowitz. Suppose I'd simply attended Rembrandt's funeral — wishing him dead already, it seems — *believing* that he was one of the world's greatest unknown painters. Afterwards, perhaps, if Anna had told me the truth herself, I might just have been able to handle it. But, me knowing the truth now, rather than Joe's artistic creation but being expected to tell her *that*; it was all completely spoiled. I wanted to disappear up my own vanishing point. I had to get out of Abramowitz's office.

It was getting dark outside already, early evening. I drove to the bar where, all that short time ago, I'd got into conversation with Rembrandt, just before his medical team caught up with him and carted him off home, with me as ambulance chaser. I'd calmed down by then, which was just as well. Otherwise, I might have drunk myself into insensibility or driven his precious Edsel over a cliff, or both.

After a glass or two of further reflection, I decided I knew what I had to do. Firm in my weak resolve, I drove the Edsel gingerly back and went to my room. The little message light was winking on my phone.

'Hello "Professor", I'm coming by the house tomorrow, late morning, to get some papers signed, if Joe's well enough. Hope you'll be there, and we can go on out. Sound good? And listen, there's a party this weekend and I sort of thought you might like to take me. We could make it some sort of celebration? Speak to you tomorrow, true love. Bye. Mwah, mwah!'

There was a spare cassette by the phone. I took out the one with her voice on it, put the spare into its place and wrapped the precious recording in a couple of Kleenex before slipping it into the pocket of my bag. Methodically, I put all my clothes in the bag except what I was going to wear the next day. Then I got into bed.

An hour or two later, I still wasn't asleep when my door opened quietly without a knock. The nubile new night nurse, who'd been giving me the eye, came in and shimmied towards the bed without putting on the light and knelt beside my pillow. 'Thanks, but no thanks,' was my first uncharitable (and untypical!) thought.

"Better come. It's Mr Rembrandt. I called the doctor."

In just a few moments, I was dressed and through there. Joe's breath was rasping. Clearly he was in pain and distress. The nurse was fixing up another drip. Rembrandt knew I was there but clearly didn't feel like speaking. Not unwillingly, I held his hand and he squeezed one of my fingers. Although I was mad at him, how I could ignore the way he'd befriended me, whatever his motives? And all this was sad and upsetting. I fought back tears. In twenty minutes, the doctor arrived and banished me. In another ten he came out, answering my unspoken query.

'Who knows? This may be it, or he may pull through. I've given him what I can for the moment, but he'll be in severe pain when he wakes up. I don't think there are any relatives so you'd better get hold of his lawyer. I wonder who inherits. Sorry, that's just American doctor talk. Ah coffee; my drug of choice!'

Manuel and Dolores had appeared bringing fresh coffee and, of all things, warm doughnuts. I wouldn't have expected to have any appetite but, in no time at all, after the first mouthful of coffee, I'd eaten a couple and was reaching for a third. Doctor and nurse were having a quiet conversation just outside the room. Dolores was tidying up and Manuel stood behind the small table where he'd put his provisions, looking for all the world like a roadside vendor. Dolores picked up Joe's discarded robe and put it in the linen basket. Then she opened the wardrobe to reach out a replacement. That was when I saw it; the small camera bag. She gently spread the clean robe across the foot of the bed, crossed herself and joined Manuel. They glanced at each other and Manuel nodded.

"We will wait in the kitchen, Señor."

The doctor asked if I would sit with Rembrandt while he made a couple of phone calls and the nurse fetched some drugs from his car. They left me in charge. When they had all gone out, obeying an irresistible urge, I stepped over to the wardrobe, lifted out the bag, took it straight through to my own room and stowed it into my suitcase. I got back to Joe's bedside with my heart racing and feeling as guilty as sin.

I sat there, thinking about what I had just done, listening to each separate breath that Joe drew and feeling sharp attacks of conscience as, now and then, he hesitated between them. The right side of my brain told me it was legitimate research; that the 'golden' key to the mystery was in that bag. It was evidence. It was a primary source. And after all, Joe wasn't likely to need it in the next few days, if ever. The left side said, 'Thief!'

The medical team came bustling back in and I went to get the number of Rembrandt's lawyers; not Abramowitz, nor Anna; I couldn't face talking to either of them, but the office in San Francisco. It was the middle of the night but an answering service gave me an emergency number. A calm but sleepy voice answered and I gave my message. The lawyer, Mr Handschumacher himself, thanked me with old-fashioned courtesy and said he would be on the road as soon as possible, in Carmel around eight or nine.

I put down the phone and picked up a writing pad. *Somehow* I had to tell her – something, anything. I'd made a 'death-bed' promise, if that's how to describe it. Maybe this was my way of paying my 'hotel bill'; of paying for what I'd been given. And for what I'd stolen? But could I, even now, tell her the *truth*. Anna had asked me to *tell* her the truth. But what, in God's name, *was* the truth? Because the truth I'd promised to tell was *Joe's* truth, a partial truth and nothing like the truth. And she had asked for *my* truth. The hell with it: the truth is only what people believe.

Believe me Anna, I wrote; pausing for thought at every other word,

This is hard. I'm writing because Joe has suffered some sort of

relapse and the doctor doesn't know how long he's going to live, and this has to be on paper now, or I might just never write it. The thing is, I promised him I would tell you something. I don't want to, but he made me promise.

Anna, if you don't know this already, Joe <u>believes</u> you're really <u>his</u> daughter. He has told me, and it may well be true, that you are his child and that, the last time he was very ill, when you were just a baby, and he was afraid he was going to die, he arranged to have you adopted by the Glovers. I just don't know if this is true but Joe swears it is.

I'm so sorry that he couldn't have told you this himself. He says he wanted to but his courage failed him, and, after all, he was very sick. My courage is failing me too. Forgive me. He certainly loved and cared for you; then, now and in the future. You're going to find out soon just how well he's planned to take care of you and then you'll be free to lead whatever life you choose. Choose well.

I've sat with Joe for what seems like a lifetime, perhaps because it was <u>his</u> lifetime, his life story. Some of it may well turn out to be a myth; much of it is still a mystery to me. What really matters is that he told me again and again he loved you.

[What else could I say to her, for God's sake?] He wanted you to know, at the end, who he really was, who he claims your parents really were, and why, for his own reasons, he never got round to telling you so himself. But you'll have to speak to Mr Handschumacher about all this.

I don't suppose being rich will make you stupid but you'd better take care.

Joe brought us together. I'll never regret that.

The truth — you wanted the truth —dammit the truth is I just couldn't handle telling you this to your face. Take care of yourself and take care of your life.

I quickly read over what I'd written, thought it was revolting but couldn't see how to make it any better, so I signed it and put it in an envelope, addressed to Anna. Not knowing where to put it for the moment, I slipped it into the camera bag in my suitcase and felt, rather than saw, the sketchbook already in there. Then I went back through to Rembrandt. He seemed, even since yesterday, to have become more skeletal, almost translucent. His breath grated painfully but at least he was still alive. It was around seven in the morning. I had to make up my mind.

Standing there looking at him, it wasn't easy to marshal my thoughts and, in any case, was I going to change the habit of a short lifetime and start making up my mind based on *logic*? Even though I was a university lecturer with pretensions, I had let myself be 'picked up' in a bar by an elderly, rich artist who seemed to have designs on me. I'd taken the kind of foolish risk that I would have mocked if I'd read about it in a newspaper; *'Missing Brit's Skeleton found under Illustrated House of Horrors'*. After all, the chances of an older man inviting me back to his place just to talk to me about his paintings, not even to show me them, must be in the lower order of probabilities. Yet, it had been a story of his life, his own fantasised version that I'd sat listening to. Having his own urgent intimations of mortality, had he wanted a confessor? I would never know and, in the end, what did it matter.

Then, with no warning and right in the middle of the crucial chapter of his elaborate fiction, he had introduced the heroine. But she, according to attorney Abramowitz, was the innocent evidence of the *true* story. Not Rembrandt's story.

Now, because of scruples I wasn't sure I could explain, even to myself, I was contemplating running away, in order to avoid speaking to the first woman to whom I'd begun to think I could simply and truthfully say; to whom I really *wanted* to say, 'I love you'. Why? Why shouldn't I just accept, let's call it, a pension? Often enough, I'd filled in and greedily returned those endless invitations from *Reader's Digest* to win enough money in one prize to set me up for the rest of my life. Now here I was, within reach of more than I'd ever dreamed of earning and owning, and all of this by the simple expedient of falling in love with an apparently willing heiress.

What was sticking in my throat, and to my 'Doris Day' conscience, was that Rembrandt had picked me out to be told his own, glamorised and *completely fictional* account of his life which he now wanted me to tell and sell to Anna. Why? Why? Why? I was to be his ghost writer or, if you prefer, I was to paint a portrait of Joe Rembrandt the way he wished to be remembered by his own daughter. Anna was not to be the price of my silence so much as the prize for brazenly trumpeting his false story.

Anna might even be in love with me now but, when she was well and truly rich, would she still feel that an indigent Englishman, a down-at-heel scholar rather than a well-heeled furniture salesman; and moreover, someone who had tried to tell her a pack of second-hand lies for gain; was the right choice as a life partner? If she was going to have doubts, did I want to sit around and watch them develop? Besides, I knew from all my life experience so far I did my own best work when I was up against a deadline; usually a financial deadline that made me get up early and get on with the work. I could remember, by contrast, the occasions when, having banked my latest grant cheque, I headed off for the lounge bar rather than the library; arguing that the library was more likely to be there tomorrow – such is the well-known transience of lounge bars. Temporarily solvent from my legacy hadn't made me permanently stupid, but it seemed to have unhinged me for a while. What might permanently rich do?

Hold on a minute! What the hell was I thinking? I *was* a scholar. I could *learn* from the mistakes of others; from the lessons of my past. Surely I could distance myself from Anna's wealth. That was hers, and her responsibility. She was a lawyer, and she could afford a raft of other lawyers and accountants to manage her affairs. All we had to do was manage our relationship. That seemed to be the answer I wanted to hear, but … even as I thought of it, I knew it was an illusion. How could a wealthy young American woman lawyer live at ease as a humble university lecturer's wife in some English or even French provincial town? And as I thought of the 'necessary' compromises I would have to make – such as feeling 'obliged' to live in America, allowing her to buy our house which would have to be much bigger than I could afford, letting her take care of the 'little things' like medical insurance, children's school fees, holidays, cars, groceries and on the list would go – I realised that there wasn't any meaningful way in which I could accept Anna as my prize for telling lies except on what would amount to *her* terms.

Crazy as it might seem to someone who has never had to make such a choice, I felt if I couldn't take her without the money then it seemed like I wouldn't take her at all. Some people are born crazy; some people go crazy and, in my case, I was driving myself insane. I went back to my room, took out the letter for Anna and picked up my suitcase.

I put the letter on the kitchen table and asked a baffled and unhappy Manuel to get out the Edsel and run me to the Greyhound Bus Station. I hoisted my case into the back of the bus and climbed on board. Within thirty minutes of leaving the house I was leaving Carmel and Rembrandt and Anna. As the bus began to move, I was in agonies of self-doubt. But within a couple of days I was on another continent.

Do I regret what I did?
 Of course I damn well do.
 All the bloody time!
 How could I have been so stupid?
 I could have coped, even managed quite well, with wealth.
 My own, and other people's.
 Look at me now!
 It could all have been so completely different.

---

1   I was hearing this at just the right moment. In working out in my own mind what had been Golden's approach to the development of his work, I had been struggling more than somewhat but now, just listening to Joe, it was all falling into place for me. I felt waves of gratitude. What can I do for you in return, Joe? What can anyone do for a dying millionaire benefactor that doesn't seem sycophantic? Whatever it was, I would surely do it. Just ask me!

6

Back in a Bayswater basement, and the fuggy cubby-hole that was mine at the Foundation, I fill my mind and my eyes with the works of Alexander Golden. This is shit or bust. The Director has not broken the rules on my behalf, but an expert art historian can see where they have been dangerously bent. Golden produced his masterwork while living and working in Paris, having abandoned his painting shack on Edinburgh's South Side. On that slender ground he had been designated an honorary French painter until either I wrote an acceptable dissertation, or left to 'pursue other interests'. I have less than six months now, and it's going to be hard work, mentally and physically.

Physically, I'm drafting my thesis in illegible longhand and one of the Foundation's more psychic typists is then converting it into double-spaced typescript. This only reveals even more clearly the gaps in knowledge, fact and logic, the weakness of the argument, the manifest errors and multiple omissions. Using some of the cultured pearls Joe has scattered in my porcine path – to sustain his own fairy story – I am able to find material about early Golden that, now and again, allows me to compare and contrast the earlier with the later artist, two-thousand words or more of grist for my slow-moving mill. I track down the particular Delaunay exhibition he must have seen and dig out the catalogue and press comments. That's good for over three thousand words and four very apposite illustrations; very helpful padding. I don't know if assessors actually check the weight of theses but they certainly count the words as well as weighing their significance.

Then, while still forging ahead with the later sections, (Did I write 'forging'? I had better watch my language!) I go back and do a 'hatchet and patch it' job on the unsatisfactory parts of the earlier text and send them back for retyping. The typists keep a complete set of carbons, in duplicate, so that I can always go back to my original if I need to. I am allowed to take one set out of their office but the other is considered as inviolable as the typists themselves. The second draft now shows up the lacunae, the *non sequiturs* and the laughable but unfunny English prose style that I adopt in times of stress. You may have noticed! And every day, another page drops off the calendar.

Mentally, I am wrestling with, and writing within, the vocabulary of art history and criticism. Like all other disciplines, there are acceptable, not to say obligatory, turns of phrase; mantras even. I can't simply say that something 'looks three-dimensional'. I have to talk about modelling, plasticity and, here and there, slip in the word *chiaroscuro*, always, at the Foundation, double underlined so that the printer will put the word in italics. Images can't be simply sharp or blurred; they have to be either hard-edged or painterly. 'Scumbling' is currently the 'in' word. Tonal range, the make up of Golden's palette, and where, if anywhere, to find the picture plane all have to be discussed. At the end, I have to reach an inescapable and satisfactory *academic* conclusion – and then go back and rewrite the introduction for the umpteenth time to make it seem like I had always been purposefully and, as all the world would surely now agree, inevitably heading there. And underneath all of this surface noise, I am having to get to grips with my own understanding and reinterpretation of the work of a minor but, if I can just persuade my referees it is so, rather more significant than previously realised, contemporary artist. The sum of all my efforts, after one all-night session with pen and Tippex, is finally delivered to the Foundation's printer less than twenty-four hours before the absolute deadline. Only then, when it's all done, delivered and there is no going back – and no going on – do I realise, with genuine surprise, how much I have been enjoying myself. This is very much my scene. Three more months later, I am summoned to the Director's office.

This is not a good sign. Good news from the Foundation tends to be despatched by second-class post in a fairly matter-of-fact way, quite often over a Bank Holiday weekend but the bullet and its intended victim are usually brought more swiftly face-to-face. My thesis is lying on his desk, as solid and digestible as a brick or, more likely, the concrete block that is about to be laid in front of, if not dropped on top of, my career as an art historian.

'Maguire.'

'Professor. Good morning.'

'Maguire. In all my years...'

'Yes, sir?'

'In all my years, I have seldom read a dissertation to compare with this.'

'No, sir.'

'No, Mr Maguire. This is not only scholarly but you seem to have achieved a seminal insight into Golden's whole approach to his work; an insight, which, in the unanimous view of the assessors, amounts to a radical reappraisal of the quality of his work and a deep understanding of his complex, personal symbolism.'

Some of these phrases are direct quotes from my thesis, but I am not about to accuse *him* of plagiarism.

'Professor!'

'Yes, *Doctor* Maguire. It's not official for another week but you may rest assured that your DPhil is, to coin a phrase, in the bag and, what is more, an offer of the post of Reader in Modern and Contemporary French Painting will be in the post. Congratulations, young fellow. I confess to having had doubts initially, but you finally put your shoulder to the wheel. Now, what about getting back to Poliakoff? Don't you think he's due for a revival?'

Bingo! Ker-pow! Success! Everything is now for the best in the best of all possible worlds. I even shook hands with him. My grin is so wide that, in a light breeze, the top of my head might well blow off.

The Director encourages me to go out and celebrate. Good idea; but who with; sorry, with whom? I've been distinctly anti-social, not to say anti-sociologist, over the past year. If ever my thoughts stray in that direction, I can't stop myself wondering about the lovely lawyer. I've not heard a word from that quarter since my flight from the scene. Nor should I expect to, after the way I had behaved. Rembrandt would have been disappointed, never mind her.

Every young woman, in some way or other, seemed to remind me painfully of Anna: for example, the Foundation's lissotrichous librarian. Such thoughts had been distracting me only the day before while she leant revealingly over her card index then straightened up and caught me staring.

'There's nothing here, but the Courtauld might have the sort of thing *you're* looking for.'

I went straight back to my bed-sit and had a shower, something my stint in California had given me a taste for, even if English showers are rather Aprilish, compared to the mordant midsummer needles fired from American faucets. In need of a clean shirt and the better of my two pairs of jeans, I opened the wardrobe. I'd done so twice a day for over six months but that afternoon I could no longer avert my gaze from the camera bag. It was my guilty secret. I had so far felt too ashamed even to touch it; even made some sort of fetish of not touching it; afraid, perhaps, that something in there might deflect me from the true path to my dissertation. Now I hauled it out. Could this even be the bag that the Director said my DPhil was in? Big joke.

It wasn't heavy. I hadn't stolen a camera, thank goodness. Unzipping it on my bed, I was almost afraid to lift the flap. Instead, I slowly slipped my hand in. Inside, I could feel the hard sketchbook and the metal spiral; the one I'd seen Rembrandt holding but which, at the last moment, he'd slipped out of sight. With all I'd heard from Abramowitz, I'd convinced myself he'd just been using it like a conman's prop, something to add an 'air of reality' to his elaborate fiction. I hesitated for a couple of moments then slid it out.

The first thing to hit me was the curious drawing on the cover; a pen and ink sketch of a tin trunk, not remarkable in itself but carefully lettered on the trunk were the words 'Alexander RIP.' Was this Rembrandt's ghoulish homage to the late and long-lost Alexander Golden? Then I turned to the first page.

What I saw was nothing more than a pencil sketch with splashes of gouache, but the colours, the shapes and their interrelationships leapt off the page and punched me in the eye. I've had no comparable experience in the whole of my life, not even sex. The effect was so powerful that, when I tilted my head to look up at the ceiling, the images, chromatically reversed, were projected there, as large as the Sistine Chapel.

Unmistakably Golden! Remember, I'm an expert, indeed, come to think of it, I'm *the* expert. *Yet, I'd never seen any canvas like this.* Transferring my gaze to the wall opposite because my neck was getting sore, I experienced a renewal of the original image in full colour. I wasn't sure if I was strong enough but I picked up the sketchbook and had a second, long look at the page that had so stunned me. Then I turned in awed, almost fearful, anticipation to the next page.

It took me an hour or more to work through the book. I'm an art historian, not a painter, but if anything could make *me* want to paint it was that succession of images, wave after tempestuous wave of them, rolling out from the pages and crashing on the shore of my imagination. What on earth, what in Heaven's name, had I walked off with? Were these really the next phase of Golden's development, as described to me by Rembrandt, a Rembrandt who, as far as I knew, had never met Golden?

Then reality cut back in. However brilliant as a collection of commemorative postage stamps, these were, in fact, the 'back story,' the cunning fabrications of a self-confessed master forger, and con-artist, created by someone whose whole house was filled with fakes on every flat surface and who must have devised this many years ago as part of some elaborate sting?

And now; was I guilty of looting an 'Art Treasure', or simply stealing an artistic curiosity? Either way, the sketchbook didn't belong to me – but what to do with it? Not a simple question. Whatever its provenance, right now *Dr* William Maguire could not make public use of it, not even admit its existence, without some risk to his promising career? In the classic British response to any real dilemma, I shelved, or rather wardrobed, it, and covered it with my laundry before going out for a pizza. Still thinking about Rembrandt and his gorgeous little gouaches, I went into Casa Roma.

The pizza was dreadful, as was the Chianti in the plastic straw covered bottle, forgeries both of them. Thinking about Rembrandt led me on to think about Anna. Nowadays, it was mostly a dull ache. If my head wasn't sore from thinking about her, my backside ought to have been; from kicking myself. Didn't I 'sincerely want to be rich' like it said in those enticing adverts for the Dover Plan?

Rembrandt, by the evidence of my own eyes, had managed to create while under the influence of considerable wealth. Some imaginary Margot (or even a genuine Gilly) may even have unleashed his creative drive. Until she met up with him in his fairy story, he'd been no more than an expert illustrator and highly talented 'frigging little forger'. Had she made him, or helped him to become, a master forger, a Rumplestiltskin to his princess, turning linen canvas into golden thread? But, the real question was, did she (assuming for the sake of argument she had ever existed) *prevent him* from becoming an original artist? Had she been able to infuse and enthuse him with the ghost of a Golden from beyond the grave? A post-mortem transfusion. Well, that's how I'd heard it from Rembrandt. It would make a great Dracula story if it weren't for the one bit of garlic that stopped all this 'she' nonsense dead in its tracks. That authenticated arsehole, Abramowitz – I could personally vouch for his existence, however much I might wish he had been a hallucination.

Sipping a coffee that could have put a shine on my shoes, until the first shower of rain, I reminded myself that several other people in the story definitely existed, like Fancy Dress, for example. I'd *seen* him. Then another scale fell from my eyes. I had never *spoken* to him; so his role in the story was entirely created by Rembrandt.

But Abramowitz existed (God alone knows who created him), the illustrated house in Carmel was real, and Rembrandt existed, or *had* existed. I'd seen them and touched them. Joe had, on several levels, touched me. I'd seen him, like a magician with nothing up his sleeve, transform a plain white surface into a paddy field full of water lilies. Like the suspicious Strauss, I'd touched them while they were still damp. That smudge on a leaf in the corner of the painting was mine. His voice had rasped the rust clean off my imagination and etched a story on it that I had found, at one and the same time, incredible *and* believable. My own notebooks and tapes – primary sources which I had deliberately (and in breach of regulations) not lodged in the Foundation's library, to conceal my Rembrandt connection – were real. Who was I then to criticise Rembrandt? Now this sketchbook in my hands was a reality. And those powerful sketches were supernaturally real.

Who, and what else, was real?

Only Anna.

Instead of *in* my arms I had held that palpable reality at arm's length and, on some bizarre impulse, some twisted logic of reasoning, some Pop Art psychology that Lichtenstein would have laughed at, I had let it all go. Had I *really* been afraid of failure? That was at least a working hypothesis. In my own past, there had been one other relationship – although, in today's use of the term, I can scarcely call it that – which seemed, at the time, to have been as meaningful and – sudden sickening realisation – I had done the same thing. Maybe I'm human after all. That, at least, would be something.

We were on the eve of a visit to an aunt and uncle deep in Norfolk. Without telling or asking my parents, I'd applied for a passport, providing all the necessary signatures, including theirs. I was only *just* eighteen. I'd already left for school before the post came so, when I got home, my mother was waiting to ask me what this was all about.

The fact was I'd been nursing the idea of hitch-hiking across Europe – because that was what people 'did', some people anyway. Maybe I knew that I wasn't really ready for this or, more truthfully, that my mother wouldn't let me go (humiliating thought for an eighteen year old). And ironically, the next year, my father, against my mother's wishes, actually *sent* me to France. So I'd said nothing, probably realising subconsciously that it would all come out and I'd be prevented from going; and so prevented from failing which, now, I could even believe was what I'd wanted in the first place.

Instead of Europe, after putting my shiny blue, gold-blocked passport in her handbag, my mother allowed me to go youth hostelling, with a Harrogate Toffee tin full of pennies. I even had to demonstrate to her I knew how to use a public telephone, how to press Button A and Button B, before my uncle drove me to the outskirts of Norwich, and, no doubt on cue, offered me a last chance to change my mind.

In those days, private cars and lorries would actually stop and pick up hitch-hikers. My first lift took me right into Cambridge and I was waiting on the doorstep of the youth hostel when it opened; opened by someone of my own age who, in my then fairly limited experience, was the most beautiful girl in the world. This isn't her story so the facts can be swiftly told.

She was less taken by me than I was by her. She already had a boy-friend back home. Even so, she was flattered by this persistent, instant suitor. She was on a holiday job and supposed to be using the hours during the day when the hostel was closed to study for her Maths A-level resit. So when she asked if I could pole a punt, I lied at once – after all, it *looked* so easy – and arranged to take her out. After my few fruitless attempts and fearful of our losing the pole, she took over and I had the pleasantly humiliating experience of letting her do it while I lay back and thought of her letting me do 'it'. As it turned out, she wouldn't.

Yes of course, we kissed. We both liked that and, fleetingly, my hands touched her breasts and grazed her thighs but anything 'more' was beyond reach. After three nights, YHA rules made me move on. I went to Stratford-upon-Avon to mark time before coming back for one night to Cambridge. This time she told me to move swiftly on. She was getting black looks from the hostel manager. But she did give me her address.

Taken aback by the fact that I pursued her there and had an ardour her other boy-friend seemed to lack – probably because he didn't have to fight his way across England to demonstrate it – in a secluded September hayfield, she stripped to the waist and embraced me. My eyes popped from their sockets as two bright pink nipples tumbled out of their padded pockets. After ten minutes of playing with them, with my priapic pain so obvious, she said, "Come on then", and began to tug at the zip of her skirt. 'It' at last!

At that pivotal moment in my life, a combine harvester started up in the next field but one and, in an instant, my mood was shattered. Lust was immediately overwhelmed by fear of discovery. Mentally and physically deflated, I mumbled something about not having any French Letters. She turned her back and dressed without a word. I left that afternoon. We never met again.

My Casa Roma reverie was interrupted by the waiter presenting the bill, pushing it under my nose on a grubby saucer. Back home, I was reluctant to open the wardrobe again and dropped my clothes on my one chair and went to bed. I slept badly and was in a less than cheerful mood when I turned up for work to find a letter stuck in my pigeonhole; still quite a rare event for me. It had French postage stamps, and the return address, printed on the envelope, was the University of Montpellier.

Would I be free, they wanted to know, to stand in at short notice for a lecturer on Contemporary French Art who had broken a leg while skiing, or some other inconvenience? The Director, who had already been sounded out, was willing, but only for one term. Forget the dream world. This was the real one, the one I had always wanted. And here it was, being handed to me on a palette. Next day I packed everything I owned and/or had stolen.

It was delicious to wake up only three weeks later, after a few lazy 'working' days in Paris to realise that, as I'd been dozing, the train had crossed the great divide and every river I could see from the carriage window must, literally, be flowing towards the 'centre of the earth', the Mediterranean. I opened the window and was rewarded with a belt of warm air, laced with 'country' smells and diesel smoke.

Montpellier was marvellous. My course went well. There were some real young talents taking the programme. I had my eye, in a not too serious way, on one or two of the more talented. However, I managed to keep my mind on my work, remembering that what I ought to be taking advantage of was not my students but the fact that I was where I had so long wanted to be, in Provence. I was where the great Alexander, my Golden hero, had probably spent time after fleeing from Paris. No, there was no academically acceptable evidence of that, even if it seemed the logical place to look. Didn't all the pale-skinned northerners, like his fellow Scots, Fergusson, Peploe, Cadell, and Anne Redpath whose paintings I was getting to know and love, follow the sun and acknowledge what the Parisians took as a matter of course: light and life were better, cheaper, and warmer in the Midi?

And that was how, or that's as much explanation as I can give you, I found myself standing late one Saturday mid-term morning in the centre of Arles, looking around and wondering which of the many Van Gogh memorabilia was the most vulgar. My vote went finally for an ashtray in the shape of an ear.

I was hungry and strolling round the square looking at the restaurants but in one shop window a word caught and held my eye: *Locations*. I didn't *need* a place to rent but that was when I began, somewhere deep in my unconscious, to admit to myself why I'd really come there: that fatally attractive, gilt-edged, glistering fiction still had its hooks into me.

In I went and found myself saying (fiction being infectious) that I wanted to find a 'modest' farmhouse in the vicinity of Arles, where my (non-existent) brother could spend the summer painting, while I sat out on the patio writing *belles lettres*. The proprietor soon assembled a batch of literature and even offered to take me on a conducted tour. Knowing I was a fraud and a fantasist, I began to back-pedal, saying I planned to have lunch first. He pressed forward, telling me he was shutting up shop anyway and would be delighted if I'd join him so that, straight afterwards, he could show me round a few of the better properties. A free lunch is a free lunch, I mistakenly thought, so I let it all happen.

At times, as he drove me from one potential den of theses to another, I dozed a little. He'd chosen an excellent wine and I'd willingly drunk more than my fair share of it. My line was I needed to see a place that had just the right atmosphere and then I would have to consult my brother and bring him down to make the final selection. He was up in Paris at present (and so on, and so on – I'll leave you to elaborate). The estate agent seemed to find all this quite believable, or maybe he just lived in, lived on, or lived off hope.

I liked every place I saw. In fact, I was even beginning to wonder, in a fraternal kind of way, whether my brother might just stay up there in Paris while I rented somewhere rustic and restorative, as my study base after I finished the teaching programme in Montpellier. Why not? Basically, because I couldn't afford it; at least not for more than about two or three months, on my present stock of capital. Out of consideration for my chauffeur, I kept that calculation to myself and, besides, I hadn't 'seen' the precise, non-existent place I was looking for. But would I know it if I ever saw it? I really was well into kidding myself.

In one of my more wakeful moments, I riffled through the bundle of leaflets on my knee. We had seen all but three. As we arrived at the next one, I was looking at the description, a panegyric in the peculiar patois of estate agents world-wide. I looked out of the window and saw that the place we'd come to was surrounded by an agri-industrial complex that, somehow, wasn't obvious in the soft-focus background of the leaflet's photograph. I shook my head, he shrugged, and we set off again. Now he began to signal the delayed onset of disillusion, glancing with ostentatious surreptitiousness at his watch, and saying that, alas, he had time to take in only one more place and, anyway, he wasn't sure if the one remaining property after that, some way out from town, was currently available; it just might have been taken off the market in the last month. It had been on one or two rivals' books as well. Three-quarters of an hour later, a rather disappointed estate agent dropped a rumpled and dyspeptic academic in the main square, saying he would give me a call at the University next week.

Feeling still a nagging curiosity, I walked into the Tourist Office and asked how I could get to the last unvisited place on the list. I had to complete the tour, and get this whole project and fantasy out of my mind. On the bus to Fontvieille, (*'où se trouve le Moulin d'Alphonse Daudet'*), I stared at the single leaflet, having binned the rest.

The bus deposited me in a village cut off by a by-pass which, in turn, had been circumnavigated by the autoroute and now, dreaming perhaps of the rather surprising Daudet revival that did eventually come, it slept all the year round, opening an eyelid once a week for a market. It wasn't market day and there was scarcely a soul in sight. I walked up to one elderly gent and showed him the leaflet and asked where the property was to be found. He jabbed a finger along the road and, in the nasal Midi accent, said something like *'sangkeemet'*.

The sun was warm and I was carrying a small rucksack, with, as ever, too many books in it. I hoisted it on my back and set off. Nearly an hour and *cinq kilomètres* later, I came round a bend and there it was, easily identifiable from the photograph. The ground sloped up behind it into a neglected vegetable garden. Clearly, it hadn't been part of any working farm, or even working farmhouse, for donkey's years.

To get my breath back, I sat and looked at the place for a few minutes then walked the last couple of hundred yards to the gate.

There seemed to be no one around and no car parked beside the house. Ignoring the sign – *'Propriété Privée – Défense d'Entrer'* – I pushed the gate which swung open, well-oiled, on its hinges then back again behind me with a metallic clang. There was no sudden baying of alerted dogs. If there had been, I think I would have vaulted the gate. I was committed now. I walked up to the front door. The windows were clean and shining, the paintwork fresh. Someone was looking after the house but there seemed to be no one at home. I looked through the nearest window into a large kitchen, with plates, pots and pans as much on display as in use. Very *Maisons & Jardins*.

By this time, I was a cocktail of conflicting emotions. The Nosey Parker instinct of most people, not least academic researchers, was mixed with a typically English embarrassment at being somewhere one ought not to be. But there was a third element, like a flavour in a recipe one can taste and smell; one knows but can't quite put a name to. I moved on round the house. At the side, there was a shiny new dustbin but I wasn't feeling enough of a detective to lift the lid and rummage.

The ground sloped up while the house was set back slightly into the hillside and I could see down into a bedroom at the back. It had windows on two sides so the light coming in from the back of the house revealed, through the side window, a double bed and counterpane, but only one pillow. The tidy room looked feminine.

A path led up into a kitchen garden, or rather the remains of one. The shapes of plots and paths between were still there and patches of currant bushes. I pushed on a little higher in order to look back at the house and the view. It was a two-storey building with a high, steeply pitched roof, and at one end someone had let into it a vast skylight, facing north. Stepping backwards to get a view over the house, I thought I heard a car in the near distance and this distracted me. Careless of where I was stepping, I snagged my foot and tripped, falling backwards. My fall was cushioned by ample vegetation although I felt the impact of woody stalks in my back. I scrambled to my feet. There *was* a car coming; by the sound of it, a Citroën 2cv, and it had come up to, paused, and then come through the gateway. Now, my very English dilemma was whether to run down to the gate, probably giving the impression I was running away, or stroll down in a leisurely fashion and give whoever was arriving, and already making towards into the farmhouse, the fright of their lives. I chose to walk steadily down the slope but calling out, 'Hello! I say, hello!'

If I'd intended to sound reassuring, it certainly hadn't worked. Whoever had got out of the car now stood rigid, mouth open, key in hand, at the front door. It was a woman. A young woman. And not just any young woman. I dropped my rucksack; she dropped her key. As I ran towards her she flung her arms open and we collided on the doorstep with enough force to knock most of the breath out of us. We hugged tightly. Snatching some air, we looked at each other for an instant then embarked on a long, sweet and silent kiss that said every bit as much about forgiveness as it did about love. Perhaps I tried to speak at some point. I certainly opened my mouth. But she laid a gentle finger on my lips and shook her head.

'In case this is a dream, don't wake me yet.'

Holding tightly onto my hand, she crouched and picked up the key. She put it in the lock and I turned the handle. Together we went inside and she pushed the door shut. Holding both my hands, she stepped back to look at me then wrapped herself round and kissed me with even more passion. Then, silently, she took me by the hand and led me through to the bedroom.

Without another word, except perhaps our names, we undressed each other longingly, climbed under the counterpane, made love, slept and made love again. It was dark outside and she was cradled in my arms before she spoke.

'We certainly postponed this as long as we could!'

'I'm so sorry for…'

'No, honey! Don't say anything. We can do all that at leisure. Just tell me you love me.'

'I love you.'

Then later, much later.

'I don't know how you found me here but anyway, next week, I was coming to find *you*.'

'Find me? Where?'

'Montpellier. At the University.'

'How did you know I was there?'

'We lawyers call it "discovery".'

'You were *looking* for me?'

'Of course! You left without saying good bye and, besides, I thought you were worth a second look.'

'Anna, I feel ashamed and more than a bit embarrassed. I don't think I behaved very well to you; never mind him.'

'Bill! It's *way* too late for the two of us to feel embarrassed and, for that matter, you're the one who's due an explanation, if not an apology.'

'Explanation? Apology?'

'Tell me first why you left and then I'll fix us some dinner. My story's good enough to keep.'

My own limp and lame story stumbled out, and did not improve with the telling. Nor did the selfish and, on the face of it, irrational curiosity that had me hunting for a fictional farmhouse. She shook her head and smiled at me very tenderly.

'Let me skip through the bath; then you can have a leisurely soak while I take care of things.'

Yes, her explanations could wait while I lay in the bath in a state of near bliss. But, as their moment approached, I could not suppress a certain apprehension.

20050202 (Somewhere over Canada on the Great Circle route)

Although I am surprising myself with my own candour, as I wing my way towards Abramowitz, this next bit of the story will test me. Given the numbers of people I know, worldwide, and the different *milieux* between which I now seem to move with ease, I value the (oh dear, I can just feel this one coming) 'golden' opinions I have won. I have no wish to be thought any kind of a heel or a cad and in my own mind I am quite convinced that, in the time that followed, from stepping out of that bath, I behaved decently towards Anna. More than that, I believe I was in love with her. Who could resist falling in love with a beautiful girl who had given herself to me so generously and excitingly and who, demonstrably and daily thereafter, showed how much she loved me?

In that limbo between the hot and sweaty warmth of her bed, the delicious and restorative warmth of the bath she had run and the golden[1] glow of her smile as we sat at the kitchen table, I let all my thoughts wash through my head as the water washed over my body. What was going to happen now? I had been pursued as ardently as, and with even more success than, I had demonstrated in my not-too-distant youth. Once again, I seemed to be about to let my libido determine my life choices and, just at that moment, it didn't seem such a daft thing to do.

I told myself that, even if the Foundation were unhappy and I had to give up the Readership, the Head of Department at Montpellier would give me a job. I was better qualified than many of her staff and spoke better French than quite a few of them. French academic salaries weren't brilliant (although the social security was amazingly good) but I was planning to write several books and, already, there was the sniff of television programmes – about Golden of course, and several other more-French, French artists. My ability to do my pieces to camera in two languages was no disadvantage. This all sounds so very mercenary but this isn't the moment to edit things out. The other point to make is that I was telling myself, as I towelled dry, that, given this second chance, I would play it totally straight with Anna. If she loved me, I would love her right back. We would make a go of it. Now she was here and with no hint so far of needing to rush back to California (after all, it's cold and it's damp) I could surely persuade her to become one half of a cosmopolitan and cultured, Anglo-American couple who did their globe-trotting during the long vacations when I would have to fit in conferences, deliver papers and thus build my academic reputation.

As I climbed into my clothes, the fact that they were not crisp and clean but somewhat rumpled and in need of a change reminded me that I had still to build a substantial part of the west wing of my academic reputation but I was sure I could exchange my research and its results for all the materials I would require. I had confidence in myself and, after all, the subsequent results show I was justified. The crucial thing is that, as I left that bathroom, I felt, in all but legal title, a married man going to meet his wife who, only a few hours earlier had been his eager and unblushing bride.

Who can tell where the rot set in and whether I was wholly, or as I still want to believe, only partly responsible for what transpired.

Who says that machines have no soul? As I make my way, in memory, through to the farmhouse kitchen, my laptop cut in to back-up all I have written so far onto another disk. Fortunately, I have a supply of blanks in one of the amazing number of pockets of the carrying case. My computer guru has warned me that the laptop will play up if I don't feed it these disks. Now, on a split screen, I have brought up the notes I made over the next couple of days as I struggled to get my head round what Anna told me. The more I look at them, the more I think that, since I am wide awake, it would make best sense if I turn them into *her* account, her version, her stab at the truth.

Well what did you expect me to do when I got your note, Bill? Like you told me to, I spoke to Nathan Handschumacher. He's such a sweetie but, Oh my God, razor sharp.

We had a real heart to heart. He said Joe wasn't so much a liar as a born-again and again fantasist, and, for certain sure, he'd concocted another of his dream autobiographies for you. But, what with Joe dying and all, it was time for me to hear the truth. And it *was* the truth, so help me, because he, the family lawyer, had been in there sorting out the many messes and paying the big bills for much of Joe's life.

So when I was sitting there with Joe, I knew before he said anything he'd been up to his life-long tricks. So I just sat there, and told him I loved him, and promised I would stay with him until … That was the hard bit, but when you've not so long ago lost both your parents, you have a little experience to go on. He heard me all right and smiled back but, most of the time, of course, he couldn't speak. On the second day tho', he rallied a little bit and talked about what he'd been saying to you, and why. That's when he said he was sorry, for not talking to *me* before. Next day he could hardly speak at all. All he said was "Trust Nathan. He knows what to do." He said that more than once. So, my much-missed Englishman, ladies and gentleman of the jury, I need to tell you the facts, leastways the facts according to Nathan Handschumacher.

Sure, Joe did come from Pennsylvania. But his parents never owned a steel mill, or worked for anyone who did, like Gerry Abramowitz told you. And his real name wasn't Rembrandt. His mother was a Hoofmeyer, a real swell, with a place up the Hudson River, rock-rib Republican – not that that's a bad thing – and his father's family came over on the *Mayflower*. Their name was Peel.

Frankly speaking, Joe was a bit of a snob; found it too darned ordinary to be plain Joe Peel. So, sometimes he called himself Joseph Pilkington and then, when he found out about some famous American painter family I'd never heard of before, he decided to become Joseph *Rembrandt* Peale. It was when he moved to Carmel he trimmed that back, or ramped it up if you will, to Joe Rembrandt.

Seems like, all his life, Joe's imagination used to just take him over. He turned himself into his own inventions: he became a character in his own stories. And that cost his family quite a bit. Fortunately, they were pretty comfortable. His father had invented something that made carburettors work better, whatever a carburettor is, and managed to get a patent on it. So, even after Ford bought him out, he still got royalties for years and years. Joe's Edsel was the last new model that used a carburettor with the Peel patent device.

Anyhow, old man Peel was totally obsessed by all things mechanical and you can bet he wanted his only son to be an engineer. He had the walls of Joe's bedroom covered with framed drawings of real exciting things, like piston rods and cog wheels. Can you imagine? But some of it must have rubbed off. Joe could draw as well as any engineer, but he never seemed to want to do anything with it careerwise. Nathan says the war rescued him.

He went into the Navy and, at first, they had him painting battleships. He told Nathan he'd suggested painting them dark blue and green to camouflage them better at sea – but that was probably just another of his inventions. Then he got posted to a Hydrography unit and the Navy got real value. Most of their charts of Southern

California are his. Shame he didn't sign them. On second thoughts, maybe just as well, in case he 'invented' some of the shoals. But then peace dumped him on the beach.

His father had just died and, on the road to Damascus, Maryland, his mother had gotten religion. All of a sudden, tho' she'd never lifted a finger all her life, she discovered the Puritan work ethic, and told Joe he had to find a job if he expected to get any more from her by way of allowance, never mind inheritance. He managed to get work in advertising. He could draw real well but pretty soon they found he couldn't be trusted near clients.

He told one he was the illegitimate son of Orville Wright. The guy was so intrigued he invited Joe home to tell him more. Joe kept that story in flight until they caught him one night making a three-point landing on the daughter. The agency lost the client and Joe was grounded. He managed to keep all this from his mother but when he began masquerading as Henry Ford II's half brother it all came out and she told him to reform or he'd be removed from the family payroll. That's when Joe thought he might go off to Europe.

Mrs Peel reckoned that was far enough away to keep him out of the local papers, so she made a generous contribution to his removal expenses. What with his allowance, and the amount a dollar could buy in those days, he could afford to rent a decent apartment and hang around in art galleries. And that's how come he met the daughter of some Paris gallery owner and, it so happened, one of the galleries handling leading contemporary painters. And the line he was shooting then was that he was on a discreet scouting mission for his distant cousin, John Paul Getty, who was just 'toying' with the idea of doing for Malibu what Solomon R Guggenheim had done for New York – always a grain of truth in Joe's stories!

Her father invited him to take a trip to the South of France and meet with some of the artists they represented. He stayed with them in the family farmhouse. By now the dealer had told him, in confidence, he needed finance for a major exhibition but was still short several thousand dollars to finance the massive illustrated catalogue he wanted and, even bigger deal, cover the insurance costs. By the time they'd gotten back to Paris, Joe's generous offer to buy up the farmhouse had been accepted, and Joe took up the reciprocal offer to manage the gallery day-to-day, while the dealer concentrated on getting his exhibition together.

Joe beavered away during the week but, every three weeks or so, it seems he would disappear off for a real long weekend. He'd come back with photographs of the way the farmhouse was being transformed; kind of bitter-sweet for the dealer you can imagine. Apart from putting in a large skylight to give his new studio a decent north light, and having the whole building painted inside and out, he had gotten in a contractor to turn the yard at the front into a flower garden, and behind the house, there was to be a vegetable garden; the pride and joy a huge asparagus bed. The dealer's daughter didn't care for these disappearances too much because, by then, she and Joe were steady dates.

One week, they had a row. She more or less demanded to be invited down and he bluntly said no. That weekend she told her father she was going to visit a girl friend in Orleans. Instead, she caught the train south and simply turned up at the farmhouse, unexpected and uninvited. The fact he hadn't cleared up from previous meals made it look like there were two places set at the table.

He came charging down the stairs and said she couldn't come up. She was so angry she tried to scratch his eyes out and managed to get past him and rush up to the studio. There *was* a naked woman on a bed up there; two in fact, but not quite what she expected: side by side on two easels, identical paintings, by a painter the gallery represented.

'There's your rival then, Ghislaine,' he said, real quiet.

'You stole these from the gallery. How could you?'

'Not stolen; only borrowed one of them. Question is; which one?'

He went over to the wall and turned round several more canvases, identical to paintings she knew couldn't possibly be there. He finally convinced her he had an obsession with other men's paintings and simply satisfied his craving to be a real artist by making meticulous copies of other people's work, borrowed from her father's gallery for the long weekend.

She was so relieved there was no human rival they finished up in bed together which, for a well brought up French Catholic girl, was just a terrible thing to happen; especially because Ghislaine pretty soon figured Joe didn't really love her. Anyway, Joe being no better than a lapsed Protestant, and not evenly remotely French, marriage would have been a total non-starter. But by now, Ghislaine was pregnant and her parents found out.

Ghislaine's father was probably the most upset of all. Having felt obliged to fire Joe, he no longer had his helpful manager, or his cosy retreat in Provence. Joe 'retreated' there himself. When Ghislaine blurted out what he'd been up to down there, her father said he wanted to drive down to Arles and check it all out. Ghislaine sent a warning telegram but Joe said he never saw him. In fact, the dealer's burned-out car was found, a day or two later, on the outskirts of Orange, which just happened to be where his mistress lived. So when the police found out that the dealer's business was on the rocks, their suspicions moved on to some sort of faked disappearance.

Joe did go to see the wife, Ghislaine's mother. She threw him out in a big rage but, six months later, looking ruin in the face, her lawyers persuaded her to accept a really mean offer from a firm of accountants who said their anonymous client had always wanted to own a gallery. By this time, Ghislaine had been packed off to friends in California and had her baby. Seems it was a difficult pregnancy. Then the child needed a great deal of medical attention and that's where Joe comes back into the picture – pun not intended. He was over in America to see his mother.

He told her he owned a business in Paris now which dealt in 'modern art reproductions'. Mrs Peel pronounced Joe suitably reformed and the consequence was that when she died, only a few months later, the religious sect collected a lot less than they'd expected, and Joe one helluva of a lot more than he'd feared. So, after giving his mother a suitable send-off, Joe did a couple of things.

First off, he tracked down Ghislaine and paid off all those medical bills. The American friends were mighty pleased, I can tell you. All they'd been asked to do was give house room to the pregnant daughter of old Parisian acquaintances and oversee the planned adoption. What they hadn't expected was to be landed with large medical bills the girl's mother couldn't pay and a young woman who wouldn't be parted from her sick baby.

Second thing, Joe offered to do the honourable thing, but Ghislaine did the brave thing, and turned him down. She knew perfectly well he didn't love her. It wasn't the basis for any kind of successful relationship. Joe put a lump of money aside for his daughter's medical and health bills and, probably without telling her, fixed for Ghislaine to get the offer of a job.

And that was where she met the sweetest, dumbest, most lovable man in the world, a wonderful person but a hopeless organiser, called Bob. Ye Gods, he was dumb but, oh boy, was he kind with it. Actually, it was Nathan who introduced them. I think she came to love him very dearly. Seemed they couldn't have any more children but he was really proud of his adopted daughter, not least because he'd been adopted too, and never knew his natural parents. His one blind spot was he didn't want to be told anything about the money in back of their relationship. Ghislaine once wrote secretly to Joe and told him she 'needed some money for "things" for the baby'. That's all she told him; all she really needed to tell him. A banker's draft came more or less by return mail. She wrote to thank him and to say she'd never ask for anything more. And by this time, Joe was back in Paris, well on his way to becoming a successful art dealer.

He'd begun developing connections with galleries back in America. Not the fashionable ones in New York, or on the Coast, but the raft of places in between where people were getting hungry for Art with a capital A, and wanted paintings for social a tad more than artistic reasons. Some galleries were tapping this market and serving up real garbage. Joe talked to small-town dealers who had clients looking for something with a little pedigree. His technique was simple. There he was, an established gallery with a half decent reputation and triple-A insurance. He was able to get some of real the top-flight Paris dealers to *lend* him paintings he told them he hoped to sell to one of his better clients. Then Joe would get a friend to come in and ask in a loud voice to see 'the new Picasso' and be instantly shushed, but just too late to prevent the mark overhearing and asking, in an awed whisper, for a sneak peep.

The genuine Picasso was never for sale but, not long after, Joe would let it be known that he had a 'previously unknown' painting by some other famous artist, offered at a fire-sale price by someone with less money than matched their urgent needs and high standing in society but, it had to be understood, any deal would have to be handled 'with the utmost discretion and in complete secrecy.' The sting worked like a charm and, over the years, quite a few Middle American living rooms were turned into secret shrines.

Every couple of years or so, Joe would get to talk with Ghislaine but she never allowed him to see his daughter. Then, one time, Joe comes over, books himself into the Hyatt like he usually does, and arranges to meet Ghislaine in the lobby. He's early, and while he waits for her, he begins to feel ill, but very ill. He has a tremendous pain in his gut and such an urge to pass water you just wouldn't believe. He staggers to the men's room but simply can't perform. When he comes out, he's ashen and people are looking at him. That's just when Ghislaine comes in.

She catches him as he collapses and stays with him while they call an ambulance. Of course, she walks with the stretcher out through the lobby and onto the sidewalk. She kisses him and says she'll visit him in hospital. And that just happens to be the moment when Bob's half-brother Wilbur is cruising by.

Now Wilbur, let me put simply, is a prize shit. His middle name is jealousy and he hates Bob, for all kinds of reasons, like being the adopted cuckoo in his private nest, and Wilbur is cunning with it. He *sees* that kiss, sees where the ambulance comes from and steps into a phone box to make a couple of calls before abandoning his plans to visit his bookmaker and goes to Mount Zion instead, claiming he's a relative. His plan, if you want to call it that, is to see what he could get out of Ghislaine as the price of his silence about her 'affair'.

Wilbur bides his time and finds out all he can before he makes his next move. Meantime, Joe's been diagnosed with cancer of the prostate, goes into surgery and everything else besides, beats the odds and, only three months later, gets himself shipped down to a clinic in Carmel to convalesce. He gets better slowly and Ghislaine has the chance to come and see him two or three times. On the third visit, Wilbur simply walks in unannounced, in his loud clothes and manners to match.

It was Joe who rescued the situation. He told Wilbur he'd taken over Ghislaine's father's gallery (literally true) and been trying unsuccessfully to persuade her to run the American end of the business (not true at all). By the end of their conversation, Joe had hired Wilbur to work for him in the States. He was to manage the 'new gallery' in return for a salary, commission, expenses – and silence. Joe reckoned that if, later on, Wilbur ever figured out the real relationship, he would be in too deep.

But Wilbur was dishonest to the core. There he was, set up in a little gallery in San Francisco, the 'Golden Gallery of Contemporary Art' would you believe. He was earning a good salary and getting commission on what he sold plus another commission for people he sent over to the Gallérie Américaine. But Wilbur knew he wasn't making as much as Joe and, after only a year or two, he thinks he knows all anyone ever needs to know about contemporary art. And, by this time, he has an artist boy-friend.

The boy-friend, Alexander, wears black studded leathers and paints the most awful canvases you could ever imagine; sadomasochism and Third Reich symbolism. Joe makes a brief, unscheduled trip over and finds Wilbur prominently displaying the awful Alexander's paintings in the Golden Gallery. Metaphorically speaking, Joe kicks the dishonest shit out of Wilbur and tells him to take down Alexander's canvases. Imagine how this plays with the artist. He just won't get a handle on the fact that it isn't Wilbur who owns the gallery and yells at him he's going to fly to Paris and 'demand an apology' from Joe. When he discovers that Alexander has actually left for the airport, Wilbur buys a ticket on the next possible flight and, like some French farce, all three of them finish up together at the Galérie Américaine. Wilbur actually gets there first; because, unlike Alexander, he doesn't grudge the cab fare from the airport. So, he's waiting on the sidewalk when Joe arrives for work, which meant they were just a tad better prepared when Alexander made his carefully staged entrance. But, after an hour or so, even Joe can't get it across that Wilbur doesn't call the shots at the Golden Gallery. Alexander keeps on insisting on his First

Amendment rights, and threatening that he and his 'friends' will make the most God Almighty stink in San Francisco if his work isn't shown in 'Wilbur's gallery'. Now *that* kind of publicity, Joe can do without so, finally, he suggests Alexander take a look around the gallery while he and Wilbur go next door for a coffee and try to 'work something out'; tho' what the hell that can be neither knows. Each has the goods on the other but it's like nuclear stalemate. They just have to find a disaster-free solution. They're trying to do just that when Alexander comes smirking up to their café table and drops his own bomb.

He's been wandering through the unattended racks behind the gallery display area and, to put it simply, has come on *three* near identical paintings by Chagall. Within minutes, there's another row going on in the gallery and, this time, Wilbur has ganged up with Alexander – expressing mock shock-horror at being involved in something 'questionable'.

Joe, who's still a semi-invalid remember, feels unable, physically or mentally, to fight the pair of them any longer, and just shuts and locks the door. Before he goes home to rest he agrees to relocate his own American operations, and to hand over 'artistic' control of the Golden Gallery to Wilbur and Alexander; all this, of course, in return for silence and now, of course, complicity. Poor Joe, I really felt for him when Nathan told me this bit.

Then Joe suggests to Alexander, now he's here, he might like to spend some time over in Paris and, if he's really keen, travel around Europe and take in some of the contemporary art scene; at Joe's expense, of course. Alexander thinks this is a really *great* idea. Wilbur isn't so keen so there's another mini-scene. Wilbur has a major client he *must* see the following week with several thousands of dollars in commissions at stake. So, it finishes up with Joe driving the pair of them out to Orly for a tearful farewell before he escorts Alexander back into Paris, gives him enough money to live on and proposes a really exciting travel itinerary. He told Nathan he'd suggested Berlin, Amsterdam and Vienna just for starters. Then Joe hauls himself off for a long rest down at the farmhouse. Now listen up: it gets more complicated, or, depending where your sympathies lie, maybe it just gets simpler.

Either way, what happens is that Alexander never comes back to Paris. The police are called in, but apart from a dubious sighting of him buying a ticket at the Gare de Lyon and an even less convincing one about being seen kissing some man in the car park at the railway station in Orange, he never turns up again; to no one's regret, except I guess Wilbur's. And I guess his disappearance isn't all that helpful to Joe either. Wilbur has the real goods on Joe and no longer has the Alexander encumbrance. His price is steep. He gets complete control of the gallery in San Francisco and rechristens it, of all things, 'the Alexander-Golden Gallery'. Fortunately, the demand for original Alexanders has dried up just as fast as the supply and anyway Wilbur finds it just too painful to keep the dear departed's remaining paintings on display.

Joe buys a new place in Carmel – he took you to lunch there. With his galleries in Carmel and Paris being well enough looked after he can spend a lot more of his time in Arles: he told Nathan he'd started painting again and was producing his best work so far – but whose work his best work was, I've no idea. That's Joe for you.

And that's how things went along pretty much until, out of left field, Ghislaine begins to behave kind of odd and forgetful. It isn't too long before they diagnosed the cruellest thing; pre-senile dementia – which is pretty much when Bob started drinking. Pretty selfish, because it meant the money for her medical bills was going, either, down *his* throat, or, on drying him out. Their daughter started talking about giving up on going to school, to stay home and nurse Ghislaine.

That was when Joe decided to sell the Gallérie Américaine in Paris and give the deeds of the Alexander-Golden Gallery to Wilbur, in return for a signed and sworn affidavit he had no further claim on Joe, nor ever had any reason to think he had. Joe bought a triple lot in Carmel and Bob found himself in charge of building a house there, although he never knew who the client was. That kept him in funds and he agreed to hire a nurse to care for Ghislaine. Nathan had the job of keeping tabs, and told Joe he'd fixed everything and just to take life easy. The daughter did go off to law school after all, and everything began to settle down.

But Bob didn't always come home at weekends, like he was

supposed to. Most times the nurse simply stayed on without being asked but, one time, she had specially asked for the weekend and Bob had promised faithfully he would be there. Who knows whether he forgot, or got drunk, or whatever; he just didn't show and, some time during that weekend, Ghislaine wandered out of the house, and stepped off the sidewalk in front of a truck.

Sorry, sweetheart. I'll be better in a minute. Just hold me. Please, don't speak yet. There's more. No! No questions. Ssh!

I'm fine now. Just fine! No: sit where I can look at you.

Things got held up, you can imagine, but, eventually, the house got finished. Joe started living there, but whenever the builders came by to work on the snag list he would slip out to the gallery. That's where he got a call one afternoon to say he'd better come home because the builder had just had a stroke.
 No! Don't ask me to spell it out just yet, sweetheart. We'll get there. Trust me.
 The daughter's back at school, after the second funeral, in her final year now, and she gets a call to go to the bursar's office where she's told her father hasn't paid her fees up front like usual. She calls the family lawyer, the only person she knows apart from a gay uncle in San Francisco.
 A couple of days later, she gets another call, this time from a shifty sounding bursar who says he's sorry but it's all been a big mistake. Not only have the fees been paid, they've actually been paid *twice* and, since her father has died, it would be simplest if the overpayment was returned directly to her and nothing more said. She's used to Bob's hazy money management, so she just accepts this.
 The daughter graduates and, straight way, she's offered a job by these lawyers in San Francisco and, six months later, up comes the chance to work in the office they're just about to open in Carmel. What a great life! Except the guy who heads the office is a bit of a jerk, the slime-ball son-in-law of Mr Handschumacher, and he's always going on as if he *knows* something but won't say what. On a

day-to-day basis, she gets to look after the affairs of some wealthy old guy who lives in a funny kind of house where the walls are covered in paintings.

Don't speak, my darling please! Just listen.

She reckons, at first, he might just be some sort of pervert as well as rich. He keeps looking at her and then snapping his head away. But he never puts a foot or a finger wrong and, after a while, she doesn't even notice his quirky behaviour because, basically, he is a seriously nice old guy. He's a gallery owner; it's off of Junípero and he goes there sometimes. The gallery manager wants to open a coffee bar and the old guy urges him to go one step further and make part of the second floor an up-market restaurant. Christens it himself; 'Art on a Plate'. She gets to handle the licence applications and all. It's quite the hit of Carmel; very, very fashionable. Her client eats there himself about once a week, but most days he just potters around his house and paints pictures on the walls. He paints all kinds of things, and when he gets tired of them he just paints the wall white and, a little while later, starts all over again.

He hasn't been too well and has to have full-time nursing and plenty bed rest but, once in a while, he still goes out eating pizzas and peach ice cream in a real dump of a saloon instead of the healthy diet that I – that *she's* – gotten his live-in help to cook for him.

Then one day, he does something real crazy. She comes to the house and finds he's picked up, or, frightening thought, maybe even been picked up by some young man, an Englishman, quite good-looking too, but nobody knows anything about him except he's just breezed into Carmel saying he has to talk to Joe about something. Since she's been told her gay uncle tried before to have people spy on him she's suspicious, but Joe says not to worry and he's just someone he finds interesting, and maybe useful, to talk to about art and stuff but, if she's worried at all, why doesn't she check him out. So she does just that and finds he's genuine, some sort of soft-boiled egg-head. They talk. They have dinner. They swim in Joe's pool. They look at each other; and every time she looks at him he gets that little bit better-looking. And, just when she admits very privately to him she just might be capable of falling in love, complicating her personal life more than somewhat, Joe has a sudden relapse and the mystery Englishman writes her a real pompous letter then simply up stakes and flies away.

So there she is, sitting with Joe for several days, holding his hand until he finally dies, and hearing him all the time chuckle about how he'd told 'the new Bernard Berenson'[2] the latest version of his life story. Never mind. The pompous letter meant she did speak with Nathan, who told her more than a thing or two.

First thing, he doesn't trust his son-in-law, so he's quite seriously misinformed him about Joe, *and about her.*

Second thing, he confirms that Joe wanted her to be told she's *his* daughter, and that, to the best of Nathan's belief, it's true.

There was a third thing – but he didn't tell her that until a day or two after Joe died.

By now, I was in shock. Anna's story was confusingly recognisable, strangely credible, yet completely new. It made me feel very, very wary. I wanted to believe *Anna* – but I wasn't at all sure I could believe her story. I had to admire, if that's really the right word, Joe's powers of invention, his skill in embroidery – no, that's the wrong word; let's call a spatula a spatula – I mean forgery. And this new structure was so fragile I scarcely dared breathe, for fear it all came tumbling down or, worse, I woke up.

But after I'd heard it all, there was a ton of unanswered questions, starting with the most fundamental. Okay, there was no Margot, and no Scottish cottage, but there was a farmhouse and apparently there was a Ghislaine – or so Anna told me. There was no crock of Golden Rembrandts at the end of the rainbow after all, but there *was* a sketchbook – full of blistering, or was it glistering, *croquis* – whose existence I had still to reveal to Anna. When had Joe created that, and for whom? Maybe he had been planning yet another elaborate con: that would be my bet. Had Joe seen me not so much the mark as the innocent, the gullible and slightly greedy expert, like the ones that used to get the good wine in the best restaurants – more my role, I think? Only that must have been a fiction. No, it was probably true, just that it happened in Paris or Carmel, not Rome or Florence. And who was this woman sitting opposite me? Had she inherited some of Joe's guile along with his genes? Whose farmhouse was this? What was I doing here? I'd recently been reading and enjoying Le Carré – was this some sort of 'honey trap' but then why would I be worth trapping?

Throughout Anna's recital of the Authorized Version, she had seldom let go of my hand or risen from the table, except to bring and serve food or pour wine, but I cannot recall what we ate or drank. Now she let go and got up, walking to the open kitchen door. I followed her, put my arm round her shoulder and we gazed together up at the vivid Van Gogh stars. I too must be mad.

'But *why* did Handschumacher *tell* Abramowitz such a story?'

'He never liked his son-in-law. The guy ran off with his only daughter, or maybe it was the other way round. Then she bullied her father into making him a partner. Nathan didn't want him in the practice in San Francisco so he opened the office in Carmel, just to put him in charge there but ring-fence him from the rest of the business. Apart from the way any father's leery about a son-in-law, he felt in his bones that Gerry wasn't one hundred per cent kosher. I don't know the details but, more than once, it seems, the old man's had to sort out expensive mistakes. When he gave *me* a job, and said I was to look after the so-called 'Rembrandt' account, he had to give Gerry just sufficient reason to believe why Joe would want me, rather than him or anyone else, to do the job. It did mean Gerry couldn't go on and on about wanting the 'Rembrandt' file transferred to Carmel. Now it had been; just not to *his* desk. He didn't like it, but he was afraid of his father-in-law because he wasn't protected by his wife any more.'

'Explain.'

'She left him after only a couple of years. So now Gerry's entirely dependent on his father-in-law's goodwill.'

'Good for her. I didn't like Abramowitz either?'

I held her tightly but, as well as growing feelings of love, was there the tiniest smidgeon of regret that I wasn't, after all, embracing Golden's granddaughter? Then, another question came to me.

'How old are you, Anna?'

'Twenty-five next month.'

'Not twenty-seven! So, another *two years* before you collect the trust fund.'

'There *is* no trust fund.'

'Hell, that's rough. After all that; not a penny then?'

'After all that, sweetheart, *every* nickel and dime. That was another thing, the thing Nathan didn't tell me until after the funeral. Joe left all his money to Gilly, in fact – Nathan had it all sewn up – but, in his will, there's the usual clause that, if she dies first, the estate goes to her 'heirs and successors'. Apart from a legacy, he specifically wrote Bob out of the will. I guess he might have contested that but, poor Dad, he didn't live long enough and, anyway, he never knew. So it's all mine now. Including, can you believe it, this farmhouse, which it turns out he really *did* own.'

'Can I *believe* it? No! Not yet, anyway … . Sorry, Anna. I'm forgetting myself. Congratulations. I hope you'll be very happy.'

'I am now, Bill. And I plan to stay that way. Help me work on it?'

Pause for a delicious embrace.

'Bill, you do realise if you hadn't written that letter he wouldn't have had the strength, the courage I guess because he had no strength left at the end, to talk to me.

'He told me he'd been having a wonderful time – pretending to be all the things he might have been, like a genuinely creative artist, and telling them to you, but that if I wanted to hear the real *truth* about him then I should speak to Nathan up in San Francisco. Nathan did tell me some things, and I nosed around a bit and found out some more. Like, my mother's family name *was* Moreau and they did come from Roubaix originally. She had an elderly aunt who married an Englishman and lived in London. Joe met her on one of his trips to London and she even sent him up to Scotland to look at some painters there. Then he was in a nasty car accident with some drunken French art dealer in the south of France. You see, Joe took bits of his personal kaleidoscope and shook them up especially for you.'

'He was one hell of a storyteller. A real professional fight arranger. I can still hear him telling me about a night up in Scotland when he and Margot got drunk.'

Anna was grinning.

'There's something lurking there behind that smile. What is it?'

'I'm only an amateur arranger, my darling. My first idea was to lure you back to the Illustrated House, and then jump out from behind an easel and surprise you. It turned out your idea of surprising *me* was much, much better. I'd tracked you down to the Foundation but they told me you'd just taken off for Montpellier. That was too good to pass up so I came down here to open up the farmhouse. I was planning next week to come and surprise you at the University.'

How could I be mad with her? All the myths were exploded now and I had no reason to go on feeling curious about the loose ends of Joe's story. I could stop worrying about his clever sketchbook forgery because that fitted in neatly with what I had just learned about his life in Paris. I wondered how long he had needed to spend in the Orangerie to work that up and who the mark might have been. Now, I had other, and it seemed to me, much more important matters to sort out in my life, in *our* life.

Just over two weeks later, we were installed *together* in the farmhouse and I'd fired off a swift letter to my landlord in London, giving notice and saying I would be back in a month or so to collect my belongings. The letter to the Foundation's Director took longer to put together.

He eventually agreed that, for the rest of my two-year contract, I could divide my academic year between London and France provided I did an irreducible minimum of post-graduate teaching *and* delivered the monograph on Poliakoff by an agreed cut-off date. Which was fine; it was still important to me – call it *amour propre* though it was becoming somewhat overwhelmed by straightforward *amour* – to have a career and to make a mark for myself in my own specialist field.

Anna, the rich young American abroad like Isabel Archer[3], just wanted to keep me happy – it was mutual, of course – so she readily agreed to the working arrangements and I was more than happy with her ideas for creating *two* rooms upstairs out of the big studio, a writing room and a fabulous bedroom, complete with *en suite* facilities to 'American standards'. We called in the local builder.

He came and sniffed around the place, shrugging and mumbling and not measuring a single thing; a cartoon Frenchman, complete with beret, blue dungarees and Gitane. Despite her very limited French (disappointing when you think she had a French mother), Anna insisted on handling everything at the farmhouse, while I taught my classes at the University and the Foundation. It was her idea the builder sketch out what he was trying to tell her as he pointed vaguely at the ceiling and waved his hands in the air.

What the sketch showed was a pump plus a new water tank, to regulate the supply of water to the bathroom on what Anna insisted on calling the second floor (and I schooled myself to call 'upstairs' so as not have rows with her at this stage in our relationship). He agreed to go off and work out a 'rough' price for the whole job, including new plumbing and wiring throughout, plastering and painting, and a *vast* new septic tank. It only took us three months to get that out of him. The proprietor of our favourite restaurant in Fontvieille, Mme Picot, assured us this was a record in itself, but the real problem would be getting him actually to do the job. She reckoned without Anna.

She simply camped on the builder's doorstep and got her message across to his wife who was captivated by *les jeunes mariés*. The following week, her husband turned up, with his tools and the bits and pieces, and came into the house with expressions of grudging admiration for *la belle américaine* and ostentatious and salacious envy of 'Monsieur Eengleesh'.

We took ourselves out of doors while he began ferrying copper pipes and glass-fibre cisterns up to the studio. We began to talk about restoring the garden to some semblance of order. I was keener on vegetables than flowers. It seemed to me, being a Yorkshireman, you ought to get some kind of return for your investment from a vegetable patch, leeks of course, and some rhubarb.

Anna wanted flowers, all kinds of flowers, and all the year round. I was beginning to get worried about who was going to look after all of this. It might seem more pleasant to garden in Provence than Pateley Bridge but it could be just as time consuming. I felt I had to establish the fact that I was an academic and writer, not a gardener. It was a pleasant enough argument and we were just beginning to enjoy it when the builder asked us to come back into the house.

When we got up to the studio, I could see that he had taken a panel off the wall, high up in the corner of the studio, exposing access to the loft space where the new pump and cistern would be going. A light hung inside from a nail driven into the rafters. I could see, hanging there almost out of sight, the top half of a block and tackle. His taciturn Gitane gestured I needed to take a look. Something was causing a problem, and something else was already beginning to disturb *me*.

Very gingerly, I began to mount the ladder. Not my scene at all: I can get nose-bleed just looking down at my shoes. When I got to the top Anna called up in alarm – asking if I'd seen a ghost.

It's no use trying to recall now what I was expecting to see. What I *did* see were literally dozens of canvases, identical in size, stacked, row upon row from joists to rafters. I was almost swept away by a jumbled flood of recollections and anxieties and had to cling onto the ladder.

I inched my way down again.

Suppressing my palpitations, I asked the builder to bring everything out of the attic, then I took Anna, or more truthfully she helped me, downstairs and poured us both some cognac. When I told her what I had seen, and my guess that this could well turn out to be Joe's production line just as she had described it to me – masterworks of minor artists or, just possibly, the other way round, minor works of major artists – she poured us both a second cognac. What we finally did see was more; far, far more than I expected.

The builder's mate came to summon us and we trooped upstairs again. Ranged round the walls were oil paintings and as my eye hit the very first one, I couldn't conceal a gasp of recognition. I was looking, as it were *again*, at the first sketch in the book, the images that had poleaxed me in my bed-sit some months previously, but now with even greater impact. The colours on the canvas vibrated, and the scumbled texture of the paint created light and shade and variations that hummed, buzzed, fizzed and, here and there, cried out with energy. But I had no time to stand and stare: I was too full of cares and they crowded in on me, because parked in a corner beside the paintings was the last thing they had brought down and what had taken them so long – a large, tin trunk, grimy from years up in the loft. Under the grime they had partly wiped off, I could see the neatly lettered words. 'Alexander R.I.P.'.

Saying *demain, demain, demain* like some demented parrot, I pursued the two workmen out of the house and stood there until they'd driven off, shrugging and shaking their heads. Then I went back to a puzzled Anna.

Fetching the camera bag up from our bedroom, I zipped it open and silently showed her the first sketch and then the drawing on the cover. We shook our heads in silence and looked from book to canvas to trunk and back again. Then I turned the page of the sketchbook and another powerful image leapt out at us from off the page, as if I'd released a second genie from the same bottle. Maybe that wasn't too inapt. There, against the wall, was its simulacrum; a fully worked up oil painting. That got us going. An hour or two later, we had matched up every sketch with a canvas of such strength and beauty that I felt completely breathless. Each canvas had its matching sketch and there were actually four sketches left over, not yet, it seemed, turned into paintings. They were patently all the work of one man. But who, or rather which? *The paintings were unsigned.*

What were they doing up in the loft and why had Joe carried the sketchbook round with him? Anna felt sure we had stumbled on Joe's personal artistic statement. I had to agree that was what it *looked* like. In all the stories he'd told, there had been his constant theme of unfulfilled creativity. Was this Joe's apotheosis as a painter? Or could it be, just conceivably, the second coming; a dramatic late flowering from the long lost, Alexander Golden? After all, what else would he have done, even in hiding? But what had Joe, the con-artist, been working at during all these long weekends down in Provence until illness had caught him short? This was a task for experts. Having worked so long and lovingly on the Golden Month, I was some sort of an expert but – and this was the crucial point – so too was, or had been, the perversely talented Joe Rembrandt. A battery of tests on canvas, paint, brushstrokes – the whole kit and caboodle – would be necessary. The selfish but seductive thought, which I kept to myself, was that, with Joe dead and gone, this discovery could be the making of Dr William Maguire, art historian and specialist in contemporary

French painting. A book, a series of books, profusely illustrated, several television series, visiting Professorships, they all seemed to flow from this. All this; Arles and Anna after all. Up yours, Abramowitz!

Feeling puzzled but, even so, very pleased, with our wonderful discovery we took ourselves off to the village that evening and ate an excellent meal Chez Picot, washing it down with something better than the usual rough, red plonk. As it turned out, the builder and his wife were eating there with friends and we strolled out into the warm evening past their table saying, this time in more welcoming tones, *demain, demain, demain* and crept in our petty pace out to the car.

Happy and teasing each other, asking who was more in love, she or me, we only just made it back to the farmhouse. We'd decided to hang the paintings all over the house and, for a while at least, turn the place into some sort of shrine to the memory of the man who had brought us together. (Another Musée Margot, I drunkenly reminded myself.) It seemed like a good idea to stagger up the stairs. We wanted a last look before going to bed.

The impact was still very powerful. Electric light made the pictures look different but no less dramatic.

'Come on, Bill; let's see what's in the trunk.'

She wobbled over to it. There were no padlocks but the latches holding the lid down were stiff. I got on my knees beside her and worked on one of them while she clawed at the other. I got mine open then had to give her a hand. At last, we yanked up the squeaky lid.

I can still hear her scream.

---

1   I've got some kind of fixation, that's obvious; or I'm just a ham writer, which I deny. I'll really have to go through this stripping the gilt from the prose.
2   A real back-handed compliment that; when you knew what kind of a fraud *he* was – but he may have been right.
3   Oh God, I've just realised what that allusion makes me – Osmond. Fortunately, I have no previous Madame Merle to explain away. Actually, I see myself as more of a Caspar Goodwood.

7

In front of us, crammed into a foetal position, head turned to stare up at us, was a mummified body, in the remains of a studded, black leather jacket and trousers; with picture wire wound tightly round its neck and a wooden plug, like a cheroot, stuck bizarrely between its teeth. It took us about half an hour just to calm down. It may *sound* farcical but this was neither thrilling nor funny.

Prosaic ideas like Anna's first intention of calling the police got short shrift from me. The thought of the protracted hassle, the unwanted publicity *and what that might do to my career*, steered me to the simple, shameful but obvious course of action: the trunk couldn't be there in the morning – and it was already after midnight.

'Anna, my darling, just think for a couple of moments. Whoever it once *was* in the trunk is beyond help now and has been that way for a long, long time. But *Joe* owned this place. *Joe* lived and worked here. If this becomes a police investigation, it can only harm the reputation of the man we both love. And that's damage he couldn't recover from.'

'All I can think about is that *thing* up there. We have to get it out of here.'

'Agreed.'

'Out of here and *tonight*, Bill. I'm not sleeping under the same roof.'

'Agreed.'

I went upstairs alone and knelt in front of the tin coffin. About to lower the lid and snap the latches, I was staring into the face of – that was the question, who? Whoever it was, or had been, was grinning back at me because of that wooden plug. It was grotesque and I wanted to do something about it. Gingerly, I twisted it to and fro and eased it out before slipping it into the pocket of my jeans and shutting the lid.

It must have been a really tricky load to get down out of the loft but even harder to get up there in the first place, even with the block and tackle. My guess is the body and the trunk went up there separately. But why hadn't whoever-it-was simply buried the body? The probable answer came to me as I lugged and twisted the trunk down the stairs with Anna trying to guide the other end. Whoever 'buried' the body in the loft must have been afraid that recently turned earth in the garden would lead anyone hunting for a recently missing person straight to his resting place. A boarded-up loft, as hot as a crematorium in summer, and behind all these paintings, was so unlikely a grave as to be ignored by all but the most nosey sleuth and, after an interval, even the nose would have had no more clues.

It took us twenty minutes to manoeuvre the trunk down to the kitchen. We collapsed and sat together getting our breath back. Anna had been reading my thoughts.

'I think I know who he is. I think we've found Wilbur's Alexander. But how did he get up there?'

'Probably collected from the train at Orange and brought down here.'

'You mean... Oh, no!'

'It looks suspiciously like it.'

'But what shall we do? Oh Bill, what shall we do?'

'Anna, my darling, apart from disposing of the evidence, we just do nothing. Otherwise, it could blacken Joe's reputation forever; just as we've discovered *his* paintings, the culmination of his life's work, and all that sort of thing.'

She nodded miserably, and began to cry quietly.

Feeling like every kind of selfish and dishonest bastard, I comforted her and led her, unresisting to the bedroom. Setting the alarm for five, I lay down beside her under the duvet. Surprisingly soon, she slept – but I didn't. My mind was racing. I was having fantastic, waking nightmares. It's easy enough now for me to blame Joe; for putting ideas into my head. But what one can never really do, without literally losing one's mind, is forget ideas, wonderful ideas; selfish, shameful but seductive ideas. At a quarter to five, I crawled stiffly off the bed and switched off the alarm.

Morning is my best time creatively but that day my mind was on destruction, selective destruction of the evidence. I didn't dare wait any longer, in case anyone came past on the road. I woke Anna. She began crying again before we got as far as the kitchen.

Together we dragged, heaved and humped the trunk out into the front yard, and then round the back and up, up, up the North Face of the vegetable garden. Anyone who thinks I'm exaggerating the strain and the pain has, presumably, never dragged a corpse up a slope in a tin trunk. Be grateful! It took us nearly thirty minutes to get it into position, screened from passing view by fronds of asparagus fern.

We went back down to the house together. It wasn't yet five thirty. I rooted around in the lean-to, found a spade and fork, and took them up to where the trunk sat before I could feel relaxed enough to drink a mouthful of the coffee Anna had prepared. It tasted like shit.

Anna wouldn't hear of staying down at the farmhouse alone while I began to attack the stony earth. She sat miserably, with the occasional sob, on a couple of sacks. I had no breath spare for sobbing. The sun was just coming up. It was going to be a beautiful day, and I had a grave to dig.

By half past six I had a hole that seemed more than big enough, and I was impatient to get the trunk out of sight for ever. Anna helped me drag it alongside the trench. I had decided, for no good reason, to bury the trunk on end, in a narrow, deep hole and this had meant some hard digging once I got below the top soil. The topsoil itself hadn't been all that easy, full of tangled roots. I slid the trunk over the lip of the trench and it began to topple. And of course, the bloody thing immediately jammed at an angle, right at the top, because I'd cut it all far too neat. We had to haul it back – a hundred times harder than pushing it in. The trench would have to be much larger than the trunk to allow for manoeuvring.

Around seven o'clock now, with the workmen likely to arrive at anytime between then and nine, they were so erratic; I was frantic to get the tin coffin into its tomb. The blisters on my hands, pains in my arms, my back and my groin, and my tight chest were agonising but I was supersaturated with adrenalin. Attacking the soil savagely, I began to cut another slice out at one end of the narrow grave. About two spade's depth down, I struck something. Expecting another root, I picked up the fork and rammed it in a little behind the spade cut and levered with all my strength.

Backwards into the trench tumbled a spadeful of earth – and what seemed at first like a human skull which rolled neatly into the opposite corner, tilted upwards to grin and mock at us. I thought I could even see the creamy circlet of the top of the spinal column sticking out of the soil from where I had decapitated it. I climbed laboriously down to investigate. Anna began to have hysterics then fainted clean away.

Death was all around us. I was so worked up I had already imagined this specimen was the Parisian art gallery owner and Anna's grandfather, or even, who in Heaven knew, the earthly remains of Alexander Golden. Jesus Christ, *now* what was the truth?

But the 'skull' turned out to be a cannonball sized boulder of limestone; nothing more sinister.

I looked at my watch, then began again, frantically excavating the hole, but at the other end. It was seven fifteen. Anna was conscious but totally collapsed on the sacks. No other 'human remains' turned up as I hacked and shovelled. Finally, I pushed and heaved the trunk to the edge of the hole and a little bit over the lip. With a quick flip, I managed to drop it neatly into the hole. I had one moment of grim pleasure realising it had dropped right on top of the 'skull'.

By the time my watch gave its inane bleep, signalling eight o'clock, I had the soil back into the trench and tramped solid. Somehow, I managed to help Anna down the path, dragging the tools in my other hand. I propped her against the wall and stowed the tools in the lean-to. Then I had, more or less, to carry her into the house and through to the bedroom. I bundled her onto the bed and wrapped her in the Primrose Bordier counterpane.

Starting the bath running, I stripped off all my clothes and rammed them into Anna's frilly laundry basket. In ordinary circumstances, a hot bath after hard work would be something quite sybaritic, something to linger over. That morning, it was simply more hard work as I scrubbed the filth off my hands and arms, rinsed the traces out of my hair then flushed the muddy residue down the plughole. As I was climbing, stiff and damp, into clean clothes and putting on my shoes at a quarter to nine, I heard the builder's pick-up outside. Telling them wearily that Madame was ill, with a hangover I implied, and sleeping it off, I left them to tiptoe upstairs to get on with it and went back into the bedroom. Madame wasn't asleep but she really was ill.

Staring wild-eyed at me she said we had to get away from this awful place. She would sell it; even *give* it away. But that short time in the bath had given me a chance to do still more selfish thinking.

'Not for a little while, Anna. You wouldn't want someone else coming in here and, how shall I put it, making any unfortunate discoveries. We need to make sure there's nothing, or no one else, hidden away and we need some time to let things grow over the bare earth in the garden. Then, perhaps, we can get away.'

I fixed her some coffee, which was all she could be persuaded to have, and held her in my arms until, an hour or so later, she fell asleep again. The builders let me up into the loft and I shone their powerful torch into its every recess. It was bare. For a moment I felt relief, then the thought that I might have to prise up all the farmhouse floorboards came rushing in to alarm me.

Although it hadn't been what they were going to do next, I arranged for the builders to cover up the paintings, where I had now stacked them at one end of the large studio with dust sheets and then several layers of plastic, and to go and get the materials to erect the partition wall that was already planned. While they were away, I looked in and around every cupboard and then went down into the small cellar and hauled out the empty wine rack so that I could tap the wall. It sounded reassuringly solid. Finally I cooked myself an enormous fry-up, wolfed it down and realised with a guilty belch that I had not thought about Anna for nearly three hours.

I took a tray of toast and tea into the bedroom and suggested we pack up and go and stay in Montpellier while the workmen got on with the new plumbing and everything. And to give us time to come to terms with what had happened, I even agreed, since she was paying, that we stay in one of the swankier hotels. And, to begin with, it seemed to work.

It took a few days, a couple of weeks in fact, but we began again, at first tentatively but very soon passionately, to make love. It was wild, frantic, mind-numbing love on Anna's part and, while we were engrossed in it, there was little room for other thoughts. However, we weren't making love all the time and I couldn't stop myself thinking about those paintings. Anna, by contrast, had stopped thinking altogether, or had switched off in order to shut out the experiences of that frightful night.

We resumed our former life in the farmhouse a couple of months later but we did not yet use the upstairs bedroom. It became my temporary study where I got down to the most important project of my academic life so far. I could see, in her every gesture, hear in her every word, that Anna was not reconciled to being there and very far from being happy. She would rather have been almost anywhere else.

But, as I explained, very patiently it seemed to me, it was an urgent and absolute academic necessity to study, photograph and carefully describe every one of the canvases; using all my professional skills and, of course, bringing my hard-won knowledge of Alexander Golden (and, for that matter, Joe Rembrandt) to bear. Apart from just sitting and looking at the paintings, one by one and then in their subtle 'sets' of six, I would have to take samples of the canvas, the paint and even the wood of the stretchers to establish a clear date for them. Come to think about it, I would be wise to check out the age of the sketchbook.

Today, of course, these things are much more scientific and, if I'm honest, for me, already too much a question of chemistry and physics rather than sound, old-fashioned aesthetics and hard-won expertise. At least one canvas would need to be x-rayed to confirm that there was nothing, no ghost of Golden past, lurking underneath the visible surface of the paint, but that would have to wait until I felt I could arrange this without taking someone else into my confidence; which, to be frank, in the academic world, is the equivalent of premature ejaculation.

Anna would smile; a watery smile, the kind of smile that should have warned me clearly, and much sooner, how unhappy she was. To her, they were just pictures, and not very good pictures. To her, whoever painted them was dead and, to her, the presence of death, lurking just below the asparagus, was gnawing away at the foundations of our dreams; dreams we no longer discussed day and night as once we had done. But to me, this uncovered hoard was a key that I had been handed, a key to unlock my own dreams, my exclusively Maguire dreams. And in my night time dreams, I was uncovering deeper and less loving layers of myself, as well as looking deeply into the mind and soul of an American artist and consummate conman.

'It won't take all *that* long, darling, but I really must do the job carefully, so that my conclusions can't be challenged.'

Anna would shrug, a weak shrug, a shrug that I should have picked up on in the same way as, using my eyesight, my experience and my intelligence I was picking out and putting down in my notebook, preserving in Polaroids, the weird but wonderful signals that each successive canvas was sending out. Anna didn't give a damn about art or aesthetics and, what's more, she was beginning to develop a morbid fear of attics as well as asparagus. As for me, I was beginning to discover, or maybe simply uncover, that side of my personality I think I'd known was there all along – ambitious, not totally ruthless but with much less ruth than average, let's say –and which, until now, I had never had the means nor the motive to develop.

'In this sort of work, sweetheart, one can't take anything for granted. One can't make any prior assumptions. Everything has to be checked out and re-established from first principles.' I may not have sounded altogether convincing.

Anna would nod and walk outside to light a cigarette. She had agreed not to smoke in the house but there had been our first serious and long simmering row when I tried to stop her smoking altogether. But with her outside, out of sight, she would already be drifting out of mind while I went back up to my discoveries? Out of mind; now there's a Freudian remark; which reminds me, there is nowadays a psychoanalytical school of art criticism that goes gleefully pursuing the priapic amongst the paint pots.

Whatever the boffins discovered, we were talking here not only about a cocktail of chemicals but a collection of intellectually and aesthetically beautiful paintings; a collection that *seemed* to present the evolution of a number of artistic ideas to the viewer, as he or she walked slowly past, pausing at each one to give it its fair share of attention. In my mind, I was already composing the catalogue of the first exhibition: I could just hear it. Would I be discovering 'a convincing reinterpretation of Golden's iconography in Rembrandt's vivid images' or might I be finding 'surprising pre-echoes of these new canvases in the *original* Golden Month?'

Could we really be talking about writing a new chapter, or at least a significant segment of a chapter, of the history of post-war contemporary art in France? Had the magnet that drew Golden to Paris and then Provence been just as much a pull on Joe Rembrandt, expressionist, illusionist, fantasist and now revealed (or would 'hitherto concealed' sound better) as an artist of the first rank. And was it now exerting its strange attraction on me? If Golden could go through a mid-life crisis to be reborn artistically, if Joe could acquire the Midas touch, then, academically, might I just lay my greedy hands on it too.

'Bill! Supper's on the table.'

On my side of the table, I was brimming full of ideas, flashes of intuition and fascinating insights and wanted to share them, or even just unburden my busy mind. On Anna's side of the table there had been, especially these past few days, only brooding silences. Subconsciously, I had been aware of the growing problem but, ever since we had come back from our 'practice honeymoon' I was so anxious to get to work on *my* discovery that I wasn't finding any time for *her* problem. Besides, as I tried to rationalise it, Anna was not interested in art just as I'm not interested in law; just as I don't know how the internal combustion engine works, or how lift, miraculously, exceeds drag when an aeroplane takes off. All useful stuff but …

'Bill, I want to go back to Carmel.'

'Of course, my darling. Just as soon as …'

'I've called American Express.'

'Perhaps in another month …'

'Day after tomorrow. They're holding two seats.'

'But Anna, I've got so much work to …'

'Jesus, you selfish bastard. Stay if you damn well like but I've got to get away from here. I've got to get back to California. I'm going out of my mind thinking about all that must have been going on here.

Murder and mayhem. And now the things *we've* done. Dreadful things, dishonest things, *illegal* things. And besides, I need to see my doctor.'

'They have doctors here in France.'

'Damn you to hell, Bill Maguire, I think I'm pregnant.'

8

20050202 (Approaching San Francisco)

I am ashamed to write this, deeply ashamed of myself, contrite – *now*. The trouble is we're talking about *then*. It was, in all probability, that 'enforced' stay – Anna mostly at the hotel in Montpellier, while I worked on at the farmhouse on the paintings and taught at the University, as well as reading up on Poliakoff, that stay which she finally agreed to only because she didn't want to fly on her own – that undermined Anna's health. By the time we finally left, nearly four months after the events of that dreadful night, she was well into her nervous breakdown. And she'd lost the baby. I can't write any more just now.

Later, when she was well enough to come back to Carmel, from the sanitarium (as Americans call it and misspell it), she told me she would *never* go back to Arles, with its several secrets, revealed and concealed. But I was just as convinced she should never sell the place. Suppose, for example, it came into the hands of a property developer, or someone keen on home improvements, or even just an enthusiastic amateur gardener?

Our discussion was fraught. I hadn't intended to get into it on the very day she came home but, as I escorted her into the bedroom, intending she should rest while I busied myself preparing a light meal – Manuel and Dolores long since pensioned off – she looked at me sideways.

'Don't think you're climbing into *bed* with me.'

'Anna, sweetheart! I do love you, but that wasn't the first thing on my mind.'

'If you love me then tell me why you told Nathan not to go ahead with selling the farmhouse. You had no right to interfere.'

I took a deep breath, reminded myself I *did* love her, and spoke quietly.

'I asked him to wait until you came home from hospital; to let me have a chance to speak with you.'

'Why?'

Illness had affected her temper. She could hardly bear to be contradicted and, now that she was significantly wealthy, there was really only myself who had sufficient access, opportunity and motive to do so. Does that make me sound like some sort of criminal? If the cap fits, Bill Maguire!

In my *rational* mind, it seemed to me that while Joe, bearing at the last the names he had been born with, had been laid to rest, or rather dispersed to the winds across the waters off Salinas Point, his — dare I use the word, judging him on limited but very damning evidence — victims, dead and alive, were beyond receiving any meaningful recompense. The principal living victim, his newly-discovered daughter and heir, was sick, but at least she had the solace of all the medical and legal help that money could buy — always assuming solace was for sale.

As for me, William Maguire, BA (Hons), DPhil, FRSA, I still had a promising career ahead of me, but one that could be severely damaged if anyone, anytime in the next fifty years (longer even, remembering that damned mummy is in a solid *tin* trunk!), ever decided to grow asparagus in the wrong place. Most of this, but with as little emphasis as possible on my own career concerns, I tried to talk through with Anna, unemotionally. Underneath, I was seething with the strain of trying *not* to upset her, while *she* — I know I'm being unfair — was simply spoiling for a fight.

'You *want* the farmhouse, don't you? You can just see yourself there; *very* comfortably installed. You've told me often enough where *you've* always wanted to live, and what *you* want to do. Where do *I* fit into all these plans?'

'Since you-know-exactly-when, you've been an integral part of all my plans. You know that.'

'"An integral part of your plans!" You're sounding like the pompous professor again. In *that* farmhouse? Never! Never in a million years.

Bill, are you crazy? Why are you looking at me like that? Are you waiting to hear me say, "Are you crazy too"?'

'Sweetheart, we don't need to live *there*. We can let it as a holiday home. We just need to live within reasonable reach of it, to keep an eye on things.'

'For Chrissake, there are things I never want to see again, never mind keep an eye on. And I don't intend to *live* within a thousand miles of the place.'

And she began to sob. Fortunately, I was able to persuade her to swallow her medication and she let me lay her on the bed and pull up the coverlet. I sat on the chair beside the bed, not daring to kiss her lest she felt I was making 'advances'. In five minutes, she fell asleep. I went out onto the patio. The pool had as many leaves in it as the Monet on the wall but before picking up the pool rake, I picked up the phone and called Nathan Handschumacher.

We'd met several times since he collected us from the airport on Anna's first homecoming. He had smoothed over a multitude of minor problems – for example, while Anna was in hospital, I had no money at all, no 'green card' to get a job, no authority to do anything at the house, and so on. He had been kind and helpful: a father-figure as well as a well-connected lawyer. It seemed to me that if – dreadful thought – her illness and its aftermath was wrecking *my* relationship with Anna, the only person who could speak to her without risk of destructive consequences was Nathan. We talked on the phone for half an hour and, next day, he turned up in Carmel.

I spent that morning raking more leaves out of the pool while he raked over the coals with Anna. It was obvious from the look on his face – on both their faces – that she'd told him more than I thought wise. Well, it was done now. And she seemed calm.

'I'm going to take Bill down to the office, *liebchen*, and go over what we've discussed before I get things knocked into shape, document-wise.'

When she looked at me a momentary flash of anger crossed her face, then the calm returned and she nodded. She even managed her watery smile.

'I had to tell him, Bill.'

She let me give her a gentle embrace but it was a million miles from a hug.

'I'll be back as soon as I can. Will you be all right?'

I had to force myself not to glance sideways at the pool.

'Yes, Bill. Don't look so worried!'

Nathan and I set off. Ensconced in Abramowitz's office, while its usual occupant had been told, to his obvious annoyance, to take a hike, we talked. Since Anna had told what she knew, I recounted the whole of Joe's fantastic story to him as well. It was almost amusing to see the range of expressions that crossed his face as I took him through each different version of events. Then we got down to the business discussion. Put bluntly, it was my reasonably generous pay-off.

I could go back to France and resume my disrupted academic career. I could have a year or more of exclusivity and, more importantly, secrecy in which to complete work on the paintings. There would, of course, be no editorial control over my academic freedom to publish whatever I wanted about them – I had to insist on that – but, when I was through, the whole kit and caboodle had to be shipped over to the Gallérie Américaine in Carmel for disposal. My advice, to use one of the London auction houses, was firmly overruled. Meanwhile, all the expenses of running and owning the farmhouse would be taken care of and I would have a generous 'allowance'.

It would be romantic and roses-round-the-door to suggest that I pleaded with Nathan, and then with Anna, for one last chance; or that I argued that we could surely make a go of things if we truly loved each other. No, let's confess it: I was by then so eager to get back to Arles I simply shrugged, sighed, signed and (yet again?) settled for failure. My mind was on other things.

20050206 (Return flight; one hour out of SFO)

The details are not important but my encounter this time – couldn't really call it any sort of meeting, least of all of minds – with Abramowitz and his wife was, to put it mildly, a disaster. I don't feel like writing about it just now. I just need to get back to Europe (meaning both London and Arles) and figure out what to do. What I do now will be, of course, a direct if delayed consequence of what I did then. Meantime, I'm going to get my money's worth out of this aeroplane's wine cellar.

It was quite a juggling act. My secondment to the University of Montpellier was over but I'd kept up my connections, especially with their laboratory. There was still talk of an appointment, in a year or two. I retained and in some senses enhanced my connections with the Orangerie, not least with its ever sympathetic Curator. I worked hard on Poliakoff to keep the Foundation sweet. I bought a vacuum cleaner, a large bottle of white spirit and a litre of linseed oil. All this to a purpose.

The Orangerie was particularly helpful. My earlier work had renewed interest in their Golden Month and they trusted me. I was allowed to take a dozen paintings out of their frames, those unattractive frames that the gallery was actively considering replacing. From each of them, I took samples of the canvas, the stretchers and then, very, very carefully under the supervision of their conservator, a warm and affectionate woman with whom I went on to enjoy (occasional) close contact, some minute shards of paint. I let her put these into separate, sealed bags for me but I wrote the reference number on each. The key to these references was written clearly and dated on a sheet of paper which I tucked into my Moleskine notebook.

Back in Arles, I repeated the process, leaving, as I intended, some very discreet, but visible evidence of where I had done so. Then I wrote out a request to the laboratory in Montpellier, asking them to analyse some samples with a view to dating them. Dropping the hint that I might just have made an interesting discovery, I explained the samples were not identified beyond a simple reference number so that there could be no suggestion of my trying to influence their results.

In my rural research centre, I made careful experiments with both white spirit and linseed oil, leaving them at least a day before I applied my fingernail. It seemed that, in their lofty hideaway, the now-revealed paintings had baked for years in the dry heat of their Provencal roof space. The heavy impasto was harder than one would ordinarily have expected in the time since, presumably, they'd been painted. There was a sort of pre-senile craquelure that would not have disgraced much older work. Clever Joe: master chef as well as everything else.

I worked on half a dozen canvases, laying them flat and using cotton buds to tiny areas in the very top left-hand corner of each. Every few hours, over the next couple of days, I would gently press my thumbnail against the paint and note carefully how readily it took any impression. The results were not at all encouraging.

By way of relaxation, for I was not a dull boy, I would exercise my French and widen my experience of local gastronomy. One old man who often sat in the corner of the bar in Chez Picot would talk to me for hours when gently plied with wine and the occasional cognac. It didn't take too long to figure out that increasing the ratio of *eau de vie* to *vin de pays* tended to increase the rate at which he told me what I wanted to hear. We used to talk about the artists who had flocked to the area between the wars, renting places to live and work; how there had been lots of foreigners, from all over Europe; Russians, Germans, Spaniards, Americans and yes, M'sieur, English everywhere. And very true, M'sieur, there had been some resentment because, well you know what artists are like, they had tended to get off with the local girls and freeze out the French. Now and again, sad to say, there had been some violence but, generally, it was hushed up; *crime passionnel* is hardly a crime, *n'est-ce pas?* Names? No, he couldn't remember any, it was so long ago but, yes, that *might* have been one. Late one evening, I showed him a photograph and after only one (or two) thought-provoking sips he was pretty sure he recognised the blurry face. In any daytime break from my researches, I searched the local churchyards but found nothing, nothing at all, to my intense relief. The golden sun of Provence was evaporating at least one myth.

Up in Paris again, I went to the street where Golden had once rented his atelier and painted for that frantic and now faraway month. Intriguingly, there was still an artist's materials shop operating but it had changed hands several times and was no longer selling any Chinese artefacts, ink or brushes. Two doors along, I bought a sander from a junk shop, and took it back down to the farmhouse. There, in wide sweeps but very, very lightly, I ran its abrasive disk across the backs of every one of the canvases and sucked up the dust into the vacuum cleaner bag. It was time-consuming and tedious but I thought about Joe all the while. Then I brought in some of the distinctive regional soil from the garden outside and scattered it over the kitchen floor. I let it dry overnight, walked over it time and again in my heaviest shoes, then emptied the canvas dust all over the floor and, finally, sucked the whole lot up again. I carried on with my thumbnail tests but, on the evidence, I was not moving towards a satisfactory conclusion.

In due course, the lab results came in the post, confirming that all the samples appeared to date back to pre-war, though hard to say exactly when, and that they also appeared to come from the same sources, in terms of the canvas and paint types. I went into Arles and had several photocopies made of the results – there would be quite a few letters to write – and, on my way back to the farmhouse, I carefully disposed of those samples I had *not* sent for testing. That evening, I wrote up this part of my research, making sure that everything from the lab tallied with what I had now written into the space I had previously reserved for them in my Moleskine notebook.

After weighing up the various options, I decided to drop a line to my Director at the Foundation, apologising for my unexpectedly delayed return but saying that, apart from his being pleased I had now finished the Poliakoff, I was fairly sure he would find what I had to tell him on another topic even more interesting. While that made its way ahead of me to London, I took small handfuls of the vacuum cleaner cocktail and, with a stiff brush, carefully worked it into all the crevices on the back of every canvas. Finally, I was ready for the final experiment.

Selecting different paintings, I applied what I seemed to be the right strength of white spirit to the top-right corner this time and, after twenty-four hours, went to the drawer where it had lain all this time and brought out the wooden plug prised from the jaws of death. Taking a deep breath, I pressed it very gently against the paint for no more than a few seconds. Alas, despite the thickness of the paint Rembrandt had applied, there wasn't any more than the faintest, partial impression of the cipher that Alexander Golden used to paint with such neatness on his pre-Parisian paintings and, in a more 'impressionist' form was to be found, but only on a very few of the Golden Month canvases, pressed onto the bottom right-hand corner.

The paint would not soften and I had already made one botched attempt that looked as though someone had been doctoring the paint surface. On an impulse, I slipped into Arles and bought a tube of Winsor & Newton's 'Permanent Rose' which was, by far, the nearest to the colour used when that corner of the final canvas was first painted. In that top corner, the paint was several millimetres thick and there was a small surface-of-the-moon crater. Using the smallest palette knife, I applied a skin of new paint. Only a tiny amount was necessary to allow me to, how shall I put this, create the right impression. I sat for nearly a week, waving a hair drier across the corner of the canvas. Then, I crated it up with one of the earlier canvases in separate boxes and loaded them into my car, another recent status acquisition. Then I put the mummy's plug in the heart of the kitchen fire and sat saying good bye to it for some time, glass in hand. The stage was now set. Two scripts were written. The choice of ending was mine. That die had still to be cast. Two days later, at the Orangerie, under the widening eyes of the curator and the admiring gaze of the friendly conservator, I would give my first performance.

They would realise, I patiently reminded them, that given all that I had uncovered during my original trip to Carmel, a visit I made as a direct result of the curator's very helpful introduction (smiles all round), I was very much minded to consider the forty-four canvases, unexpectedly discovered by my acquaintance, Ms Glover, during refurbishment of the property she had inherited – no, not from her sugar daddy as has been at first reported but her natural father; information he had entrusted only to me – as nothing more than meretricious pastiches, *à l'instar de Golden* – my goodness, how they sat up – painted, there seemed no doubt by the late Mr Peel/ Peale/ Rembrandt/ whatever and it was in that frame of mind I had set about my examination – interrupted, alas, by Ms Glover's most unfortunate illness. In confidence, her mother did suffer from pre-senile dementia. (I may have seemed to go all round the houses but, in reality, it was a well-planned journey.)

They could imagine my surprise, no greater than theirs no doubt, when the lab results came back and, *without exception*, indicated that the new paintings dated from *before* the war; plus or minus ten years, say the mid 1930s. (The die was cast: there was no going back now for Bill Maguire.) Here, for their information, were the lab results and the key was in my notebook here. Yes, they were welcome to photocopy the notebook too; why hadn't I thought of that? I had to thank the Orangerie for allowing me to take some samples from authentic Goldens, half a dozen of which, chosen at random by the conservator (more smiles of mutual admiration), had been used as the control data for these analyses.

These very unexpected and dramatic results had, I explained, sent me back to look again at the canvases I had been rather neglecting, while I concentrated on my teaching programme and the Poliakoff monograph on which I was working for the Foundation. They had been sitting under wraps all this time. I was, I frankly admitted, quite ashamed of my initially dismissive approach, and rather hoped they would not now hold that against me. In the typed notes which I had prepared (and which I thereupon produced with a restrained flourish from my briefcase), they would see that there was now at least a possibility, based on the way they seemed to dovetail so seamlessly with the iconography of the 'first' series, and the other stylistic parallels, that the paintings were not, in fact, by another, lesser hand. I had, as yet, held back from the growing conviction that they might, in fact, be by Golden himself. With their permission, hungrily granted, I then opened the box and revealed the painting I had brought with me. I let them look at it and gasp. It was the conservator who, scanning the canvas with her professional thoroughness, suddenly started and pointed, speechless, to one corner. The curator followed her gaze and let out a cry. I asked desperately for an explanation.

'Golden has *signed* it. Look there.'

And they directed my gaze to the top right corner where, almost hidden in a hollow of the thick paint, one could barely make out just a hint of his cipher.

'You're a better art historian than me, Mademoiselle. If you are *right*, and the other evidence tends to confirms it, *you* may have solved one the mysteries of the century.' The conservator blushed modestly, but the curator and I were insistent in giving her credit.

'I have to go on to London tomorrow morning but, as soon as I come back, I suggest I get in touch with the legal representative of the owner and discuss how this should all be handled. Do you think I could possibly have the use of an office here? My own facilities in Arles are somewhat basic. Meantime, can I rely on your total discretion?'

Pleading an early start, I declined the curator's invitation to dinner and, instead, had it sent up to my hotel room where I shared it, and much besides, with the conservator.

Dr Johnson was right. The imminence of a hanging does sharpen the mind and loosen the tongue. Still, I'm glad I've set all this down even if it is only for my own benefit.

The Foundation's Director was more or less waiting on the steps for me and rushed me from my taxi, helping to carry the crate up to his office. He locked the door and turned to me with a manic look.

'Gaston has been on the phone, Dr Maguire. Cut to the quick. Let me see, let me see! Oh my God, this will be the making of us!'

I heard a dead man whisper in my ear, 'Who the fuck is *us*?'

Once the Director was moderately calm again, and had allowed me to close the crate and make arrangements, in his name, for it to be put in the Foundation's air-conditioned vaults, I reminded him that the paintings actually belonged to a young woman of uncertain mind and disposition with whom, he needed to understand, I had had an affair that, alas, had not turned out well, and who now seemed to have a certain animus towards me. I held out hope, however, that I might be able to deal with her more pragmatic and pleasant legal representative, a European like *us* and, as it turned out, something of an art lover and patron.

'Then set about it Dr Maguire, Bill, dear colleague. I'll speak to our Chairman at once and maybe have a word with the Tate; that is, if you agree? After all, he may have painted in France but the man is British, through and through. But it's your show, dear boy, your show.'

'There's bound to be a battle with the Orangerie, and if Gaston has phoned *you* then I don't doubt he's already having lunch at the Ministry of Culture. But unless the Minister bans their export, all the paintings will very soon have to be shipped to California. Director, do you think the Foundation's budget would stretch to an air fare to San Francisco?'

'Be on the next flight, William, business class, even if I have to serve Empire wine at our next graduation. Don't waste a second.'

'I need to get back to Arles first. Now that the Orangerie have discovered what Gaston is calling the "long-lost Goldens", I need to move them from the farmhouse. I think they'll be safe in Montpellier's hands for the moment. I've seen their storage facilities; very much state-of-the-art.'

'Couldn't you simply hire a van and drive like hell for the Channel?'

'I'm sure you're not serious, Director, but if you were then I'd have to say that I have my own reputation to consider.'

'Well, well; I was joking; just letting my enthusiasm carry me away. Do what needs to be done. You have *carte blanche*.'

As in Paris, I arranged a decent office and a direct phone line.

'Bill, do you know what time it is? I haven't even had my breakfast! Are you calling to ask about Anna? You are a good boy and I wish I had good news but the fact is her physician has had to step up her medication. She is one *sick* woman.'

For a while, my unfeigned concern allowed me to sustain the illusion that I had, in the first instance, made one of my now less frequent transatlantic telephone calls to ask how his ward was getting on. When I broached the other matter, he readily agreed to meet me at the airport whenever I was able to fly over.

It was clear from the outset that no British gallery would have sufficient funds to purchase all forty-four paintings. The National Gallery of Scotland did try to get a consortium together. Alas for all of them, they were not the property of anyone who might have been willing and able to negotiate a deal with HM Treasury in lieu of Estate Duty. The rules under which the galleries operated also meant they were unable to sell off, as someone suggested wickedly, a couple of Rembrandts to put themselves in funds. Apart from the single painting, which I immediately removed from the prying eyes and poking fingers of the Foundation's technical experts, there was nothing on British soil to give the Art Fund any standing in the matter. Names like Thyssen and Getty were freely bandied about. The noise they all made was heard far enough afield to raise the estimated price now put on the collection by one whole order of magnitude.

The painting I'd left, with some trepidation, at the Orangerie, and its more travelled companion, were now driven, under police escort, to Montpellier. Making the point loud and clear that the French State owned the first Golden Month, the Minister of Culture then announced a ban on the export of the 'second Golden Month pending negotiations with its purported owner'. French experts and critics given privileged access were surprisingly unanimous in seeing and confirming the links, in terms of both continuity and development, between the two 'Months'. According to the newspapers and other media whose reporters thronged the village, overran the farmhouse and thrust microphones, cameras, notebooks, drinks and sometimes money in the faces of the local population, quite a few people, notably one rather animated alcoholic who was best interviewed not too long after he woke in the morning, clearly 'remembered' at least one English artist of the 1930s. He *might* have been called Golden, 'like the apple'. Either way, he had certainly behaved no better than any of the others and had 'dozens' of *petites amies*. Accounts differed but, certainly, there had been some feuding and fighting, then, quite suddenly, the Englishman and one of his more intimate friends had disappeared. Such things happen and, with a war looming, there were other, more important matters to think about.

The farmhouse had belonged to some now defunct local family then some Parisian had owned it and that Englishman had stayed there. After the war, an American had owned it for a while: they said he ran a gallery in Paris and came down at the weekends. He had never had any *petites amies,* or even *amis*: not so far as anyone could recall anyway. The builder was on national television and, for quite some time, his frustrated clients were in more despair than usual of ever getting their extensions built. Most of the French papers had it in for the young American woman who was claiming, merely on the strength of owning the house, to own its contents too. These surely belonged to 'the people' and they should join their older brothers and sisters in the Orangerie. Nathan was agog. Naturally, he turned to me for advice and treated me as his friend and confidant in preparation for the negotiations.

'Maybe the French government's not on solid legal ground regarding title, but I might have to send in the Marines to secure actual possession, Bill. The Minister probably has the power to expropriate them, in the national interest. We're into a real poker game. You might even persuade me to fly back with you and have some fun negotiating. I was supposed to be retiring next month but this could give me something to do in my old age! Besides, I really would like to have an opportunity to see the whole kit and caboodle, and actually handle some of them.'

Nathan Handschumacher, for some years now a widower, in his very late seventies, with a paunch that he kept well wrapped in high-waistbanded English worsted suits, sat across the dinner table at which I was his welcome guest. I hadn't been aware of it until my second visit to Carmel, with the very unwell Anna, but Nathan had begun, as soon as he had some spare cash from his thriving legal business, to buy, very selectively, early German Expressionists. It had given us some common ground and meant I hadn't been dealing with a Philistine when it came to asking for time to study the discovery 'Anna had made in her attic.'

Now he was looking at the photographs I had brought with me and, although he had dropped out of buying his favourite artists as their price went beyond what he could afford, it was already obvious he wouldn't mind parting with a small fortune to own just *one* of the new Goldens.

'The Foundation think I'm here negotiating for them and the Orangerie assume I am on their side but, do I need to say Nathan, where my heart really is?' (Worthy of Iago, I thought.)

'*Leiber* Bill. I know you really loved Anna and I am so sorry that, as they say, you did not "get the girl". But life can be cruel sometimes. What would you propose we do?'

'My feeling for what's possible tells me that the Orangerie have the best hand but our tactics should be to encourage the Foundation to get the Tate and the ICA wound up enough to cry foul. Then, as Anna's lawyer, you could keep saying you want the California galleries to be allowed to bid, and the sale to take place in New York. I'd also suggest you hire a PR agent in New York to wind up the critics and a few of the wealthier patrons.'

'And why should we go to all that trouble when we know where they will finish up?'

'It should mean that the value the saleroom put on the paintings sold singly, or even better as one colossal lot, will go through the roof. Then, even if they *are* expropriated by the State for the Orangerie, they'll be obliged to pay a half decent price.'

'That rather kills dead the hope I might own just one of these – for old time's sake, as well as everything else. I don't think Anna would want one.'

'You'll be negotiating. What about one each? Make that your deal-breaker.'

20050211

Now, a fair and full number of years later, I am sitting on a warm evening at the door of my comfortable and well-appointed farmhouse, looking in at the paintings that are round the walls and out at the well-stocked flower garden. Round the back, I have rather let things go: I call it my nature reserve, protecting the environment and so on. My housekeeper doesn't live in. I prefer to have the place to myself in the evening but she *has* prepared a meal. She's such a good cook that I let her do it, but no more than three days a week. On other evenings I generally go to the quiet restaurant where the late and much missed Mme Picot used to queen it. Now a chef with Michelin stars in his eyes practices there on his patrons. Tonight, my housekeeper has prepared tripe, in the Provençal style. It's a secret favourite of mine and I might as well enjoy it while I can.

At the beginning of next week, I must fly back to London where one of my staff at the Foundation, a very zealous but otherwise quite attractive young lady whom I have recently begun to think might be worth inviting out to dinner, has asked to see me as soon as possible. From what she has hinted at in her *courriel* (the French neologisms are always the best), I rather fear she may have some disturbing news. I have replied, asking her to keep matters strictly to herself.

Almost certainly, I shall advise that the painting be withdrawn from sale; there isn't time to do much else. Much more difficult, however, how am I going to explain all this to the owner's legal vulture? The one person who might have helped me and urged calm and reason is gone now and, in consequence, is the *reason* for the problem. This makes it almost impossible to predict the response, other than scabrous, and I am getting to the stage in life when I dislike unpredictability. Alternatively, could I afford to buy it myself and hang it once again beside its companion? I rather fear the answer must be no.

And what exactly *is* her disturbing news? Not to know, and yet to fear that I *do* know, is the most disturbing part of her news. Meantime, the oven timer has gone off and my glass is empty.

20050214

I do not, these days, need to change planes in Paris. In earlier times, it was not only a necessity but a distinct pleasure. Alas, I did not attend the curator's last rites since I was, at that time, on an extended lecture tour of the Far East. Now, it's only for my annual lecture at the Orangerie's new *Pavillon Golden* that I can bring myself to visit the place.

The independence that a significant amount of capital; given to me quite a few years ago by the then Trustees for the Administration of the Glover Estate, together with that one painting now behind bars in my moated grange in Monken Hadley; and a substantial income from my books and television films; haave all meant that I have enjoyed not so much a charmed as a charming life, despite a recent grumbling appendix. It is a function of wealth that it affords its possessor choices that are not available to the less fortunate. Naturally, I have also accepted the significant salaries for the succession of posts to which my academic knowledge and my skills in art administration have progressively and relatively swiftly elevated me. To sustain the lifestyle of a successful, well-known and, some do say, popular art historian requires not only initial outlay but substantial upkeep. I have been, for three years now, the youngest ever Director of the Contemporary Arts Foundation. My name is even being mentioned as a potential future Director of the Tate and if that ever happened surely I could finally persuade the French authorities to let me stage the very first exhibition of the entire Golden oeuvre outside the Orangerie. What pleasant daydreams.

20050215

Belinda Cornish presented herself in my office, blushing as I sat her down and poured the coffee myself. She had a folder with which she fiddled continuously, until I gently took it from her ring-free fingers and laid it on the low table in front of my Magistretti sofa. It was half-past eleven and I had already been thinking it was rather too long since I had been seen at The Ivy.

'Pour out your problems to me, Belinda.'

She blushed even more deeply, composed herself as best she could and drew breath.

'Director, it's about the checks for Shepherd's in advance of the sale. You know all about that.'

[I knew so much more than she realised. Abramowitz, in recent years, having made things up with his wife, the pair of them had ingratiated themselves once again with a sentimental and terminally ill Nathan; the artistic consequence of which had been that the couple inherited his house and its immensely valuable art collection. Nathan's daughter's taste in paintings, such as it was, tended more towards kitsch than de Kooning and, besides, she had a smart accountant.

In some measure, this was due to the accountant having acquired as client and, later, friend, Anna's elderly and now semi-retired, semi-respectable, semi-uncle Wilbur who was acting as some sort of art advisor. It was very likely down to the Wilbur connection that Abramowitz began to make quite insulting suggestions, in front of his wife too, that I had been in some way – no, he didn't say 'in some way', he said, in effect, 'directly' – responsible for the chronic illness and now total incapacity that made Anna a ward of his legal practice, the lawyers for the Trustees who were now acting as her guardians. I did not remain long to be insulted but so far forgot myself (again) as to catalogue for him some of the faults that Anna had found in him back in Carmel.

At this time, London auction houses are in a slight ascendancy over New York but I suspect Abramowitz insisted that Shepherd's sell the work more or less across the road from the Foundation, just to press home the point that he hated not just my guts but all of me.]

'Where do you, I, we come into all of this, Belinda?' And a still small voice in my head silently asked me who the fuck were *we*?

'It's slightly embarrassing, Director, but I was one of the team checking over all the German Expressionists for Shepherd's, although they are of quite indisputable provenance, but the auctioneers are being so careful these days. So anyway I was using the UV lamp and had just finished them when there was the Golden right beside them and I was already running the lamp over it before I realised. And in the corner, around the impression of his cipher, the UV picked something up.'

'What sort of something?'

'Well, just a different refraction, very small but it seemed peculiar so – and this is the embarrassing bit – without getting anyone's permission, I took some tiny samples of paint.'

'You did *what*!?'

My quite legitimate over-reaction masked my real feelings.

'I do apologise and, if you wish,' she added miserably, 'I will resign immediately.'

'But why did you take a sample? What was it for?'

'Director, you know my first degree is in chemistry and I'm particularly interested in the history of pigments. I wanted to see if I could date the paint chemically by identifying the pigment.'

'Had you some reason?'

'Apart from that curious UV reading, none, Dr Maguire, but I have been making a whole series of tests recently using partition chromatography and I simply went ahead and added it. No one at

Shepherd's knows, and no one here either – apart from yourself now, of course.'

'Tampering with another person's property without their permission? You do realise what sort of trouble we would *all* be in, if that were to become known?' And I did not mean the royal 'we'.

She hung her head in abject surrender; face, neck and arms scarlet with suffused shame, waiting for me to deliver the well-deserved blow.

'And what did you find?'

'Quinacridone.'

'Ah! Really?'[1]

I took a couple of deep breaths and a mouthful of my cold coffee.

'I think I am being rather hard on you. I know you are a diligent researcher and, if you were a little bit carried away, that's not perhaps a fault in someone of your age. I think we need to discuss all this in a more relaxed atmosphere. Is that the folder of your results? I'll lock it in my desk for now and we can chat together over lunch.'

Her gratitude was touching.

Once I had established the crucial details, I think I did most of the talking. I was also thinking furiously while acting the generous and ever so slightly flirtatious host. We had a table in an alcove where she could not be seen by the rest of the dining room. Why did I feel that everyone was looking at me? I topped up her glass and forced a smile.

'I should have said that was only the first result. There are still some others to come from the other corners. But I asked them to give this one priority.'

The whole dining room must have heard me gasp. 'You certainly should have said, but no matter. When do you expect them?'

'Early next week. I took samples from all four corners.'

'Then there's nothing to be gained by rushing into hasty action. Tell me, Belinda, how is your dissertation progressing?'

We talked and drank, or rather she did, while I sipped and silently sorted things out in my mind. This, as only I knew, was the first time that the new Goldens have been subjected to any kind of chemical test of their paint; whatever the published record might show. If they were ever to be tested in this way, I have every reason to be apprehensive. All I can think of doing now is to delay what seems an inevitable discovery. But, in this life, nothing is inevitable and for as long as I can keep a lid on the release of one piece of information, I have time to go on thinking and hoping that something, or better still nothing, will turn up. As I poured the last of the second bottle into her willing glass, an idea came to me.

'You've never seen the place where the new Goldens were discovered, have you?'

She gave me a very tipsy smile.

20050226

The fact that I helped her unresisting into a taxi, took her unprotesting out to Monken Hadley, carried her uncomplaining upstairs and put her, partially undressed but completely unmolested into my own bed, and laid not a finger on her all night, seemed to convince her that I was that contemporary rarity, the perfect gentleman, and predisposed her, I'd like to think, to accept, wide-eyed, my invitation to fly down to my farmhouse for the weekend and enjoy my hospitality, a tour of some significant galleries and still be back in London for the arrival of those other results. My own plan was simply to keep her out of circulation and away from dangerous conversation with others.

It was for me a completely new experience, and surprisingly pleasant, when, on the Sunday afternoon, *she* took the initiative and seduced me. This is the twenty-first century after all. As we parted at Heathrow the next day, she promised faithfully to keep everything to herself and come straight to me with the results and, with a giggle, not to ask my secretary if 'Willy' wanted to come out to play!

By Wednesday, the results, from the lab out at Croydon, had still not arrived but I told her not to phone them up as if she were anxious, and this meant my flying off to Milan for a television shoot with the intention of continuing on from there to Arles. One look at her face was enough to have me succumb and invite her to join me: as if I didn't have troubles enough, but what else could I do? It would have been imprudent for her to call me while I was in Italy but, in what now seemed only a postponement of the inevitable, I agreed she could break the news to me when I reached Arles on the Friday afternoon before she caught her budget flight to Marseilles. My piece to camera on de Chirico was not my best, but I didn't have the energy for more than two takes.

This afternoon, when I got here from Italy, I went up to what is now my study and as I looked round for more paper for the printer, I saw, lying beside the sketchbook on the shelf where I keep photographs of Joe and Anna, a single tube of oil paint. As if removing traces of a former mistress, lest the current one should be offended and leap to unfortunate conclusions, I slipped it in my pocket and went for a stroll. For the first time in, literally, years, I walked up past the waving fronds of asparagus fern. There, with a spoon from the kitchen, I dug a tiny hole – though even that gave me some unpleasant feelings – and dropped into it the scarcely used tube of 'Permanent Rose', trusting that it would not take root and flower.

When I arrived back in the kitchen, the message light on the phone had started winking. Although I would have to drive to Marseilles, I still poured myself a brandy before I sat down to listen. What I was about to hear, I had no doubt, was going to spell the end of my career. Not only was I about to be thoroughly discredited, exposed as a fraud and a *poseur*, lose my job, my prospects of the next plum post and all that I had been building towards but the reputation of the Foundation and all its other honest staff and students would suffer considerable damage.

Well, what did it matter? I even found myself grinning quietly at the thought that I, that we – and I know who the fuck 'we' are in this context – might even disappear just like the originator of all this mystery, the long-sought Scot, Alexander Golden and that the whole cycle might start all over again. Why not? I had no intention, wouldn't have the nerve even, to contemplate slitting my veins in the bath or some such melodramatic gesture. Even in Paraguay they must have at least one decent art gallery. I could perfectly well take all my wealth and go off, far from the public gaze, to the ends of the earth, or even, if it came to that, Australia. I might find that the buxom, and astonishingly talented, Belinda would not want to go and live in South America. I might find, of course, that she would want to go anywhere with me, in all the circumstances and to that I was perfectly reconciled. Pouring out another small snifter, I sat down and pressed Play.

'Professor Maguire? Bill? Aren't you there yet? I'll have to go off for my plane straight away because they've called it and it's fully booked so I don't want to get bumped… . Humped I might like but not bumped… . Are you there? Yoohoo, yoohoo… . Oh dear, Willy I only have a moment so I really must tell you and put you out of your misery but I don't think you're going to be able to understand this any more than I do.

'I've got all the results and, really and truly, I think they just make matters even more difficult to explain. It does seem certain that someone must have tampered with the painting but how they managed to add back his cipher I just don't know. I think we'll need to get every one of the new Goldens checked out, just in case whoever it was has touched any of the other canvases. The things is, I've got all the results back now – they'd gone to the Courtauld by mistake and they took ages to send them round – and they don't tie up at all.

'The samples from every other part of the painting show no trace of any pigment that wasn't available in the 1930s when Golden was painting and they tie up absolutely perfectly with the tests you did yourself at Montpellier. You know I did begin to wonder if we were looking at a clever forgery but these tests mean, beyond a shadow of doubt, it's a genuine Golden.'

---

1   The absolutely crucial detail, the detail that would crucify me anyway, was that the paint sample, taken from beside the faint impression of Golden's cipher, covering only about a square centimetre perhaps, certainly not two, the spotting of which had been the convincing clue discovered by the late conservator, had shown traces of an identifiable pigment; a synthetic pigment – and as experts we *both* knew this – that had not been developed until the 1950s by Dupont, and, more to the point, not included in their range of oil paints until 1958 by the ever enterprising Winsor & Newton. Thus, whatever one might say about the whole of the rest of that canvas or the other new Goldens, this *tiny* spot could not have been painted until then – and that did not fit in at all with the art world's present belief that every individual daub had been applied to its surface by the long-lost and presumed late Alexander Golden. But if it was not by Golden then, by a process of ruthless elimination,

there was only one other person whose name was in the frame, pun not intended. And that begged the further and most unwelcome question as to how that person could have imagined in the first place that the paintings were by Alexander Golden – and that 'person' was *me*.

PUBLISHER'S AFTERWORD

Readers will be aware that the manuscript of this book – as dramatic in the story it has to tell as in its frankness and self-revelation – came to the world's attention thanks to the bold but agonising decision taken by its author's widow, Dr Belinda Maguire.

In the few years since Professor Maguire's untimely death, his reputation as a critic has been hotly debated in the art world and in wider intellectual circles.

As the man whose persistent and diligent researches uncovered the missing second Golden Month and who subsequently wrote a whole new chapter in the story of abstract expressionism, he was assured of one enduring reputation. Nor should one overlook his works on several other French artists of the twentieth century; notably Poliakoff, Kijno and Lanskoy. His hair-raising adventures in Tahiti, rescuing a purloined Poliakoff while making a television programme made him known to millions.

He was too a talented administrator who maintained, sustained and enhanced the reputation of the Foundation he so ably directed. He had seemed to many to be destined to progress further.

However, the revelations in this manuscript that Maguire actually judged the canvases of the second Month to be fakes and that, taking advantage of the recent death of the man he wrongly believed responsible for painting them, he then went to extraordinary and, frankly, dishonest lengths to 'pass them off' as original Goldens, has ensured him a second quarter of an hour of fame as the art expert who managed to pass off originals as originals, while himself believing them to be forgeries.

Blinded, it seems, by a loyalty to the now entirely discredited Joseph Peel, he did not want his friend's reputation damaged by the suggestion — only too credible — that some major art forgery scam had been in preparation. Curiously, all the evidence now suggests that this was exactly what was intended — not, however, the scam that Maguire supposed.

The work done by Dr Belinda Maguire has persuaded many that Peel, who never received the recognition he craved as an artist in his own right, discovered the cache of canvases, realised their colossal significance but, perversely, devoted many years to preparing a hoax that would have had the world believe, after his death, that he, Joseph Peel, painted them as some sort of bizarre homage to Alexander Golden.

As his widow wrote, 'My husband was torn between his own instinct and training and the wonderfully convincing yarns that the fake Rembrandt had spun about him. While his head believed the paintings to be genuine Golden, his heart wanted them to be forged Rembrandts. That Bill's head turned out to be right, but for the wrong reasons, is one of life's major ironies.'

Despite, and at the same time because of, the tragic death of Professor Maguire on his honeymoon just that kilometre too far from hospital when his appendix ruptured, and which shattered her happy new world, his widow has decided to publish the manuscript which she found among the back-up disks of Professor Maguire's computer and which, without doubt inadvertently, survived his earlier unexplained destruction and burial of his laptop in the asparagus bed of his beloved Provençal farmhouse.

Royalties from the sale of this book will go to a trust fund established to benefit the Maguires' infant son, Joseph.

Lightning Source UK Ltd.
Milton Keynes UK
UKOW050021271012

201288UK00002B/2/P